WHERE THE LIES HIDE

Visit us at www.boldstrokesbooks.com

By the Author

Epicurean Delights

Stroke of Fate

Where the Lies Hide

WHERE THE LIES HIDE

by

Renee Roman

2019

WHERE THE LIES HIDE

ISBN 13: 978-1-63555-371-0

THIS TRADE PAPERBACK ORIGINAL IS PUBLISHED BY
BOLD STROKES BOOKS, INC.
P.O. BOX 249
VALLEY FALLS, NY 12185

FIRST EDITION: AUGUST 2019

CREDITS
EDITORS: VICTORIA VILLASENOR AND CINDY CRESAP
PRODUCTION DESIGN: SUSAN RAMUNDO
COVER DESIGN BY SHERI (HINDSIGHTGRAPHICS@GMAIL.COM)

Acknowledgments

Len Barot, thank you for making Bold Strokes Books a safe haven for writers and a place we can escape to as readers. I owe my deepest gratitude to my editor, Vic Villasenor, for showing me the ropes and explaining the whys, and why-nots, of this craft we call writing. Cindy Cresap, thank you for your patience and encouraging words. Hopefully, you only pulled out a few hairs this round. Cover artist, Sheri, I am in love with this amazing cover. Sandy Lowe, thank you for working through the rough spots with me. I know it's not always easy, and I appreciate your kindness. And to all the behind-the-scenes folks at BSB, thank you for the hard work and dedication you show every author. We couldn't do this without you.

To Shel Lee, for your investigative insights during the conception of this project. You were the jump start I needed. Thank you, Detective Sergeant Dan, for your procedural input and explaining precinct ranks, among other things. Stick around. There's a police story that will need you down the road.

To my friends and family—when I told you I was being published I think I surprised you all. Your love and support are a gift to me.

To my wife, Sue. I know it's not always easy living with a writer wife and I am grateful for your endurance and understanding.

And to my readers, there are pages, chapters, and books ahead. I hope you enjoy reading them as much as I enjoy crafting them.

Dedication

To my BFF, Sandy.
When life is a series of road bumps,
remember to enjoy the ride.
Thanks for always taking that ride with me.

CHAPTER ONE

Dear Investigator,

I'm contacting you because my wife has been acting rather strange of late, and working a lot of overtime without any evidence in our bank account...

Camdyn Stark drummed her fingertips on the desk while reading the latest email addressed to Stark Revelations. The organization only consisted of three people—her, one green investigator, and a crackerjack assistant—but she was proud of the work they did.

She'd much rather help someone who was at their wits' end with nowhere else to turn than follow cheating spouses.

Cam was about to close the window on the screen when she heard the ping announcing the arrival of a new email. Convinced it would be another boring case that she'd end up taking just for the sake of keeping busy, she sighed. Perhaps it wouldn't be the usual. Maybe it would be a case that would hold her attention; those did come along occasionally, and she loved unraveling mysteries.

The plea was from a middle-aged couple whose father had disappeared. They'd filed a missing person report with the local police, but without more information, there hadn't been a lot to go on. Now they were desperate to know what had happened to him. Sometimes she lucked out with missing persons cases similar to this one, though when it involved the elderly, it could be a much grimmer outcome. Especially if the family wasn't aware their loved one had dementia or Alzheimer's, which happened way more than it should. She hoped that wasn't true in this case, for their sake, though it would be a good learning experience for her new hire, Kevin. She'd sit in on the initial interview and make sure the investigation headed in the right direction. He had good instincts, but he didn't always ask pertinent questions.

As for the suspicious wife, she'd deal with that one. A few hours of snooping might reveal the individual was having an affair. Another scenario that baffled her. She never quite understood why people didn't just talk about their feelings. But then, she wasn't exactly an expert on emotions, so what did she know?

She picked up her desk phone.

"Hey, boss. What's up?" Maggie answered in her always upbeat tone.

"We might have a couple of new cases. I'm going to send you the emails. Can you start a file and contact the people to set up interviews?"

"Standard procedure?" Maggie asked.

"For now. Thanks, Mags."

"Sure thing. I'll get right on it."

❖

"Hi, Sarah. What's up?" Lisa asked.

"I...uh, can you come over?" Sarah barely got the words out, her voice betraying her.

"On my way."

Lisa was her best friend. They'd known each other since the first grade and had both returned to their home town after graduating college, and even when more than a thousand miles separated them, they'd still found time to talk. Sarah's awkward teenage years had been an emotional rollercoaster. She hadn't thought about her preference for the company of girls over boys until her hormones kicked in, leaving no doubt where her attraction lay. Lisa had been the first person she'd revealed her lesbianism to, and she'd hugged Sarah fiercely. Their relationship had grown closer after the revelation, and she trusted Lisa with her highest joys and her greatest fears.

Sarah's hand shook as she put the phone down. She tried to focus on the picture of her and her parents hanging on the wall over the buffet table. Her eyes filled, blurring everything in front of her. *This can't be real.* There had to be a mistake. She picked up the white envelope, her name neatly written on the front in her mother's familiar handwriting. She should have known something was wrong when the first sentence following the salutation was, *"This isn't going to be easy, but it's something you need to hear."*

She couldn't read it again. She had to wait for Lisa to get there. She needed moral support and to know she wasn't going crazy. She paced through the small rooms, glancing out the front window every few minutes. Relief washed over her when the familiar red Beetle whipped into the driveway. Sarah raced down the few steps to greet her on the walkway. Lisa's strong embrace calmed her.

"Let's go inside and you can tell me everything. I brought reinforcements." Lisa held up a bag from a local dairy, and Sarah knew it contained a quart of their "dire situation" go-to food. Rocky road ice cream.

After Lisa scooped out two generous bowls and joined her at the table, she met Sarah's stare. "Does this have to do with Anne's death?"

Sarah shook her head. "No. Well, yes. Kinda." She wasn't making any sense. But as usual, Lisa didn't rush her or ask a million questions; she just waited while Sarah gathered her thoughts. She took a deep breath. *Where do I even begin?*

"I was going through the stacks of papers lying around, you know, to sort out the junk, find bills. The will." She shoved a spoonful of the decadent treat into her mouth, instantly feeling better. "Anyway, I came across this." She reached for the envelope with her name on it and handed it to Lisa.

"You want me to read it?" Lisa asked around her own mouthful.

"Yes," she croaked, fighting against the lump in her throat.

Lisa took her time, reading it once before looking up, then read the first page again. She set the letter reverently on the table, then reached out to Sarah. "I don't know what to say."

"So, it's true. It wasn't something I imagined… I have a twin?"

"It seems so." Lisa glanced between the papers and Sarah.

"I don't know whether to be angry or happy." She pushed away the bowl, her appetite gone. "All these years thinking I was an only child." Sarah snatched the pages and shook them. "Why didn't they tell me?"

Lisa's expression softened. "I'm sure they didn't do it to hurt you. They loved you so much. Maybe they were afraid you'd resent them for not adopting your brother, too."

Sarah's anger flared. "Cowards."

"Now, hon, you know that's not how you really feel about the only parents you've ever known. I'd say they did their best for you from the first day they held you. Haven't you said it yourself a million times? That you were so lucky to have two people who loved you unconditionally and never made you feel any less than their own flesh and blood?"

She pursed her lips. Lisa was right. She had been blessed with two amazing parents and she couldn't imagine what her life would have been like without their love and support. She just didn't know what to do with the news.

"Of course, you're right. You've always been my voice of reason." She pulled the bowl of melting ice cream in front of her, stirring the contents. "What do I do now?"

"What do you want to do?" Lisa asked.

She rested her chin in her hand before she downed a few more spoonfuls as she contemplated one of the most important questions of her life. What *did* she want to do with the information? After making the funeral arrangements and contacting her mother's agent about the life insurance policy, Sarah hadn't expected any surprises.

"When Dad died, my family shrunk to two. Then Mom died, and I came to terms that I was truly alone in the world." She met Lisa's hurt expression and hurried on. "Except for you. You know what I mean?"

"I do."

"But now…everything's changed. I'm not alone. I have a brother. Somewhere on the planet someone shares DNA with me.

All those years growing up, I wondered what it would have been like to have a sister or brother. I knew Mom couldn't have children, and by the time they had enough money saved to afford adopting another child, they were older. So I accepted I'd be an only child, and I was okay with it." Sarah didn't want to seem ungrateful. Still, the prospect of finding and getting to know her sibling was exciting.

"I think I want to try to find him." She dropped her spoon in the empty bowl. The hollow sound reminded her too much of how she thought of herself. "Is that wrong of me?" She glanced up. She'd asked herself the same question over and over since reading the letter.

Lisa smiled at her. "I think it's courageous. Tell me what you're thinking, and we'll make a list."

CHAPTER TWO

The weekend had been a blast, but expensive. Cam had gone a little overboard wining and dining the hookup she'd met at Kevin's friend's bachelorette party. Jackie's hourglass figure had her mouth watering, and she'd made the mistake of flirting with her. Cam told her she'd like to show her a better time, but of course she'd been joking. What was she to do when the woman called her bluff, saying she had her suitcase in the car and nowhere to be? As the night wore on they'd drank a bit too much, the alcohol lowering any inhibitions the woman might have initially had. Cam had to admit the sex had been spectacular. Way more than any fantasy she might have imagined. The things they did were on the far edge of kinky and exactly what Cam had been craving. The carousing was familiar territory from her teen years, a mechanism by which she could pretend the person she was sleeping with cared about her when the darkness threatened to close in on her.

Now she had to find a way to recoup the grand she'd spent on drinks and a room with a hot tub at the nicest hotel in the city. Jackie had been worth every penny. And then some.

It was time to get back to business. Kevin was working on a case of identity theft. It wasn't her preferred type to handle and could take a lot of man-hours, but it was a great learning experience and would provide him with a ton of on-the-job training. She didn't want to have Kevin follow her around for months. Every investigator had to develop their own way of doing the legwork, and she'd seen potential in him from the start. He was eager to learn and well-mannered. Plus, he didn't have her jaded views of some cases, like deadbeat dads and people who failed to take responsibility for their children.

Cam made a stop at the always ready coffee pot in hopes the caffeine would soon kick in before she knocked on Kevin's open door.

"Hey, got a few minutes to go over the Stillman case?"

Kevin glanced up and smiled. "Absolutely, Cam. I was just finishing a few notes on what I'd found."

She sat at the round table in the corner of his office. He soon joined her. He was organized, which she appreciated, and came up with logical assumptions based on leads he was able to follow. Thirty minutes later, she was satisfied with the progress he'd made.

"Good job. Keep at it. These people tend to fall under the radar and you don't want him slipping away."

Back at her desk, she scanned the six emails that had come in overnight. She'd finished her last case before calling it quits on Friday. It was time she moved on to a new one. If only she could find one worthy of challenging her skills. Her mood darkened and her chest tightened. A lot of those skills had come from looking for the woman who'd abandoned her. She didn't want to go there. She opened her inbox and prayed she could lose herself in her work.

❖

Sarah studied the listing of private investigators in the mid-Hudson area. She hadn't been sure about Lisa's suggestion, but having nowhere else to turn, she figured it wouldn't hurt to see what was out there. She laughed out loud at the "specializing in" categories. Background checks. Civil investigations. Surveillance. Insurance scams. Fraud. Corporate investigations. Accident reconstruction. Domestic. Infidelity.

Her heart sank. If she were a betting person she would have thought missing persons would have been near the top of the list. Following the categories was a general description of each. Her chest froze when she reached the last line under "Civil." Missing persons.

She hadn't had all that long to make sense of the revelation left behind by her mother. Now she had the option of acting on the news. It wasn't that she didn't believe her mom, but Sarah couldn't understand why she had waited until *after* her death to drop the bombshell in Sarah's lap. But then, the letter's explanation was believable. After her father's death from a series of heart attacks, her mom had stewed over telling her, weighing the pros and cons until she thought she'd cause her own demise. She wrote that she couldn't face telling Sarah the truth. The guilt she'd lived with for twenty-eight years was too much for her to handle, so she'd written the letter and hidden it, knowing Sarah would eventually find it.

So, here she was. Staring at a screen listing PIs in the vicinity and contemplating how much she wanted to know. She didn't have the time or energy to do it on her own; she wouldn't know where to begin. She would explain to whomever she hired, *if* she hired someone, that she just wanted to confirm he existed, that he was still alive. Maybe her twin lived in another country. Maybe he'd died in some freak accident. Maybe there'd only be dead ends and she wouldn't know any more than she did today. But she'd be no worse off. Not trying wasn't an option. She had to try. But she didn't *have* to meet him.

Certainly, if he knew of her he would have searched for her too, right? She huffed at the idea of the two of them unaware of each other for all this time. She sucked in a breath. What if his adoptive family preferred he not know about his sister and had covered it up like her parents had? Sarah shook her head. He was old enough to make up his own mind now. His parents couldn't stop him even if they wanted to.

The easiest thing to do would be to close the screen and forget everything her mother had struggled to explain, to pretend she didn't know about him and save the remainder of the insurance policy for something she really wanted, instead of on hiring someone to search for a total stranger she might not even like. She could buy a newer vehicle. Or take the vacation she never made time for.

Even as each of the reasons for not looking passed through her mind, she moved her finger along the scroll bar as it traveled down the list of names. The vibration of her cell phone across the table startled her.

"Hello."

"Well?" Lisa asked.

"Well what?"

"Did you do it?"

"No," Sarah said.

"Have you changed your mind?"

"No, but…I'm trying to find the right one."

"And how do you plan to do that?"

The tease in Lisa's voice eased the tension in her shoulders, and she laughed. "I honestly don't know. Dartboard? Name out of a hat?" She chewed on her lower lip. "It should be easy, right?"

"Honey, if I've learned one lesson in life it's that nothing is easy, except love." Lisa certainly had a way of stating the obvious. "Knowing you, you probably have a spreadsheet with details and plot points."

"I do not." Sarah tried to sound offended, but how could she be? Making a spreadsheet was her next option.

"Oh, I called too soon in the process." Lisa's laugh was infectious.

Sarah tapped her pencil on the paper in front of her where she'd written the names of investigators specializing in civil matters and missing persons. "There's more than I thought there would be."

"That's kinda sad."

"I know."

"I'm going to leave you to it then."

Lisa was silent for so long Sarah checked her phone to make sure she hadn't lost the connection before Lisa spoke again.

"Sarah. Trust your gut. You've got good instincts. Let them do the work. I'll check back later. Love you."

"Love you, too."

She glanced from the screen to the list and back again. *Trust my gut.* At this point, what choice did she have?

❖

I should hire a bookkeeper. Cam slit open envelopes and stacked them in a neat pile. It was time to pay the bills that kept her business going. From the first day she'd opened the doors until today, she'd taken on the additional duties of all the financial transactions. Balancing the books in and of itself could be quite a feat, especially the months when business was a little slow. Since she'd hired Kevin, there was even more to do, and it was beginning to eat into her investigative time. Maggie could handle the extra workload, but she wasn't sure she wanted anyone else privy to the books except for her.

The pinging of her email notification drew her attention away from the ledger she was bent over. She should ignore it and finish what she was doing since she'd put it off long enough, but the subject line glaring at her refused to go away. It simply stated, "Lost Twin." *Who the hell loses a twin?*

"This ought to be good," she mumbled as she pushed the papers out of her way and pulled the keyboard in front of her.

The email from Sarah Peters explained she and her twin had been separated shortly after birth and adopted by different parents. Her own adoptive parents were both gone, and she wanted more information about the brother she never knew. *Interesting.* Cam finished reading the rest and checked her date book. She had a meeting scheduled with a forensic accountant on Wednesday, the information from which would most likely lead to her finding an embezzler or an outright theft of company assets. Fairly straightforward since all she had to do was follow the money. She could always get Kevin to help. It wouldn't hurt to talk with the woman and get the details.

"Mags, would you please set up an appointment this week for Ms. Sarah Peters? Her contact info is in your mailbox. The sooner the better."

"Got it. What do you want for lunch today?"

"Anything but pizza. You pick." The influx of cases gave her an appetite. The tiny hairs at the nape of her neck tingled. She'd been in a bit of a slump of late, unexcited about the same old cases. She was tired of cheating spouses and disability frauds. This would be a new vein to follow. Even though Ms. Peters had stated it was a missing person case, it really wasn't. If she didn't know her brother existed, he wasn't missing, he'd never been found. She wondered if Peters had considered she might not be happy with the results.

CHAPTER THREE

Sarah flipped back her shield, removed her gloves, then wiped her brow. She looked over the intersecting steel beams in front of her to make sure the weld was smooth. She didn't like sloppy work, but she wasn't really concentrating on the job and her thoughts had gravitated to the email she'd sent last night, wondering when or if she'd ever get a response. It would be just her luck that the investigator she'd chosen was a front for some illegal operation and she'd never hear from Camdyn Stark, the owner of Stark Revelations.

She had to admit, it was a catchy name for the business, though it seemed a little egocentric. She'd also tried to do a little detective work of her own by googling the owner's name but had found very little except that Camdyn was a woman. There were several testimonies from clients, all anonymous, who praised the agency with pulling off near impossible investigations. Of course, there wasn't any way for her to verify they were legitimate, but still... she'd been inexplicably drawn to the picture of Camdyn. Her long dark hair and confident smile were hard to ignore. Maybe it was the uncommon name. Or it was simple fatigue from looking at one screen page after another, though she didn't believe that was the reason either. Whatever had made her stop at that particular agency was of little consequence. The important thing was that she'd settled on one and sent a request asking for a face-to-face meeting. There wasn't any way she could explain her circumstances in an impersonal email. Not if she were going to trust someone with a matter that could change the course of her life, for good or bad, she wanted to look that person in the eye and see what they were made of. If Camdyn didn't take her seriously or acted disinterested, she'd know. She always knew the sincerity of a person by their gestures and the look in their eyes. She trusted her intuition and the inner voice that guided her. Her parents never doubted her abilities to overcome any obstacle, and she saw no shame in asking for help when she needed it. This was one of those times. All she could do was wait.

❖

"Ms. Peters, if I understood your email correctly, you're looking for your twin. And as far as you know, you were both adopted when you were babies. You had no idea your brother even existed until a few days ago. Is that correct?" Cam asked.

Sarah looked at her expectantly. "Yes. Exactly," she said before leaning forward. "I was adopted right away, but it's entirely possible he stayed in the system, right?" She dug around in her bag. "This is a copy of the letter my mother—"

"Your birth mother?" Cam was confused.

"Sorry. Adoptive mother. She mentions the name Mary and the sign over my bassinet was Baby Girl Jones." Sarah pushed the document toward her. "Do you think you can find him?"

She was pretty with expressive eyes though she didn't have a clue. The thought of tracking down someone who was most likely lost in the proverbial rat maze of adoption agencies, not to mention Social Services, made her think twice. She'd glossed over a couple of details on her initial read through, and now Cam regretted having been so anxious to work on something new. She glanced back up to meet Sarah's hopeful regard, and Cam sighed inwardly. She wasn't easily persuaded.

"Are you sure you want to find him? Sometimes people stay hidden for a reason." The minute her words left her mouth, Sarah's demeanor changed.

"If that's code for you not being interested in helping me, just say so. I don't want to waste your time or mine." Sarah gathered the oversized sack that probably carried everything she might need in the event of an apocalypse, then slung it over her shoulder as she stood.

Cam couldn't ignore the niggling feeling in her gut. The one that told her even if she wanted to drop this case and say good-bye to the soon-to-be client with fire in her eyes, it wasn't an option. She rose to her feet.

"I didn't say I wouldn't take the case, Ms. Peters. I just want to be sure you're aware of what *might* happen." She gestured for Sarah to sit down again.

Sarah stared at her so long the scrutiny verged on uncomfortable. She refused to succumb to the urge to squirm.

"Fine, just so long as you're as committed as I am to finding him." A look of longing crossed her face, dampening the earlier flame.

Cam fought the sudden tug on her heart. It would be a mistake to feel bad for Sarah. She was a client. She needed to remember that point. Her default barrier came up. "You'll get your money's worth." The sarcasm sounded harsh and unnecessary, but she blew it off. She was who she was, and the circumstances of the case rubbed her in a way that brought up her own unsavory past. The Peters woman could hire her or not. Either way she'd survive.

Sarah snorted. "You don't have to sound so enthused." She pursed her lips and Cam waited. "So now what?" Apparently, she'd decided to move forward with Cam at the helm.

"Now, Ms. Peters, you read the contract—"

Sarah interrupted her spiel. "It's Sarah. I'm not big on formality."

"Fine." Cam pushed the standard paperwork for a missing person inquiry forward. "Carefully read, then sign it. You can take it with you if you like. That gives me carte blanche to make standard inquiries on your behalf and with your permission. If there are extraordinary circumstances for which I may need to file a court plea, or other such document, I'll have a specific request drawn up and leave the decision to pursue up to you. Then you give me a one-thousand-dollar retainer, and I do what I do best. Find your brother."

She hadn't been able to locate her own family. Maybe she'd do better this time.

❖

Sarah pressed the gas pedal and steered through the traffic trying to slow her down. She wasn't sure what bugged her more about Camdyn Stark. Her questions about whether she was sure she wanted to pursue finding her brother, her confidence, or her borderline cocky attitude. Sarah wasn't normally attracted to looks alone, but she wasn't immune to them, either. Camdyn rode a fine line between feminine and butch. Long, wavy hair and mesmerizing bedroom eyes were the first things she'd noticed. That, in combination with her tall, trim figure, caused her to tingle in a few places she'd almost forgotten she had. When Camdyn moved from behind her desk to lean against the edge, her muscular thighs and well-shaped ass had distracted Sarah from the reason she was in her office.

The moment she'd left to talk to her receptionist, Sarah had taken the opportunity to inspect the impressive array of certificates and awards covering the walls, along with newspaper clippings of high-profile cases Stark Revelations had solved. Some dated back nearly ten years. Sarah found it hard to believe Camdyn was much older than her. While it was true they'd gotten off to a bit of a rocky start, Camdyn had assured her she would do everything she could to find her unknown sibling. For some reason, Sarah believed her, and when she'd returned, Sarah had quickly read and signed the agreement, though there was some legal jargon she didn't fully understand. Camdyn might have noticed because she ended their meeting by handing Sarah her business card and telling her to call if she had any questions.

She glanced at the folder on the passenger seat. It contained a copy of the contract, a list of documents to collect, and a questionnaire for her to complete. Some of the things Camdyn would do she could have done herself, like search the web, but to what end? Even if she found a useful clue, then what? The knowledge of her brother's existence was difficult enough without having to spend the few free hours she had collecting random threads. It was best left to the professionals.

❖

Cam tapped her pen on the form in front of her. She should be happy. The check was good. Maggie had already called the bank. The contract was signed, and she'd given Sarah a list of questions that would provide her with the basis for starting the investigation. So far, it had been routine. But nothing about the case *felt* routine. Maybe it was because of her ingrained hate for the system. Her stomach roiled again, and she reached for the near empty bottle of antacids she kept in her desk. If she were to compare herself to a drug addict, this would be her drug of choice. She chewed the chalky tablet and washed it down with a long swallow of seltzer.

Cam hadn't started out wanting to be a PI. Once she'd escaped the system, she had moved to Florida, thinking the heat and sun would burn away the remnants of abuse. From her skin. From her mind. Key West seemed like the perfect destination for a nineteen-year-old in search of herself. Living on the streets for more than a year had not only hardened her heart, but she'd taken on so many jobs involving manual labor, her body turned to chiseled granite. And the women…well, the women, especially the older ones, were willing to pay for what she had to offer. But two years of hard living and an unpredictable place to lay her head at night forced her to reconsider. The day she met Liv had changed her life for the better.

She leaned back in her chair and closed her eyes, allowing herself to fall into the fond memory…

Cam was considering her options for the evening as she scanned the room. Several of her past hookups were at the bar, including one guy who paid well and didn't ask for much, but she wasn't in a good mood, and the thought of having to smile and act like she was into what she was doing seemed too much like work. She drained her glass and stared into the bottom, wondering what she should do.

"I don't think that's the way to get a refill."

She hadn't even noticed the arrival of the older, handsome woman who occupied the stool next to her. "I'm willing to try anything once."

The woman's eyebrow lifted, a smile playing at the corners of her full-lipped mouth. "Not the first time I've heard that line." She'd stuck out her hand. "Olivia. Friends call me Liv."

Cam slid her palm into the outstretched one and was surprised to find it both firm and soft. "Marta." She tipped her head toward the occupied tables. "They don't call me that." She wondered what Liv wanted and if she could get lost in the kind, soulful green eyes that washed over her body like a soothing balm. Unfortunately, she was attracted to her, and she'd known it wouldn't take much to give in if asked.

Liv slid her fingers slowly across Cam's palm. "Who are 'they' and what do they call you?"

She looked around the darkened space, taking in the customers. Not one person she saw could be considered a friend. They were all tricks, casual acquaintances, or total strangers. She turned back.

"I don't know. No one really knows me. I don't pay attention to what they call me." She looked into her glass again, wishing she could wash down the pit of loneliness that felt like a rock in her throat. Even though she'd made her own way, she was still virtually alone, and the weight of acknowledging how pathetic her life had been ever since she could remember threatened to pull her into the abyss of despair she'd barely managed to rise above.

Liv slid a fresh drink in front of her. "Sometimes having no ties is good." She drank from her beer, her eyes never leaving Cam's. "Sometimes not."

Her line rang, jarring her back. "Stark."

"Hey, Cam. I've got some information on the Stillman case that might close it. Can I stop in when I get back?"

"Of course. I'll be here another couple hours."

The walk down memory lane had been a pleasant distraction from being preoccupied by her distaste for the system she was about to delve into. But she might not have met Liv if she hadn't been, so there was some good that came out of the bad.

❖

Sarah looked at the booklet of pre-printed pages. After she'd left the office, she returned home and pulled out every piece of family history she could find. Of course, they were her family's history. There wasn't much in the way of references to her biological mother or father, and nothing about her brother, but if she combed through the clippings and albums her family had stored in totes in the attic, maybe something would jump out at her. She wanted to get them back to Camdyn as soon as possible, especially since she told Sarah the information would serve as a starting point. Which she was sure meant Camdyn wasn't going to do a lick to find her brother until she had the papers in front of her.

"I still don't know if I completely trust her," Sarah grumbled.

For a minute, she'd almost changed her mind, thinking she'd picked the wrong person to do the job. That was before she saw all the times the phone lines had flashed with incoming calls and had heard the faint ping of emails throughout their meeting. That, along with the additional verifiable references Sarah had found, added credence to the quality of work Camdyn performed, and she believed her instincts were working. Just because the woman was full of herself didn't mean she couldn't get the job done. That was all Sarah really cared about.

After changing into lounge pants and a sweatshirt, Sarah flicked the light switch and climbed the attic stairs. Dust particles swirled in the rarely disturbed air, reminding her of happier times when she and her mother would come up to gather Christmas decorations. The red tote she remembered her mother stashing bits of memorabilia in would be in the far corner, under the eaves. She looked around, taking in items carefully stowed in plastic bags, boxes, and containers. All marked with her mother's distinctive, sweeping handwriting. Unshed tears burned behind her eyes. All of her parents' history had been lovingly saved, along with her achievements. Maybe someday she'd have a family of her own and she'd do the same thing for posterity's sake, but she couldn't dwell on what might never happen.

She dragged the tote to the edge of the stairs and carried it down to the dining table. Something was written on the top, covered by a thick layer of dust. She swiped it away and drew in a breath. Two words printed in thick black letters. My Life. Sarah collapsed in a chair, saddened that her mother's full, rich life had been reduced to one box. She did nothing to stop the tears that followed.

Chapter Four

C am?" Maggie called from the front desk.
"Yeah?"

"The Peters woman is on her way here to drop off the question-naire. You want me to close your door?"

Cam sat back and considered the question. If Sarah saw her, she'd most likely want to talk to her and remind Cam how important it was that she find her brother. A fact she was well aware of. But the thought of seeing Sarah with her feisty attitude warmed her insides, although she wasn't entirely clear why. Aside from both having been raised by people other than their birth parents, they had little in common. Sarah was anything but the type of reserved woman she normally gravitated toward. One that let her maintain control of the situation. If she were being honest, Sarah had her at odds. She should just do her job and ignore how attractive she was. Maggie cleared her throat as she leaned against the doorjamb.

"No. It's okay."

Maggie's eyebrows rose in response. Cam ignored her by focusing on her computer screen. She wasn't about to analyze it. A few minutes later, she heard Maggie's voice loud and clear.

"Good afternoon, Ms. Peters."

Cam sighed, bracing herself for what she was sure would be an interrogation from Maggie with regards to why Sarah was given the rare privilege of knowing Cam was in her office. Most of the time when a client showed without an appointment, her door stayed closed, and Maggie convincingly talked about how rare it was for Cam to be at her desk with the caseload she had. Cam wondered what she'd do if Sarah asked if she was in. It didn't take long for her to find out.

"I filled this out the best I could." Sarah sounded despondent.

"Yes. I'm sure you did. I'll give it to Ms. Stark as soon as possible." The sound of a file drawer opening and closing echoed in the lobby.

"I don't suppose she's in."

It was more of a statement than a question, and Cam rose, taking her time reaching the doorway. She cocked her hip against the casing and crossed her arms. "As a matter of fact, I am."

Sarah displayed a pinched smile, and Cam caught Maggie's eye roll.

"I brought over the papers. I'm afraid a lot of it's blank." She looked at the floor, her embarrassment clear.

Cam wanted to reassure Sarah even the smallest piece of information helped. Instead, she went to the file cabinet and pulled out the file labeled "Peters, S" with the date of hire. She scanned the sheets and her shoulders fell. Virtually every question had been left blank. She had her work cut out for her. Schooling her disappointment, she smiled at Sarah.

"If you have a few minutes, I'd like to ask some additional questions."

"Yes, of course. Anything to help."

She motioned to her office and Sarah went in. She turned and stuck her tongue out at Maggie, knowing she would have a few questions of her own when Sarah left.

Sarah watched her expectantly as she flipped to a blank page on her pad and opened the folder. Cam cleared her throat.

"Ms. Peters—" she began.

"Sarah."

"Right. Sarah, there isn't a lot for me to go on here." Cam masked her disappointment. The deep desire to give Sarah hope made her uneasy. "Do you think there may be documents you haven't gone through?"

"I suppose anything's possible. I haven't gone through everything in the attic. It's…"

Sarah was obviously struggling, and Cam wished she could offer comfort, but that would be unprofessional.

"I'll try to get through it this week."

Cam had spent more than a year trying to find her mother, and she'd started with more information than Sarah had provided. *I was looking for a challenge.* Wish granted.

She smiled. "That's fine." The typed questionnaire mocked her. There wasn't any reason to continue the meeting, so why was she stalling? A knock on the door made her look up.

Maggie leaned in the office doorway. "Sorry to interrupt. You have a scheduled meeting in ten minutes."

Sarah's cheeks became rosy. Maggie never interrupted her when there was a client in her office unless Cam had called her in. So why now?

"Thank you. If we're not finished when they arrive, offer them something to drink and have them wait."

"Yes, Ms. Stark." Maggie's reluctance to leave was obvious, and Cam hoped Sarah hadn't noticed.

"Sarah, if there's nothing else…" Sarah's intent focus on her stole Cam's breath. How had she not noticed her amazing blue eyes? But that wasn't the only thing about Sarah she was cued in on. The sprinkling of freckles across her nose gave her a youthful appearance, and if she hadn't already known her date of birth, she would have guessed she was barely in her twenties.

"I almost forgot. I wanted to give you this." Sarah reached into her oversized bag and produced a faded picture of a smiling woman holding an infant with light colored hair.

Cam studied the dog-eared photo. She took in all of Sarah's features again. Just to check for a resemblance with the woman in the photo.

"I think the baby is me. I have no idea who the woman holding me is." Sarah's eyes revealed her confusion.

Cam flipped the photo over. The April 1, 1989, on the back was close to Sarah's birthday. She would have been two weeks old. "Do you have a picture of your adoptive mother?"

"Yes, of course, but how will that help?"

"I'll scan it into the computer and do a comparison to double-check. Make sure it isn't your deceased parent."

Sarah dug around more in her bag. "I know I have it..." Her eyes flashed on Cam. "It's just..." She abruptly looked up. "I took out the pouch of important papers for policy numbers. It must be home. It has my parents' pictures in it."

Cam saw the slight tremor of Sarah's lip, though she sat rigid as stone. While she'd never known the loss of a mother's love, she could imagine how it would feel if she lost Liv, and her heartstrings tugged. "It's all right. Another time."

"I could run home."

She almost gave in, but she couldn't fall into the trap of caring for Sarah on a personal level. She didn't let women get close enough to see inside. She had to maintain her distance. "I'm expecting a client, but you could drop it off at the desk." Cam gestured in the direction of where Maggie sat in the outer office.

Sarah nodded, then stood. "Yes, okay. I've taken enough of your time." She appeared to want to say more but extended her hand. "Thank you."

Cam stood. "You're welcome, Sarah. Thanks for coming by." She hung on a little longer than necessary. Sarah nodded. The door quietly closed behind her.

Once alone, she stared down at the photo. She should remove herself before it was too late and give the case to Kevin. Adoption and Social Services weren't things she wanted to be involved with. They hit too close to home. But even while considering the option, it wasn't what she would do. She tapped the edge of the photo. This was a thread she might be able to follow. The only question was to where.

Cam rubbed her temples. She'd been looking at screen after screen of random statistics and entries based on Sarah's date of birth and the city she was born in. Since she was a twin, her brother had arrived either a little before or after Sarah, but she didn't have a time to go by, and the number of twins born had been more than she'd expected. Ten sets of twins had been born in Dover, Delaware, in the two major hospitals over a twenty-four-hour period. Of course, there was also the distinct possibility the person she was looking for had been born on the other side of midnight, so she had to check for twins with different DOBs, too. Then there was the task of finding birth certificates. Sarah had a copy of her amended birth certificate, but Cam questioned if Sarah's birth mother had used her real name in the hospital. What were the odds her name was Mary Jones? And to make matters worse, the father was listed as "unknown" in the letter from her adoptive mother.

She fought against the nausea. A migraine was starting, and there wasn't much she could do to ward it off if she stayed at the office. She needed to find a dark, quiet location. Fast. And she needed to eat, a little detail she'd neglected aside from the pot of coffee she'd nursed her way through and the bag of stale pretzels she'd found in the bottom of her drawer. Cam jotted a few notes and shut down the computer while she thought about her options. There were several restaurants on her way home, but there was only one destination that really appealed to her. She locked up the office, jumped in her SUV, and headed to her favorite place.

The sign above the door was an understatement. Dead End Bar & Grill was a hangout frequented by the locals. It was where the bored retirees and the married folks who didn't want to go home spent their time and money. She should know. She'd spent a fair amount of both here when she started the agency. A lack of clientele meant she had nothing to do, and occasionally she'd find a lonely woman looking for an escape. She didn't mind providing the service.

"Cam. Been a while." Jack, the bartender who reminded her of the well-aged bourbon they occasionally shared, stood at the end of the bar. His handlebar mustache stuck out a good four inches from the sides of his face, and his barrel of a chest gave the impression he was slow and out of shape. Looks could be deceiving.

She settled on a stool so her back was to a wall rather than the door. Slapping a twenty on the bar, she smiled at him. "You know how it is."

Jack nodded. He'd probably heard every excuse there was for why people did this or that. "You here to hook up or to drown out?"

Laughter bubbled from her throat. Jack had a unique way of conversing with his customers. "Neither. Trying to ward off a migraine. Is Connie here?" Connie made the best burger she'd ever had, and each night of the week, the toppings changed. It was an odd place to find the best of anything, but the bar was known for its ice-cold beer and stick-to-your-ribs food.

"Yep." He grabbed a bottle of stout and leaned into the kitchen doorway. "Cam's hungry."

Connie yelled back. "When ain't she...for something? Ten minutes."

Cam shook her head and watched Jack efficiently pour beer into a frosted mug. It arrived in front of her with a short head of foam, the way she liked it. The first sip was always the best. The rest wasn't bad either. She glanced at Jack as he polished glasses.

"So, what have I missed?" Her hand went to her temple, the knife edge of pain slicking along her nerve track. It wanted to take her down. She took a couple of deep breaths and relaxed the muscles in her face and jaw. Tension was her enemy.

Jack wiped the bar; the scent of bleach tickled her nose.

"Same old. Charlie fell off his stool last week. Whacked his shoulder pretty good. Lucky for him Doc was here to check him out; said he'd be bruised but okay." He leaned against the back shelf where an impressive array of libations was backlit by typical bar lighting, drawing customers in and separating them from their hard-earned pay. For not much more than the cost of a couple of drinks, they could have a whole bottle, but then they'd miss out on Jack's lively conversational skills.

Her shoulders eased from her ears. The feeling of being on familiar ground was welcoming. Jack continued catching her up.

"Mike went missing for a few days. No one knew where he was. Thought I was gonna have to call on your professional services." He reached inside the kitchen, then set the steaming plate of food and a bottle of ketchup in front of her. "He finally showed up wearing a huge smile. Apparently, he'd been holed up with a woman who'd done him right. He was wearing clean, ironed clothes. Smelled of aftershave. Told us not to worry if we saw less of him."

Cam blew on a fry and bit into it. The crispy coating was full of flavor with a bit of a kick. Blissful. "Good for him." *If only I could be as fortunate to find a woman who would look after me for a change.* She applied a liberal amount of ketchup to her burger and took a bite. Horseradish cheese, lettuce, bacon, and a bit of mashed avocado burst through the well-seasoned meat. She made a noise of satisfaction after a thorough chew and swallowed.

"Connie! You outdid yourself. This is the best," Cam yelled toward the kitchen.

Connie's head popped out of the doorway. "I know. That's why you keep coming back." She disappeared into the mysterious area where the magic happened. Cam liked to think the space was pristine, but she didn't want to find out if it was otherwise. Some things were better left unknown.

While she ate, she thought about Sarah and her mesmerizing eyes. She'd waffled during their last meeting, vacillating between composed and vulnerable. Still—there was an undeniable connection. Either way, she had a job to do, and as difficult as it was proving to be, she was determined to provide Sarah with as much information as possible.

By the time she was done eating, the migraine had receded, leaving a soreness in its wake that she would gladly deal with.

Jack took her plate and pointed to the empty mug. "Another?"

As tempting as another cold one sounded, she'd accomplished what she'd come for...for tonight. "Nah. I've got a full belly and a hot case that needs tending." Hot might have described Sarah, but not the case. So far there'd been nothing to follow. She tossed an extra five-dollar bill down and smiled. "Next time."

Sarah finished the last weld and turned down her torch, flipping back her shield with a nod of her head. After pulling her gloves off, she grabbed the insulated water bottle always hanging on a carabiner from her tool belt, and let the cool liquid soothe her parched throat. She was glad this job was almost finished. She was going to take a few days and catch up on the yard and house chores that had been neglected far too long. She'd spent most of her free time sitting vigil at her mother's bedside. The thought she might die alone had wiped away all other concerns, and even though she couldn't afford to miss work, she'd made sure she was with her whenever she could.

That was then. There was no one to rush home to now. She had to turn her focus inward and concentrate on what was important to her happiness, and her future. It wasn't that she regretted being an only child. She'd had her parents' undivided attention and they had doted on her while providing the means for her to develop a level head. With their deaths came a reckoning of the dreams and desires she'd pushed to the background while she cared for them. Dreams of finding a special someone to share the type of adoration that had been so evident between her parents. When she was in high school, she'd thought about having a family of her own with a couple of kids and a loving partner. She might even find time to seriously pursue her love of metal sculpting. She might not be able to paint a portrait, but she had an artistic flair and had sold a couple of small pieces of art over the years. Could she juggle work, a family, and her art? Did she want to consider having them all in her life? When she thought about her childhood and all of the fun and love her parents had provided, she knew the answer was yes. She did want it *all*. Even though she'd decided in her early twenties she much preferred women over men, it didn't rule out her ideal of the perfect family unit. Her children might even have an uncle if the self-assured Camdyn Stark came through and made good on her promise.

The first time they'd met, Sarah had been convinced Camdyn was a lesbian. Between her manner of dress, the confidence she exuded, and the knowing looks they'd shared, Sarah was fairly certain her assumption was correct. *She probably spends her nights hooking up.* Sarah snorted. What Camdyn did on her own time wasn't any of Sarah's concern.

Satisfied with the quality of her work, Sarah picked up her tools and climbed down the cross section of iron beams. Construction was her first love, but she enjoyed the artistic side of metallurgy and wished she had more time and resources to pursue it. Creating art centered her, like the job she was on, but in a much different way. At work, she had to be ever conscious of where she stepped. How far away the next beam was. Where her coworkers were. She didn't have a fear of heights, but she had respect for how quickly a careless moment could take her life. She couldn't be distracted like she had been the past few days. At least when she'd daydreamed about her future before her world had turned upside down, she'd been sitting and not walking the narrow intersections of steel far above the pavement below.

The short drive to the dilapidated garage that served as Sarah's studio gave her a chance to regroup. She parked on the uneven, pothole ridden driveway, and then unlocked the door with her remote. She gathered her tools and set them on the workbench. Looking around the cramped area made her sad. The peeling walls and pitted cement floor were older than she was. The overhead shop light dangled from a frayed cord; the only thing holding it up were the two chains suspended from the open rafters. She'd rented the space and used it to complete welding jobs she picked up to supplement her income. Her parents' insurance had been okay while they'd been healthy, but with her father's heart attacks and her mother's cancer treatments, the bills had skyrocketed. They'd had no choice but to take out a home equity loan. Sarah helped as much as she could by picking up odd jobs and repairing broken objects, like stair railings. Thankfully, the owner of the garage knew her parents and let her have it cheap, but there was still electric and heat to pay for. She didn't mind the hard work, and often got lost in the methodical approach to each joint soldered before polishing them smooth. She wondered if Camdyn had ever done physical work, though the muscles she'd glimpsed beneath her fitted clothes had to have come from somewhere, but for some reason she couldn't see Camdyn as a gym rat. She chided herself for letting her mind wander to a person she hardly knew, and turned her attention to the random pieces of metal she'd shape into something abstract, something that would have meaning and substance, not like her speculations of Camdyn.

Two hours and a new art project later, Sarah admired what had started out as a couple of bent rebar rods and two large, rusted industrial padlocks. She'd ground everything to remove the flakes, then heated and twisted the items until they fit in some semblance of the vision that took shape as she worked. Once she was sure all the metal was sufficiently cooled, she locked the door, then got into her ten-year-old car. It wasn't the worst she'd ever seen on the road, and it was mostly dependable. She hoped it would remain that way for a few more years. The quiet engine turned over, although that wasn't always guaranteed. She should have it repaired, but it was an expense she'd rather not deal with. She backed out of the driveway and headed for home. Unwarranted tears fell. It wasn't often she let the grief of loss overtake her. When it did, there wasn't anything she could do to stop it. With no one to go home to and no one who would miss her, she wiped the tears away and changed lanes. She needed an escape. Somewhere she could get lost in the crowd and maybe lose herself for a little while.

Ten minutes later, she parked at the end of the block. Decade's neon sign was a beacon among the otherwise drab storefronts, most of which were closed for the night. She looked in the mirror and laughed. She had smudges on her face. Her black T-shirt hid whatever dirt was there, and she knew there was plenty. Her torn jeans were still clean, even though they had a few holes in questionable locations. They'd have to do. At least she'd remembered to put on underwear today, not something she did on a daily basis. She preferred long skirts to pants, but they were impractical when welding, not to mention dangerous. The glove box held an array of items she kept for emergencies such as this. The can of store brand wipes was almost empty, and she added it to the growing list of things she needed to buy. A few scrubs and the marks were gone, leaving her skin pink and clean. She could pull off the androgynous look when she wanted to, and not wearing makeup made it easier, even if she preferred her feminine side. After a final check for her ID and money, she nodded at her reflection. *Time to get lost.*

CHAPTER FIVE

Sarah held a piece of scrap metal she'd found during her latest round of "trash to treasure" as she liked to call her foraging through neighborhoods on trash nights. A stiff wire brush would remove all the loose oxidized particles from the surface. Her cell vibrated across the bench. She read the display as she removed a glove, then swiped the screen to answer.

"Hi, Lisa."

"What's shakin'?"

She giggled at Lisa's attempt at being cool. She probably didn't realize her choice of words were outdated by a decade or more. "Playing in the shop."

"Have you heard anything yet?"

She went outside with a can of diet soda and sat in the dilapidated lawn chair she'd confiscated from a pile of trash by the road. Some of her best finds came from the items discarded by others. "No, but it's only been a little over a week. Camdyn said it would take time. I just have to be patient." Thoughts of what kind of work Camdyn was doing to fulfill their contract constantly nagged her thoughts. "I called earlier, but she was out of town." Sarah had the distinct feeling the secretary at the office didn't care for her. She'd been professional when they'd spoken, but there wasn't any warmth in her tone.

"Oh. Maybe that's a good sign." Lisa sounded upbeat.

Her enthusiasm was more than Sarah could generate. "Maybe. I pulled down the last two totes from the attic. I'll go through them later."

"Want some help? We can grab a bite to eat after. My treat."

"You don't have to do that." Lisa was aware of how tight her finances were, but that didn't mean she had to foot the bill when they went out.

"I know. I want to."

❖

"Wow, this is old." Sarah held up a yellowed document, the edges curling and cracked.

Lisa carefully took the document from Sarah. "It's Anne's parents' marriage license." She brought it closer to the light. "It's dated nineteen forty-four. I wonder how old they were."

"Mom didn't have a lot of pictures of her parents in the album. Probably because they lived in Tennessee, if I remember right. She and Dad moved to Delaware right after they were married so he could find work. I only remember seeing my grandparents a few times while I was growing up. They were kind enough, but we didn't do much family stuff together."

Sarah wondered why that was. Granted, they'd been about eight hundred miles from them, but it wasn't across the country. Though it might have seemed like it back then. Maybe they hadn't approved of her parents' marriage, or her adoption. She shook her head, wondering what had made her so judgmental. First with Camdyn, now with her grandparents, even though she didn't have any real reason to dislike either of them. She needed to get her anger under control. It wasn't anyone's fault her parents had died. Maybe she wanted to have someone to blame for feeling abandoned and alone. What she needed to remember was she wasn't alone. Lisa was there, and if Camdyn was as good as she claimed, she might even have a brother. Sometimes family kept distance from one another for odd reasons.

"What are you thinking?" Lisa tipped her head.

"Sometimes I wonder if looking for a sibling who doesn't know I exist is wise."

Lisa scooted closer. "I thought you wanted to find him?"

She glanced down at the assortment of cards, letters, and miscellaneous papers piled around her. "I did. I mean…I do, but…"

"Sarah, it's okay to question it. You can stop any time. Right?"

Sarah nodded, and Lisa went on. "Come on. Let's finish here and get cleaned up. Then I'll take you to your favorite restaurant for dinner."

As she piled the stacks back in their containers, she couldn't help feeling they'd provided more questions than answers. Why hadn't she had a closer relationship with her grandparents? Could it be they'd never joined the twentieth century and relied on letters and phone calls alone to stay in touch? Even so, there'd been very little from them in the way of birthday cards. Lord knows, her mother had saved everything else. Thinking of the threads that connected people gave her a better sense of what little Camdyn had to follow, and her appreciation grew, but just a little.

Cam held on to the sides of the toilet seat and leaned her head on her arm. The migraine she'd done her best to ward off earlier had finally won over the meds she'd taken, and her stomach lurched every time she moved. Unable to deny the need to vomit, she'd stumbled into the bathroom and collapsed next to the toilet, losing what little lunch she had left in her stomach. She flicked the handle and moved away from the rancid odor.

"Christ, I look as shitty as I feel."

She washed her face and brushed her teeth. She also wanted a shower, but she was too unsteady on her feet and afraid if she fell she'd become a statistic of accidental death. Her shirt was wrinkled beyond salvaging, so she tossed it aside before pulling a clean sweater on, then ran her fingers through her hair. Her stomach revolted at the thought of food, but with a need for caffeine, she didn't have a choice. She wished someone was there to go with her. *Where the hell did that come from?* She was quite capable of handling things on her own. She'd been doing it for years.

Her stomach gurgled again, and she didn't want to be embarrassed by having to bolt through a restaurant to the restroom. She fingered through the stack of take-out menus and picked the least offensive. The local bistro did a great wood-fired pizza, but they didn't deliver. After placing her order that included a small antipasto, she considered how wise it was to be driving in her condition, though she'd done worse things in her life. Lucky for her, she only had to go a few blocks. Dusk was approaching, but there was enough daylight remaining that there wouldn't be much headlight glare. Cam gulped down the fresh air hoping to clear her head.

"Hi. Can I help you?" The woman behind the small podium asked with a smile.

"Take-out order for Stark." Cam forced a smile in return though she felt anything but sociable. The woman disappeared into the kitchen before returning empty-handed. "It'll be a few more minutes. Would you like something while you wait?"

She thought a barf bag might come in handy. "No, thank you." Cam slumped onto the bench by the door and scrolled through the texts she'd missed while she was passed out. Maggie had sent a few, checking on her. Several clients had called, and Maggie covered for her absence by saying Cam was out of town. Maggie hated texting more than emailing. One text from Kevin with an update on a case he was working. A voice mail from Sarah. Her heart beat a little faster. She pressed the icon and listened as Sarah's hesitant voice came through her earpiece.

"Uh, hi. It's Sarah. Sarah Peters." An exasperated sigh could be heard before she continued. "I don't mean to bother you while you're away, but I was going through some papers and found a photo of a baby and a strange note. I don't know if it means anything. Anyway. If you want it, let me know."

She listened to the message again. She should be annoyed that Sarah hadn't given her much time to find info, but then again, she'd told Sarah to call her if she came across anything she thought was important. She looked at the time. It was too late for her to call, and since there wasn't much she could do in her current state, she decided it could wait till morning. As suspected, Maggie had also left a voice mail wanting to know if she was feeling any better and to give her a call tomorrow.

"Miss. Your order is ready."

Cam paid and grabbed the bag. On the drive home, she couldn't help thinking about Sarah's desire to connect with family. She'd had the same desire once. There was only one person she considered her family, and it was never too late to call home.

"Cam, how are you?" Liv's voice rumbled through the phone.

"I've been better." Cam knew no matter the reason for her call it was always welcome. She had come to love Liv in a way she never could have imagined. Not only had Liv given her a hand up when she'd needed it, but she had taught her that love came in a variety of shapes and sizes, and all she had to do was be open to it. They loved each other in a unique way. No other woman would ever take Liv's place.

"Tell me all about it and we'll fix it together."

❖

"Don't be ridiculous. I'm not letting you pay." Sarah didn't want Lisa to think she couldn't pay her own way, even if it were true. She rummaged in what served as a handbag looking for her wallet until her fingers closed around it and she pulled it out. "Ah-ha." She smiled at Lisa before glancing around. She'd spoken a little louder than she intended. The other tables seemed unaware, but her gasp that followed didn't go unnoticed.

"What's the matter? You look like you've seen a ghost," Lisa said.

All Sarah could do was point at Camdyn as she stood near the front door.

"Wow. I mean, I'm not into women, but she's hot." Lisa smirked at her, laughing.

"That's her," Sarah whispered, grabbing Lisa's hand and hoping to keep her quiet.

"Her who?" Lisa asked before she grasped the meaning. "Oh my God, is that the investigator you hired?"

"Yeah." Sarah tried not to stare. Lucky for her, they were toward the back, and Camdyn had sat down near the front door.

Lisa slid the check presenter to the edge of the table. "No wonder you have the hots for her."

"I do not have the hots for her," Sarah hissed.

"Could have fooled me." Lisa signed the bill and took back her card. "Want to say hello?"

Lisa started to rise, and she grabbed her arm, pulling her back to her chair. "No." Sarah said it a little more forcefully than she intended.

"Gee, okay." Lisa rubbed her arm. "If you don't have the hots for her I don't see the harm in being polite."

Sarah shook her head. "We aren't exactly friends, you know. It's a working relationship. It would be weird." Although the thought of being friends wasn't totally out of the question, she couldn't entertain the idea as long as Camdyn was working for her. It wouldn't be right.

"Fine. Whatever you say."

Camdyn stood and went to the cash register. The waitress handed over a brown paper bag, and Sarah experienced a minute of regret as she left. It was obvious Camdyn had ordered dinner and was probably heading home to eat alone. She knew what that felt like.

"Can we go now?"

"In a minute." The last thing Sarah wanted was for Camdyn to see her leave the restaurant with an attractive woman, though the thought was idiotic. What difference did it make if Camdyn saw her and Lisa together? It's not like she was interested in dating Camdyn.

"Whenever you're ready." Lisa stood and the look on her face told Sarah the only person she was kidding was herself.

CHAPTER SIX

Cam opened the file one more time, making sure her paperwork was neat and orderly. There were only two large hospitals in the Dover area—Kent General and Milford Memorial. She'd followed her instincts and driven to Kent. She'd tried several of the more conventional avenues of inquiry including mutual consent registries, which would probably end up being a dead end. Unless Sarah's birth mother had a big change of heart, she wouldn't have given consent for disclosure of her personal information. What was the likelihood that a baby girl Jones, born on March 15, 1989, had a birth mother named Mary Jones? The woman might have given a fake name, especially if her pregnancy had been unplanned to begin with, which was likely the case. It wouldn't be the first time Cam had discovered a fake identity, and since Jones was nearly as common as Smith, Cam's odds of finding the correct birthmother were slim. Sarah's adoptive mother had even questioned her own memory about the birth mother's first name, and Cam wasn't sure she could rely on what she'd read as fact. While she waited for a response to her formal inquiry, Cam had kept digging. Which brought her here.

The first thing she had to do was find the maternity ward. Against her better judgment, she slid her gun from its holster and locked it in the glove compartment. After all these years, she felt naked and vulnerable without it, but hospitals frowned on armed individuals. Even more so in maternity wards.

The wing she wanted was to her left. Maternity was on the fourth floor. She took a deep breath and reviewed her speech. The elevator's monotone voice announced she would be "going up." Cam disliked automation, like those nondescript voices that told her to press one for balance inquiries, two to make a payment, etcetera, etcetera. Elevators were another thing she disliked immensely. This one was dark and a bit dingy. The lights flickered and she held on to the railing as it rattled and jerked upward on cables she was sure would break any second and send her hurtling to her death. The rush of air when the doors opened allowed her to breathe again, and she nearly leapt into the hallway, vowing to take the stairs when she was done. Cam approached the reception desk, and an elderly woman looked up and smiled at her.

"Hello. May I help you?"

She read the woman's name badge and smiled back. "I hope so, Sandra. I'm looking to speak with a nurse who would have worked here in the late 1980s."

"My, my. That's a long time ago. Tell me the person's name."

She'd planned ahead for the most common questions and leaned a little closer. "I wish I knew." She showed her badge and ID, hoping it would put the woman at ease. "I'm on an investigation and reached a dead end. Any information would be helpful."

Sandra's eyes grew big, the excitement clear on her face. "Oh dear. Let me think. Ruth has been here longer than I have, and I've been a clerk in the ward for twenty-five years. Maybe she was working here back then."

"Do you think I could speak with her?" Cam's heartbeat picked up pace. It always did when she was on a trail.

"I'm not sure. She may have already left for the day." Sandra's index finger ran down a list of phone numbers taped on the desk near the phone. "Let me call and see." She punched numbers into the keypad and then looked up expectantly, her hand waving in the air in a "hurry up" motion. Regret showed on her face before she spoke again. "I'm sorry, I don't think…" Sandra began, then stopped. "Ruth, you're still here." After a brief pause, she went on. "I know, but I need to ask you something. Were you working maternity in the late eighties?" Sandra's head did that side-to-side thing one did when listening to someone drone on. She smiled at Cam and held up her finger. "There's someone at my desk that wants to speak with you…well, that's up to you." Another pause. "Okay. I'll tell her to wait." She looked satisfied as she put the phone down. "She'll be right down, but I'm not sure how long she'll stay. She's had a rough day."

"I do appreciate your help." She slid a business card onto the counter and wrote her work cell number on the back. "If there's anyone else from that time frame who might be able to help, feel free to give me a call." Cam pressed the card into Sandra's hand and let her fingers linger briefly. Sandra's face flushed.

"I certainly will." Sandra was studying the card when a tall woman with silver hair rounded the corner. Sandra proceeded with the unnecessary introductions.

"Is there somewhere we can talk privately?" Cam asked. When Ruth hesitated, she said, "I'll only take a few minutes of your time."

Ruth nodded and gestured to an open door a little way down the hall. Once they were inside, she closed the door behind them.

"I'm not sure I can help with whatever it is you're looking for. The eighties were a long time ago."

She handed over the recent picture of Sarah. "This woman, Sarah Peters, is looking for her twin brother. I believe they were born here under the last name Jones, and separated shortly after. Her adoptive parents died recently and she has no family." Cam knew it was a cheap shot to play on Ruth's emotions, but it was all she had. She pulled out another picture from the file in her briefcase. It was from a couple of days after Sarah was born. "She has an amended birth certificate and not much else."

Ruth studied the photos. "She's grown into a beautiful woman."

Cam inwardly agreed but waited while the woman's eyes briefly glassed over while her finger traced the baby picture of her in a hospital bassinet. The sign, though a bit blurry, stated Baby girl Jones, six pounds, one ounce, seventeen and one-half inches.

"The boy was very sick." Ruth looked up at Cam. "I remember them because they were my first set of twins. The girl was robust and healthy. We put them in the same bassinet and she held on to his hand when he cried. This must have been taken when her brother was having tests or being fed." She slid the baby picture across the table and picked up the one of an adult Sarah. "I knew she'd be okay." Ruth handed it over.

"Do you remember the mother's name or any other details?"

Ruth closed her eyes and took a breath. When she opened them again it was obvious she was trying to not cry. "It broke my heart when I heard they were put up for adoption. Even more so when I learned they were being separated." Her lips pursed. "Sarah?" She tipped her chin at the photos, and Cam nodded. "She was taken first." Ruth wistfully smiled. "The young couple looked so happy when they held her. I was happy for them."

"And the boy?" Cam asked.

Ruth's face darkened. "He screamed the minute his sister left. I don't know what happened to him because I was off for a few days. He was gone when I came in for my shift. I asked around, and another nurse said an agency came for him."

Cam tried to hide her disappointment, but she must have failed because Ruth touched her hand.

"The other nursery RN is retired, but she lives in the area. We're friends. Her memory is better than mine. Maybe she could tell you more," Ruth said.

Maybe there was hope after all. "Do you think she'd talk to me?"

"I'm sure she would. A little intrigue will spice up her life." Ruth winked. "If you know what I mean."

Cam wrote her cell number on the back of another card and handed it to her. "If you can give her my number I'd appreciate it. I'll be in town until tomorrow sometime."

Ruth stood as she read the information. "Stark Revelations." She glanced up, smiling. "Clever."

Cam grinned and waved over her shoulder as she turned into the corridor. She looked for the stairs and pushed through the door, glad she didn't have to endure another minute in the death trap called an elevator. She got to the first floor and pulled out her phone to call the office as she headed to her car.

"Stark Revelations, Maggie speaking."

"Hi, Mags."

"Hi, boss. How's it going?"

"I might, and that's a big might, have a lead. In the meantime, I'm calling for messages." Cam rubbed her temple. The telltale signs of an impending headache forced her to take the medication that made her groggy. She hated the feeling almost more than the migraine.

"Thank God. Sarah Peters called again. I told her you were on a stakeout and that I likely wouldn't see you until tomorrow."

Cam remembered the way she'd rolled her eyes the last time Sarah had been at the office. Then she'd interrupted them. Both were so unlike Maggie's usual behavior. Something was bothering Maggie and Cam needed to know what it was. "What's eating at you about the Peters woman? I haven't seen you like this in ages."

Maggie huffed into the phone. "It's not her, it's you."

"What about me?"

"Don't play coy with me, Camdyn. You know perfectly well what I mean. You were practically falling all over her when she showed up."

"I was not." She pulled into the parking lot, used a key to unlock her hotel room door, then flipped on the lights and winced.

"I should know. I was watching." Maggie's "Don't bull me" voice rang through loud and clear.

Whatever. "Mags, I'm medicated. Give me a break, okay?"

"Aww, poor you. Okay...for now. You want the rest of your calls?"

Cam turned out the overhead lights and turned on the desk lamp. "Please."

A few minutes later, she lay on the bed, a cold washcloth on her head. She hated these unpredictable interruptions to her life. Her neurologist told her it was a result of the two concussions she'd suffered in childhood, both at the hands of foster care. She'd lost consciousness the second time, waking up a few hours later in the emergency room. Luckily, the foster mother had panicked when she hadn't responded to being shaken and called an ambulance, telling the rescue squad she'd fallen and hit her head. The ER staff noticed unusual bruises and called in their social worker. The migraines had started a few years later, though she hadn't known that's what they were for a long time.

Her thoughts drifted to Sarah. It made her laugh to think Mags was irritated by Sarah more than she was. Maybe that was because Cam believed if she took on a case, the client deserved answers. It couldn't be because she was attracted to Sarah, even though she *was* captivating. She was just anxious to provide some answers, or not, and close the case. The sooner the better. Wanting to move on was understandable. Sarah's attractiveness had nothing to do with it. Nothing at all.

❖

"Is this Camdyn Stark?"

"Yes, it is. Can I ask who's calling?" Cam didn't recognize the number, but then, she rarely did.

"Julie Rice, a nurse from the hospital. I'm a friend of Ruth's, and she asked me to call you."

"It's good to hear from you, Ms. Rice. Would it be possible to meet? I have a couple of pictures I'd like to show you, along with a few questions about babies you took care of a long time ago."

"Well...I suppose it would be okay." Julie hesitated.

"Any public location would be fine. A diner or coffee shop. Wherever you like." People were wary these days with the state of the world and often felt more at ease in a familiar setting.

"That would be fine. Do you know Vickie's on Johnson Boulevard? It's a coffee shop and bakery. They have the most delicious pastries."

Cam had just left the local library. She'd spent the early morning poring over birth announcements in the archives of the local newspapers but hadn't had any luck. "I'll find it. Would eleven o'clock be too soon?" She did a search for the address. It would only take her fifteen minutes to get there, but she needed to check out of the hotel first. She wanted to get home by early afternoon. Sarah's wasn't her only case, even though it seemed that way at times.

"Perfect. I'll see you then."

"I'll be there." Cam almost hung up until she heard "wait" coming through the earpiece.

"Yes?"

"How will I know it's you?"

"Safety first. I like that. I'll be driving a dark gray Charger and wearing a red sweater with black pants."

"Got it."

Forty-five minutes later, Cam pulled up to the short block lined with storefronts and parked a few spaces down from Vickie's. True to Julie's description, there were signs in the window boasting the best coffee cake in town, making her mouth water. It wasn't often she treated herself to sweets, but today she felt like breaking the rules.

The little bell over the door announced her arrival, and everyone looked in her direction. She'd learned a while ago that small town residents always looked for a familiar face. Since she wasn't one, they soon went back to their conversations. All except a gray-haired woman sitting in the third booth. She hesitated for a second before motioning Cam over. Cam extended her hand.

"Hello, it's nice to meet you, Ms. Rice."

The woman's intelligent eyes took her in as she settled on the bench across from her. "Likewise. Ruth said she spoke with you."

"Yes, ma'am."

"You mind showing me some ID?"

Cam fished out her wallet and flipped it open. It held her driver's license on one side and her PI badge on the other.

Julie leaned forward, then nodded. "Can't be too careful nowadays."

They ordered coffee when the waitress came over. Cam perused the one-sided menu and added a sample plate of baked goods. Julie smiled.

"Got a sweet tooth, do you?"

She laughed. "My secret is out."

"I know how to keep a secret." Julie's demeanor changed from light and flirty to subdued.

"Do you have a secret you want to share?" Cam asked. The hair on the back of her neck bristled, a sign she thought she was getting close to a piece of the puzzle.

Julie giggled, making her appear younger. She leaned forward, her eyes flashing around the busy diner as if making sure no one was paying attention to them. "It's really not a secret, but I do love the cloak-and-dagger feel of it. You love what you do, don't you?"

Cam stared at Julie. The only person who had ever asked her that question had been Liv. "The easy answer is yes. *Why* I do has a whole bunch of connotations I can't really explain."

Julie patted her hand. "Oh, I get that, honey. People used to ask me all the time how I could take care of babies knowing some of them were going home to the worst parents in the world." She shrugged, her face somber. "I loved each one in my care. That's the best I could do for them."

"I'm sure you did." The silence between them stretched out for a long beat until the waitress returned. The aroma of strong coffee and sweet pastries filled the intimate space between them.

"You must try some of everything, Camdyn. They are simply to die for." Julie used her knife to cut each one in half.

"Call me Cam." She looked down at the platter. "I don't know where to start."

"Which one do you want the most?"

The choice was easy. "Coffee cake."

"Then leave that to last, so you can savor the flavor after it's gone." Julie winked at her.

Cam slid a pastry onto her plate. "Let's get down to business, shall we?"

Julie took a bite, and the flaky bits reminded Cam of falling snow. "It was a long time ago, but some things you never forget."

Cam agreed, though there were times she wished she could.

"There's my favorite PI. How did it go, boss?"

Cam was reluctant to tell Maggie about her rough night. "I spoke with two of the RNs who worked the nursery when Sarah was born." She didn't make eye contact and Maggie must have sensed her angst. She always did.

"You're killing me." Maggie touched her forearm. "What's wrong?"

Cam shrugged. She didn't want her to worry, but even she was concerned about the frequency of her headaches and how severe they'd become. "Nothing. I was hoping for more, but at least I have a real first name for Sarah's birth mother. The nurse I spoke to was adamant it was Judy. It's a long shot, but better than nothing." She turned for her office, hoping to avoid Maggie's scrutiny. No such luck.

"Good. About the case. But that's not what I'm talking about."

Cam finally looked up, and Maggie studied her with such singular focus she wanted to move away and slam the door on her, but she couldn't. Next to Liv, Maggie was the closest friend she had. She couldn't hide anything from her.

Maggie led her into her office then guided her to the small couch before sitting next to her. "How bad was it?" Maggie's forehead wrinkled in concern.

She'd done her best that morning to not have the lingering fatigue show during her interview. Once she'd reached the office, though, she let the bravado slip away. She slumped back, letting her head rest on the soft cushion, and closed her eyes. "Bad enough that I threw up, and that was *after* I'd medicated. Twice."

"Don't you think it's time to go see Dr. Bryant again?"

Cam drew her fingertips across her temples, the flesh beneath still sore in the aftermath of what she called a "tsunami" migraine. "For what? I know what caused it. There's no cure and I'm already on meds. Why waste the money?"

"Maybe she could prescribe something different. Or maybe there's something you can try to ward the next one off." Maggie, always the optimist.

She wished it could be that simple. From the time she was seventeen she'd been treated for them; the answer was always the same. If you feel one coming on, take your medication. If that doesn't work, get somewhere dark and lie down. Take more meds.

Drink caffeinated beverages. Blah, blah. Cam sat up and leaned her elbows on her knees.

"I don't have the time or the energy to go through it all again, Mags. I'll just deal with it."

Maggie pursed her lips.

"I'll try to get more sleep and slow down a little to see if it helps. In the meantime, I need you to set up an appointment for Sarah Peters to come in. We need to go and file a formal request in person at the Dover Office of Vital Statistics to see if they'll release her real birth certificate without her mother's name blacked out. Because of the adoption, they wouldn't give it to me."

"You want to do an overnight in Dover with Sarah Peters?" Maggie crossed her arms, meaning she was irked at the notion.

"It will be a long day trip unless there's a reason we need to stay." As much as she loved Maggie, sometimes she forgot Cam was her boss. "Just make the appointment like I asked you to, Maggie. Is that clear?"

Maggie's arms dropped to her sides. "Crystal. I'll get right on it." She closed the door behind her a little louder than necessary.

Cam sighed and walked around her desk. She wasn't sure if Maggie's reaction was a result of her dislike for Sarah, or her refusal to do more about her migraines. She didn't want to have that conversation, with her doctor or anyone else. Not again. The men who did this to her were no longer on her radar and would never be able to find her unless they discovered her current name. She and Liv had paid a hefty price to bury her old identity so deep no one would ever find it.

Every trip to her doctor was a blatant reminder of all the things she'd suffered at the hands of her so-called caregivers. Maggie was looking out for her, and she understood her protectiveness, but this wasn't anything anyone could help with. Even her own ability to take care of the headaches was limited. Sometimes they just had to run their course.

The screen showed a message waiting for her. From Maggie. "Christ. Is she that pissed?" She opened the notification and read the text.

Ms. Peters is scheduled to meet you on Friday morning at eight a.m. in the office.

No greeting. No signature. If Maggie's silent treatment continued, it was going to be a long day.

❖

Sarah wrung her hands. The refrigerator held little in the way of comfort food. A cold beer might settle her nerves. The call wasn't totally unexpected since she'd left a message a few days ago. Being asked to travel with Camdyn to Dover was the part that threw her equilibrium off. The assistant stated the sooner the better, but Sarah couldn't afford to miss work. She'd used up most of her sick time, what little there was, during her mother's illness. Vacations were also a luxury. She was up to ten days a year, but she'd been hoping to use them for an actual vacation. In light of the newest development in her life, she needed to save her days in case her brother was found. God knew where she'd have to travel to see him or for how long. It had been a stroke of fortune that the last day of work on her current construction site was Thursday. Friday was originally going to be a day of housework and chores, but this was more important. She'd get to them on the weekend.

Today was only Tuesday. She had to wait three more days to hear if Camdyn had good news. Well, she had to have news of some type, otherwise why would they need to go to Dover? Maybe Camdyn was going to bring her to her brother? Was that the news? No, it couldn't be. *Maybe I should pack an overnight bag, just in case.* The trip would only take a few hours each way, but she wasn't sure of anything except having to file a request in-person at the Dover Municipal Building. Maggie had barely said more than a dozen words. Sarah tipped the bottle to her lips again, surprised it was empty. She needed to get a grip. Certainly if Camdyn had discovered news of consequence, she would have spoken with her personally.

She glanced at the clock over the stove. Time to throw together some dinner and make her lunch for tomorrow. Then she'd go through the last shoebox from the attic that had been tucked behind crates of books from her childhood. Among them were the long-forgotten pen pal letters she'd looked forward to receiving every week. Her parents had signed her up to join the Boys & Girls Club, and one of the activities was picking a pen pal. After she started high school, the letters became less frequent on both their parts, and she missed corresponding with Kelly. Maybe she'd try to find her on Facebook.

She tucked into the corner of the couch, balancing the meager portion of leftover spaghetti on her leg. After settling on a show about travel, she pictured the page in her diary from years gone by that she'd reserved for vacation destinations. Hawaii, Yosemite Park, and the High Peaks of New York were the three she could remember. She'd hoped to have crossed off at least one by now. Sarah looked down at the remnants on her plate. She didn't want to deprive herself anymore. She turned off the TV. She was tired. It was after ten and she needed sleep to be able to function.

Sarah snuggled into the covers, willing herself to drift off, but her mind was a whirlwind of conflicting emotions. Her life was mundane with the same routine day after day. Maybe she'd look into taking a couple of art courses at a local college. She'd have to stay close to home until she got a better car. She needed to do something other than dreaming about places she couldn't afford to go. Cam's life probably wasn't routine at all. She imagined what it must be like to live in her world and wondered what had shaped her into the person she barely knew anything about. Where had she grown up? What was family life like? How much traveling had she done? She might have a few years on Sarah, but certainly she had an unfulfilled bucket list and she was curious what was on it.

The last thing she remembered was the look on Camdyn's face the last time she'd seen her, as though she were really looking at her for the first time. The memory warmed her, sending tendrils of comfort through her as she drifted to sleep.

CHAPTER SEVEN

Cam wasn't sure what she expected, but seeing Sarah in a navy blue tailored skirt and blazer, paired with a white lace shell hadn't been it. There were hints of makeup, which only highlighted her natural beauty. The woman standing in front of her desk was quite different from the one she'd first met. Gone were the peasant skirt and cotton button-down casually thrown over a faded T-shirt. Sarah's voice interrupted her musing.

"Uh…is this okay?" Sarah gestured to her clothes. "I wasn't sure, but I want whoever we speak with to know I'm serious about getting what we need." She gave Cam a knowing look. "I'm not totally without decorum."

"I believe whoever you speak with will give you their full attention. Your clothes demand professional courtesy without being snobbish. They're perfect." *Like you.*

Sarah's cheeks pinked, and Cam was again caught off guard by her extremes. One minute she was shy and demure, and the next fiery and forthright.

"Apparently, your mother hadn't prearranged your adoption, so you were issued a new birth certificate after the fact, listing your adoptive parents." Cam hoped this little bit of information was somewhat comforting. "If you and your brother had been prearranged adoptions, there'd be little we could do to get the information because your adoptive parents would have been on the original. But this is good, because it means there's an original out there somewhere. I've assumed yours was a closed adoption, since there's been no contact."

Sarah's eyes were downcast as though she carried the burden of being unwanted. Cam remembered having much the same feelings when she was old enough to realize none of the people she lived with were her relatives, and thinking no one had wanted her.

"Some states require an in-person request, which is why we're going to Dover."

Despite Sarah's anxious expression, she remained calm. "You did tell me I might need to be involved. It's not a problem." Sarah smoothed her hand over her skirt.

While it appeared to fit her perfectly, it was obvious she was more comfortable in casual clothing. Cam couldn't help taking in every detail. From her lustrous wavy blond hair, to her unbelievably light blue eyes. Her robust complexion could most likely be attributed to healthy eating, a detail she should include in her own life. Sarah's curvaceous body and the muscular calves she'd glimpsed hinted at a physical routine. If not at a gym, then some other form of intense exercise. Cam hadn't asked about her occupation, assuming she earned her living sitting behind a desk. Now she wasn't so sure.

"Camdyn?"

She shook her head, breaking the spell. "Yes?"

"Are we heading out soon?" Sarah's handbag was clutched in her lap, her knuckles white.

"As soon as I gather your file." *And get my shit together.* Cam stood and pretended to check over the documents she'd pulled together earlier. Nothing had changed, but she slid a pad of paper into the folder and made sure she had a pack of sticky notes and a supply of pens in the front pouch of her laptop bag.

"I need to use the restroom."

"Sure. Maggie can show you where it is," she said as she slid her laptop into the padded compartment. When she looked up Sarah was still in her chair.

Sarah looked over her shoulder at the closed door. "I'll find it. I don't think your assistant likes me."

Cam stiffened. It was one thing for Maggie to display her dislike for a client with Cam, it was quite another to let a client see it. *Time to have a heart-to-heart with Mags.*

"I'm good here. I should probably go too, otherwise we'll be stopping before we've begun." Cam shared what she hoped was an understanding smile.

Sarah's face relaxed. "Thank you."

As Cam washed her hands, she glanced at her reflection. She needed a trim. Sarah joined her at the sink, and, catching Sarah looking at her, smiled. She had every intention to remain professional when interacting with Sarah, but she couldn't help her desire to give Sarah a reason to smile. Every time she did, Cam's breath froze in her chest. A feeling that wasn't at all unpleasant.

They finished up and headed out to the parking lot.

"I need to get something from my car." Sarah gestured to the decade-old vehicle parked a few spaces from Cam's much newer slate gray Charger.

"No problem."

Cam had a perfect view of Sarah's backside. The three-inch stilettos made her calves flex as she walked, and the movement of her hips was rhythmic, keeping Cam from looking anywhere else. *Get in the car.* Her inner voice hadn't been gentle in the warning as bells went off in her head. The few times in her career she'd been tempted to have more than a professional relationship with a client had been the times she'd remembered how much she'd loathed the characteristic of no boundaries in others. It kept her from stepping over a line she'd established years ago when Liv had given her the tools and advice on how to be someone with integrity and pride. She wasn't about to throw it away on a whim.

However, the appearance of the bag Sarah was carrying initially threw her off. Sarah tossed it on the back seat and got in, and Cam schooled her reaction. She didn't want Sarah to think she was a letch with nothing but sex on her mind.

"All set?"

"Yes." Sarah shared a small grin. "Thank you."

Cam smiled in return. "Let's start this road trip."

The silence was deafening in the enclosed space. Once they were tucked into the flow of traffic, she ended the uneasy quiet. She couldn't help noticing how much Sarah fidgeted in her seat, tugging at the fabric and readjusting seams.

"If you don't mind me saying so, you looked more comfortable in a long skirt."

Sarah's laughter rang gently through the car. The sound was delightful.

"Probably because I am. This," Sarah motioned, indicating her current clothes, "is purely for show. I brought jeans and a shirt to change into the first chance I get."

She gestured to her own attire. The formal slacks and long-sleeved silk blouse were her usual outfit when she was in the office. "I would dress differently too, if I wasn't working. I'm glad I chose to dress accordingly for today, or else I'd have looked like a slob next to you."

Sarah's face colored for the second time. She glanced out the window, and Cam wanted to erase the awkward moment. She would much rather be looking into Sarah's eyes.

❖

Sarah stared ahead. It wasn't that the compliment hadn't felt sincere, but rather that she wasn't sure how to react without letting Camdyn see her discomfort. She didn't know Camdyn, not at all really, and the comment had been unexpected. She focused instead on the scenery outside her window and taking in the green pastures and thick stands of trees. She hadn't traveled anywhere except for work in years. *That's one thing I'm going to change.* Camdyn switched on the radio. Perhaps the silence made her uncomfortable, too. She stole glances at her every now and then. There were tiny crow's feet at the corners of her eyes, suggesting she might be older than Sarah first thought and helped explain how Camdyn had managed to have so much experience. Her brows were finely arched, and her nose was reminiscent of Grecian heritage. The full, pouty lips and squarish chin was strong, but not masculine. While definitely androgynous in many ways, Camdyn could never be described as gender-neutral.

The music played softly in the background as she ran her hand along the soft leather of her seat. Such a contrast to the worn, split material in her vehicle. Lost in thought, she almost missed Camdyn's words.

"I never asked what you did for a living."

Sarah's jaw muscles bunched. She wasn't expecting to have to explain her chosen occupation. It was silly on her part. She made an honest living at an honest profession. She turned to level a laser-focused look at Camdym. "I'm an iron worker in construction. And I do welded sculpture when I have time. Mostly from pieces of metal from things people have thrown out."

"I admire people who have the skill to do any type of trade work. Have you ever had a fear of heights?" Camdyn glanced at her before returning her attention to the road.

Sarah settled back against the door and relaxed. Apparently, she'd been wrong about Camdyn. Again. She'd anticipated some flak for her chosen line of work. Granted, it wasn't all that common for women in general to be welders, but that didn't mean Camdyn thought less of her. *Like I should care what she thinks.*

"Not really. I was a typical tomboy. I'm sure my parents didn't expect what they got." She paused, wondering what had brought on the sudden bout of insecurity. "They had their choice and they left my brother behind. I wonder if they would have been happier with him."

Camdyn reached for her hand and gently squeezed.

"I don't see how they could, but I'm sorry you feel that way."

The snort was the most unladylike thing Sarah had ever done in her presence and Camdyn's face showed her surprise. Sarah slid her hand away. The warmth Camdyn's touch brought was too easy to accept. She shook her head.

"Oh, I'm not sorry they chose me. I had a great childhood with loving parents, a roof over my head, and food on the table. I have no idea how my brother grew up, or what the people who adopted him are like. I think I did okay, and worrying that my parents weren't happy with their choice is ridiculous. It was just a moment's ponder."

"I meant I was sorry you were separated, but I agree having good childhood memories is important." Camdyn's jaw muscles tightened.

Sarah wondered what that was about. Maybe she'd grown up very poor. Or had an alcoholic parent, like some of her childhood friends. She remembered hearing her parents talking about it one night, and the reason they allowed her to have one of her playmates spend the night so often. She hadn't understood why that girl in particular until much later, but she never forgot the kindness they'd shown.

"Camdyn, are you all right?" Sarah's instincts told her something was definitely wrong, though she didn't think it was anything she'd said. Camdyn didn't blink, and when the car veered into the next lane, Sarah jerked hard on the steering wheel.

"Camdyn," Sarah yelled. She had no idea what was going on, but they were both in danger and she was going to do whatever she had to do to keep them safe. She pushed Camdyn's foot out of the way with hers and fought for control of the steering wheel until she got them off the road. Her heart hammered as she put the car in park.

CHAPTER EIGHT

Sarah's voice sounded far away, like she was in a tunnel. Pictures of her former life flashed in front of her. She might have been looking out the windshield, but her focus wasn't on the road, it was on the memory of being curled in a protective ball in the corner of her closet. The steering wheel jerked with such force her first reaction was to try to slam on the brake, but Sarah had taken control. Horns sounded around her. They were on the shoulder of the highway. Traffic zoomed by at an alarming speed as her focus returned.

"What in the hell are you doing?"

Sarah sounded pissed, but one look told Cam she was terrified. She shook her head to clear it. She needed air. The car was already in park and she moved to get out, when a steel grip held her in place.

"We aren't off the road far enough for you to get out. You'll get killed."

She put the window down and glanced out. They were barely out of traffic. She didn't remember pulling over. All she remembered was the sound of her foster father screaming as he searched the house for her. She pinched her thigh. The sharp pain blocked out the visual memories and her focus centered on the dashboard display. Numbers helped her regain her equilibrium.

"Here." Sarah shoved a bottle of water in her hand.

Cam's hands were shaking so bad, she thought she was going to end up with more on her than in her until Sarah guided it to her lips. She took several gulps. Another minute passed before she was able to speak.

"Thank you."

"Are you going to tell me what just happened?"

There wasn't any accusation in the question, and she owed Sarah an explanation. The trouble was, she wasn't sure where to begin. "I get migraines. I think I had an aura. It happens sometimes, but this is the first time it's ever happened while I was driving." She swallowed around the lump in her throat. "I'm sorry I scared you."

Sarah stared at her before saying anything. "Are you okay to drive? I can take over." She looked at the GPS blinking from where it was mounted on the dashboard.

"No, no. I'm okay." The look of genuine concern touched Cam, but she couldn't let Sarah think what had happened a minute ago would happen again. She gave a silent prayer to the powers that be and straightened in her seat, adjusting the seat belt as she viewed the readout on the small screen, instructing her to return to the road. Sarah's soft touch on her arm sent a tingle along the nerve track.

"I really don't mind."

For the moment, she was back in control, and she would do everything in her power to keep it that way. "I promise if I feel anything at all, I'll pull over. Okay?"

Sarah nodded, then slid her hand away.

Cam reached for her sunglasses and hoped they'd mask her fear of the old memories trying to terrorize her in a new way. After a pit stop and another couple of hours, they arrived at their destination without further incident. Cam was glad Sarah finally seemed to relax a bit, though she kept glancing in Cam's direction. She couldn't blame her for staying vigilant. The near accident had set her on edge, too.

The woman in the Office of Vital Statistics was forthcoming as she spoke to Sarah. The clerk didn't know if there'd been a court order sealing the information on the birth certificate until the formal request was reviewed by someone higher up. If they okayed the request, a copy would be sent to Sarah's home address within the next two to four weeks. Cam was used to the bureaucratic delays for obtaining official documents. Sarah wasn't as calm.

"Are you sure there's nothing you can do to expedite my request? I've come a long way and with work..." Her voice trailed off, and Cam knew she was close to tears.

"I'm sorry, ma'am. That's our policy and I have to follow it." The clerk looked between Sarah and Cam before continuing, as if making sure they both understood. "If you'd like, you can prepay for the copy now. It will help expedite things if your request is approved."

Sarah rummaged in the small bag. Whatever she was looking for wasn't there and her shoulders slumped. "I must have left my bank card in my other bag. I'll just have to wait."

Cam stepped up to the counter. "I'll take care of it. No need to delay things." The look of disbelief on Sarah's face made her question how she'd presented herself on previous occasions, and she wondered if Sarah thought she was unscrupulous.

"You sure you don't mind?" Sarah asked.

"Not at all. Shall we finish up here?"

"Yes. Thank you."

Sarah stood off to the side while Camdyn paid the small fee with her card. The clerk produced a receipt and made a copy of the form Sarah had completed, then stapled them together. Camdyn handed the paperwork to Sarah.

"One less thing to worry about." She gestured for Sarah to lead the way, then reached around her to open the door.

This hadn't been the first time her preconceived notions about Camdyn had been upended. Sarah had been convinced she was an egocentric, but the more time they spent together, the more evident it had become that Camdyn was much more than her first impression had projected. They settled in the car and Camdyn pulled a folder out of the space beside her seat, making a note on the inside, which contained several entries. The tab was labeled "Peters, Sarah—MP." Her curiosity won out over discretion.

"MP?"

Camdyn's mouth moved in an almost smile.

"Secret code for mild pain."

Sarah's eyes felt big and her mouth opened in surprise. She couldn't pretend she wasn't shocked at the admission. Camdyn started laughing.

"Oh my God, the look on your face is priceless." It took her a few minutes before she was able to talk. "Sarah." Camdyn touched her hand. "I just couldn't resist. MP means Missing Person. It's a missing person case."

She snapped her mouth shut and shook her head. She deserved Camdyn's response to her being nosy. After all, it was her job to investigate and give Sarah pertinent details. Not give her information on the inner workings of her business. Still, now that she thought about it, she must have had quite the expression. She laughed a bit at her own foolishness.

"You definitely had me going. I originally had the impression you were rather full of…" She felt the heat travel up her neck and looked to where Camdyn's hand covered hers.

"Myself? Egotistical? You wouldn't be the first person to think so." Camdyn pulled her hand back.

"I didn't mean to insult you. If you remember, we did get off to a bit of a rocky start."

Camdyn stared out the window.

The renewed tension between them made her wish they could go back to earlier in the day. She kept the sigh to herself. For being on professional terms, their relationship was already proving to be complicated. Maybe that was because all relationships were that way, and she just hadn't had much experience that they could be otherwise. Sarah had known cocky women before, and they'd been a turn-off. What was it about Camdyn that had the opposite effect on her? "Camdyn?"

"Cam."

"I'm sorry?" Sarah frowned.

"I'd prefer if you call me Cam. Only Maggie calls me Camdyn when she's pissed." Cam shared a wry grin. "I'm not much on formality either."

She chuckled. "Okay. Cam it is."

"You were saying?" Cam flicked her attention to the GPS.

"Thank you for taking care of the fee. I'll pay you back as soon as we stop."

"No need. I'm still working off the advance. Besides, it was minimal. Just make sure you hold on to the papers in case we need to follow up on it."

Sarah chewed her lower lip. She probably should have asked more about her fees when she'd hired her. She remembered Cam telling her something about hourly, but she'd been so nervous, she hadn't paid much attention. She didn't see any harm in clarifying it now since they were stuck in the car together for a while and she hated when they fell into uneasy silence.

"So, how much do you charge for cases like mine again?"

"My standard fee is seventy-five dollars an hour, plus expenses."

"Oh." She blinked several times. She'd missed that detail. "I'll need to give you more soon."

"Let's cross that bridge when we come to it."

She looked down, refusing to meet Cam's eyes. She really needed to pay more attention.

"Are you ready to get out of those lovely, confining clothes?"

"How did you know?" She smiled in relief.

Cam tipped her head in the direction of the back seat. "I know your bag isn't stuffed with cash."

"Ha. Hardly. I'm dying to get out of these as soon as possible."

"Can't say I blame you. There's a nice restaurant not far from here. Quaint but not fancy, if you'd like to stop for an early dinner. I could go for a cup of coffee and a hot meal."

"I think that's the best idea I've heard in a while."

After Sarah changed her clothes in the restroom, Cam took her bag to the car. When she returned, Cam asked for a quiet table. They ordered drinks and food. She hadn't realized how hungry she was until they'd sat down.

Sarah buttered a thick slab of Italian bread. "What do you do when you're not working?" Cam paused mid chew. Maybe she was being too personal. "You don't have to answer. Sometimes my curiosity wins over etiquette."

Cam swallowed and took a sip of wine. "No, no. You're fine. I just…" She looked off for a moment. "I like to read. I try to work out a few times a week, but that's more of a goal than what actually happens."

"I imagine some days are long."

"Nights are longer. And often boring as hell." Cam smiled.

She knew she shouldn't, but Sarah wanted to know more. "So no going out with friends? No wild nights on the town?"

"Ah. I see. You want to know if I ever let my hair down."

Sarah shrugged. "Just making small talk."

"Uh-huh." Cam winked at her. She had all she could do to not choke on her food.

The rest of their dinner was filled with easy conversation. Cam talked about a missing person case she'd taken on involving a fourteen-year-old girl who'd disappeared off the face of the earth for more than two years. Cam had followed every lead on that one. Made phone calls. Found people to talk to…more than once. In the end, she'd reunited the teenager with her frantic family. They'd never given up. Never stopped looking for her. Never stopped hoping against all odds she'd be found. Cam said she'd had all she could do to keep from firing a shot between the pimp's eyes when she caught up with him. The innocent young girl he'd lured into his car and driven halfway across the country had returned a used and abused adult who would never be the same. Sarah's appreciation for Cam's profession took on a new dimension.

The meal was simply delicious, and the half carafe of wine they shared the perfect accompaniment, aside from Cam. Over the last few hours, she'd gotten to see a different side of her, and Sarah liked this one. A lot.

"How was your fettuccine?" Cam asked

Sarah scooped the last of the sauce onto a wedge of bread, wanting to get every last bit. She chewed, rolled her eyes, and swallowed. "The best I've ever had."

"I couldn't tell." Cam's smile changed her looks from guarded to gorgeous in seconds. She drank some water, wiped her lips on the fine linen napkin, and picked up the wine, tipping it in her direction.

"Care to finish this off?" Cam had only drunk a short glass.

"I really shouldn't." She didn't want the wine to influence her interactions. Not that it would, of course.

"Hate to see it wasted, but I won't force it." Cam set the carafe down and signaled the waiter. "Could I have a double espresso please?" Cam glanced at her. "Would you like anything else?"

She eyed the wine and shook her head. "Oh, what the hell. I'm not driving." She emptied the rest into her glass. The waiter returned with the brew and cleared their empty plates.

"I like the way you think." Cam stirred a little sugar and a drop of cream into the espresso and inhaled deeply, her eyes closing in the process.

The look of total contentment was one Sarah hadn't witnessed before either, and she wondered what Cam was thinking. "Out loud."

Cam's eyes popped open. "What?"

"You were miles away. I wanted to know what you were thinking, so I asked you to think out loud."

"Oh." Cam set the small demitasse cup down. "The simple things in life are sometimes the most enjoyable."

"Like?"

"Like enjoying a fine meal with an intelligent, beautiful woman." Their gazes met and the storm that brewed beneath the surface of Cam's eyes revealed more to Sarah than the words she'd spoken.

Sarah's breath froze in her chest. She had never considered herself beautiful, even though her parents had said so often enough. Everyone knew parents were biased. If the circumstances were different, she would have asked Cam to follow her home and spend the night. But that wasn't their reality.

"Thank you for saying so. I've enjoyed our time, too."

Pink flushed Cam's cheeks. "That was totally inappropriate on my part."

"Does that mean it was a lie?"

"Not at all. What I meant was it's unprofessional for me to speak to you that way. You're a client. I'm sorry."

Sarah didn't want her to be sorry, but it was best if they kept things to a strictly business basis and she hid her unwarranted disappointment. Finding her brother had to take precedence over any attraction she might have for Cam. She'd been startled by Cam's admission there were personal feelings involved. She needed to ignore them. For the time being. That didn't mean she was letting Cam off the hook.

"You never mix business with pleasure?"

"No, but then, I've never had a client as charming as you, so who knows what the future holds." There was a hint of tease in Cam's voice.

Sarah felt exposed when the heat traveled up her neck to her cheeks and she wished she'd left well enough alone. There was no going back now, but she hoped Cam's playful demeanor was just that. Being playful and nothing more, though she also hoped it didn't stop the lighthearted wordplay they'd been enjoying.

She picked up her wine and finished it off in one swallow. "I guess I asked for that."

Cam sat back. "Well, now that we're done teasing each other, should we continue our journey back?"

"Okay." Sarah was sad their time together was coming to an end. Cam was delightful to be around. So much of her was a mystery, she had the impression *she* should be the one doing the investigating. It hadn't gone unnoticed that Cam had been rather ambiguous. She would have liked to ask about her childhood. What had made her decide on her profession? Where she had grown up? Sarah couldn't help but feel there were moments when they were flirting, at least on her part, but she couldn't continue. She didn't want Cam to think poorly of her.

Cam gestured for the check. When it arrived Sarah reached for it.

"This is on me." Cam slid a credit card into the folder and handed it back.

"Cam, I can't—" Sarah began.

"My treat. Not part of my fees. You were gracious enough to take the time to make this trip, and I think it's only fair. I'm sure your boss wasn't pleased with the last-minute notice."

She swiped at a few errant crumbs. "My job ended yesterday, so I'm not missing any time."

"What will you do now?"

"Work on my art until my union calls with another job. I could go rogue and pick up something on the side, but if they get wind of a move like that, they could revoke my membership. I'd end up with no health insurance and I can't afford any more astronomical bills."

"Are you okay? Are you sick?"

"Oh, not mine. My mom, she…" Sarah's eyes filled, and Cam watched as she tried to blink the tears away. "She was really sick for a while, and insurance didn't cover everything. I'm trying to pay them off, but it's daunting."

Cam moved forward and raised her hand as though she was about to comfort her, but something stopped her before that happened. Sarah wished she hadn't changed her mind. She could do with a bit of consoling.

"You aren't responsible for your parents' medical bills. Why are you paying them?"

"The only thing I have left from them is the house. I don't want to chance losing it. They raised me to be responsible." Sarah shrugged. "It's the least I can do after all the sacrifices they made." Her father had insisted she go to college, even though there was no money to pay for it. She'd gotten a few small scholarships and a student loan to cover what the income from her father's odd jobs didn't.

A fat tear dropped onto the front of her shirt, spreading like a telltale sign of her loss. Everything that had been thrown at her was becoming too much for her to deal with in such a short span of time. Cam's soothing voice grounded her in the here and now.

"Let's get out of here, shall we?"

Cam stood protectively in front of her, shielding her from the view of the other patrons while she got herself together. After dabbing her eyes and taking a steadying breath, she accepted Cam's outstretched hand. The relief Sarah felt at her touch mystified her.

This virtual stranger was the first person, aside from Lisa, who'd seen her vulnerable side. None of her parents' friends had witnessed how devastated she was after they'd both died. She hadn't let them see. What did it mean that she'd felt comfortable letting Cam see that part of her? *It's just a moment.* She needed fresh air. Cam let her lead the way, placing her hand at the small of her back. The simple gesture sent a current to her core. Like the residual effects of shock therapy for psychiatric patients, its unfamiliar feeling was disorienting. Once outside, they silently walked to the passenger side and stood facing each other.

"I'm not usually so emotional. I'm sorry if I embarrassed you."

Cam's face softened. "You didn't, and you never have to worry about embarrassing me." She leaned closer. "In case you haven't noticed, I really don't give a shit what others think of me." Cam took a step back, as if she needed the distance. "You, on the other hand, need to be kinder to yourself."

"I'm not sure I know what you mean."

"You've lost both parents in, what, two years?"

Sarah nodded.

"On top of that, you're paying off debts that aren't yours, and you suddenly have knowledge of a brother. Even without a surprise sibling, you have a lot on your plate. I can't imagine how overwhelmed you must feel."

Cam opened her door and she got in, sinking into the soft leather of the bucket seats. She was glad she wasn't expected to deny how close she was to breaking down at any given moment, that she was fighting for control on a daily basis. She was grateful for Cam's astute interpretation of her seesawing emotions.

From the driver's seat, Cam reached behind her and produced an unopened bottle of water, handing it to her.

"I replenished our goods when we got gas."

Sarah thanked her and cracked the seal, trying to wash away the taste of anxiety. She'd never been overly emotional. This was new territory for her. With her parents gone, she wasn't going to get much pampering and she appreciated Cam stepping in. Even if it was temporary.

❖

Cam did her best not to stare at Sarah while she was showing how much she was hurting. She was concerned about Sarah's mental health, remembering how it felt to be alone in a world full of virtual strangers. She'd been bounced from one foster home to another. Some of it had been her own doing and those she never regretted. She would deliberately sabotage her placement when one or both of her caregivers began abusing her, either physically or emotionally. Other times, it was simply the way the system worked. There had been fosters she adored, albeit few and far between. Unfortunately, they were usually the ones who had committed to a particular amount of time, in most cases one year. Then she'd have to move on.

Tragedy had struck the one family she wanted to stay with indefinitely when the father had been killed in an automobile accident. The mother had been left with a child of their own and had cried a stream of tears when she told Cam she didn't have any reserves left to give her. Of course, as devastated as she was by the news, Cam understood. The couple had been in their thirties, and none of them had been prepared for the unspeakable blow that rocked the small family unit.

Now, with Sarah experiencing a similar type of pain, she couldn't help wanting to alleviate it. She was about to tell her how strong she was for not only dealing with her solo status, but also in having the courage to look for her brother, when she felt it hit.

The bright white flash took all thought away. She heard Sarah curse before she could see again, and she pulled over as soon as it was safe. Once the car was in park, she grabbed her head, knowing this would be another debilitating episode. Her stomach roiled.

"Cam. Cam. What's wrong?" Sarah sounded like she was panicking.

The knife of pain subsided long enough for her to talk. "Head." She swallowed the acidic bile burning in her throat. "Migraine is coming."

"Oh my God."

She heard Sarah's door open, then hers. "Let me help you."

Sarah's hand slid along her back while the other grasped her elbow. She kept her eyes to slits. The corona of the bright setting sun was like ice picks in her orbits. She didn't want to vomit in front of Sarah, but with this much pain, it might not be a choice. They rounded the car and she dropped onto the passenger seat, leaning against the headrest. It took a few long minutes to find the strength to talk.

"Thank you."

"Is there something you can take? Ibuprofen or such?" Compassion laced Sarah's tone.

Cam nodded, and a fresh wave of pain washed over her. She hadn't meant to moan out loud.

"That's it. We're heading to the nearest hospital."

She grabbed for Sarah. "No. Nothing they can do." She took a breath before going on. "In the trunk. My medicine is in the bag."

Sarah huffed. Cam heard her rummaging around for a minute before returning to her side.

"Is this it?"

Cam opened one eye and glanced at the bottle Sarah held up for her. "Yes."

"How many?"

"One. For now."

Sarah pressed a tablet into one hand and a bottle in the other. She threw the pill into her mouth and took a drink. The only thing left to do was wait for it to take effect. There was one other problem though, and she wasn't sure how Sarah would take the news.

"Just give me a minute to adjust the mirrors and get my bearings in this beast," Sarah said. Cam heard the whirl of the side mirrors and the seat sliding along its track. "Shit. There's a lot of controls on this thing."

Cam would have laughed if she didn't feel like her head was going to explode.

"Okay. I think I'm ready."

Sarah rubbed her thigh. She closed her hand around Sarah's wrist. "There's one more problem."

"What?"

"The motion of the car is going to make me sicker. We need to find a hotel as soon as possible. I have to lie down." She hated Sarah seeing her like this, but it couldn't be helped. When Sarah remained silent, she went on. "I'll pay for a separate room for you. Or you can drop me off and drive home. Maggie can pick me up when I'm better." She cocked one eye open, needing to see Sarah and focus on something other than the explosion in her head.

Sarah sat back, looking pissed as she pursed her lips. "Just because I'm not warm and fuzzy all the time doesn't mean I'm going to abandon you." She glanced around the road they were on. "I have no idea where we are, and I don't remember seeing any signs for hotels on the way here."

Cam closed her eyes as another knife of pain sliced through her head. When it receded enough for her to think she pointed to the GPS. "Just scroll the menu until you see hotels and pick one." Time stood still, and it felt like an eternity before Sarah spoke.

"Okay. I have one. It's only a few blocks away. You need to buckle up."

She held her breath. The thought of moving and turning her head filled her with dread. She'd rather take her chances if they got in a crash. At least it would ease the pain she was experiencing.

"I can't. Just drive."

Curiosity got the better of her when she felt movement around her. Through narrowed eyes, she was just in time to see Sarah leaning across her to grab the seat belt near her head. Her breasts pressed against Cam's chest. The moan she couldn't stop had nothing to do with her migraine. The firm mounds came dangerously close to her mouth before Sarah yanked and grunted, pulling the belt free and backing away. A resounding click locked it in place. Sarah gently snugged it against her and then settled back in the driver's seat, looking satisfied. It was the first time she looked happy since before leaving the restaurant. Cam didn't try to hide the smile that forced her cheeks to move.

"Are you happy now?"

"With you buckled in? Absolutely. That you're in pain? Not even a little." Sarah turned the key and the engine roared to life. "Hang in there for just a few more minutes."

Cam had no choice. Like it or not, she was at Sarah's mercy and there was nothing she could do about it.

CHAPTER NINE

S arah pressed the accelerator, and the car lurched onto the road.

"Sorry. I'm not used to a car with this much power."

"It's okay. I should have warned you, but if you can avoid any sudden moves you'll spare me a mess to clean up."

She shot Cam a quick look. "Got it."

The GPS got her to the Hilton Garden Inn Hotel in less than five minutes. She parked in the unloading zone and put the four-ways on.

"In the console. My credit card."

Sarah was touched that Cam wanted to take care of the charges, but it was the least of her concerns at the moment. She reached in the back and snagged her wallet from her bag.

"We'll settle up later."

She sprinted inside and explained why she was in such a hurry. A couple of minutes later, the accommodating clerk provided two key cards. He offered to have the car parked and to bring in their luggage, but she thought better of it. She had no idea what Cam had in her vehicle. She reassured him she'd be okay and quickly walked to the car. She opened the passenger door, and Cam stirred. She reached across and released the seat belt.

"Cam, can you get out?"

Cam's eyes opened. Her pupils were dilated and her eyes glassy. "Drugs." In slow motion, she slid her legs around and hung on to the grip bar. "Might need help."

"I'm right here."

Sarah got Cam's arm around her shoulder and hung on to her wrist. After Cam managed to stand, she swayed and nearly fell, and Sarah tightened her grip. Cam's height had her at a disadvantage. She moved out of the way so she could shut the door with her hip, then engaged the lock.

Cam fought to keep upright. "Elevator?"

"First floor. Not too far."

"Good. That's good."

The walk down the hallway probably seemed like miles for Cam since she took small steps and her eyes were barely open. Sarah guided her to one of the queen beds in room 102 and kept her voice low.

"Lie down, Cam."

Once she was settled, Sarah glanced around. The room was clean, if sparse and impersonal, but it would serve the purpose.

"Lights, Sarah. Please…" Cam murmured.

She had forgotten that some people were light sensitive during headaches and probably more so with a migraine. After turning on the bathroom vanity light so she could still see her way around the room, she switched off the others.

"I'm going to go get our things and move the car. Will you be okay by yourself for a few?"

"I won't move an inch. Promise," Cam said with a hint of humor.

Sarah let out a relieved breath. Cam's voice no longer held the edge of pain. Whether it was from the medication or the dark space she didn't care.

On her way to the car, Sarah questioned how easily she'd accepted spending the night with Cam. Even though they'd be in separate beds, she couldn't let go of the fact sharing a hotel room wasn't what she had in mind when they took off this morning. After moving the car and grabbing their things, she slipped the key through the mechanism to their room as quietly as possible. The resounding beep made her wince. Cam was on the bed exactly as she'd left her, and she hoped she was sleeping.

"Sarah," Cam whispered.

"I'm here."

"Thank you."

She covered Cam's hand with hers. It was cold to the touch. "You don't have to thank me. Do you need anything?"

"To feel human?"

Sarah chuckled from nerves. Even in her current state, Cam oozed sex appeal.

"You're quite human."

"Glad you noticed."

Thankfully, the room was dark. Cam couldn't see her embarrassment for blurting out the comment, and she reluctantly pulled her hand away. She found an extra blanket in the closet and covered Cam after removing her shoes.

"I put your pills and the water on the stand." Sarah looked around. It was only six o'clock. She couldn't imagine being able to sleep this early. Maybe if she took a nice hot shower and turned on the TV without sound, Cam wouldn't mind.

"Do you need to use the bathroom?"

"Not right now. You go ahead. When you come out, would you bring a damp washcloth with you?"

"I'll get it right now." Sarah had no idea if it was supposed to be cold or warm, so she opted for somewhere in the middle. "Where do you want it?" She bit her lower lip.

"Just put it across my eyes. That way you won't have to worry if you want the light or TV on."

With the washcloth draped over her, Cam looked more vulnerable than before. All her earlier preconceptions began to fade one by one. Cam hadn't done anything to deserve mistrust. It was Sarah's self-preservation instincts that had clouded her judgment.

"I won't be long."

❖

Cam wished she were anywhere else except lying incapacitated in a strange bed. Sarah had been so thoughtful and caring, she was hard-pressed to find a reason not to like her more than she already did. When the shower turned on, she sighed softly. The thought of Sarah being nude and just beyond the wall separating them teased her imagination. She tried to swallow, but her mouth was so dry she coughed instead. Covers tossed aside, she swiped at the washcloth, letting it fall beside her head, and then reached out for the nightstand in search of the water. Her hand hit it and send it flying, along with the bottle of pills.

"Son of a bitch."

She didn't have a choice. She had to move before her parched throat sent her into a coughing fit, exacerbating her throbbing head. She swung her legs out and sat up too quickly, the stab of pain blinding her. Cam grasped the sides of her head as she leaned her elbows on her knees. She pressed and waited for it to subside.

"Here." Sarah took her hand and placed the bottle in it. "The cap's off."

She hadn't heard the bathroom door open. Sarah was quickly earning a spot in Cam's miniscule heavenly deity list. An angel when she needed one most. She took a swallow, then another before she attempted to talk.

"How long since I took a pill?" To her, it seemed like hours.

Sarah sat beside her, one arm protectively around her back. "I'm not sure. About forty-five minutes. Maybe an hour at most."

"Christ." Cam opened her eyes. This time she set the bottle on the stand without missing it. "Feels a lot longer." She looked around on the floor. Her pills must have rolled under one of the beds. She would need to take another dose soon if this kept up.

Sarah must have guessed what had happened and knelt, reaching under the bed. When she straightened she produced the bottle of pills. "Do you need more?"

"If it doesn't let up in a few minutes I will." She hated asking, but she needed caffeine. It might be enough to ratchet down the throbbing. "Would you mind going for coffee? I'd do it myself, but I'd probably make a mess." She tried sharing a grin. It felt awkward and stiff. Like her neck. Her head felt twice its normal size.

"What do you want in it?" Sarah asked as she rummaged through her bag, then pulled on a zippered hoodie. It was then that

Cam noticed she was wearing lounge pants and a T-shirt, minus a bra. The stir low in her belly would have led to arousal if she wasn't fighting just to keep upright.

"Black." She thought about how strong the coffee might be if it had been sitting for a while. "If you don't mind grabbing a couple sugars and creamers in case it's horrible, that would be great." Cam stood and her world tilted on end. The wad of money she produced from her front pocket and shoved in Sarah's direction felt more like a payoff than an offering. She winced at the cliché. A beautiful woman in a hotel room and a handful of cash. Could she be any more pathetic?

"The coffee in the reception area is free," Sarah said while helping her sit.

"Snacks. Or food. If I have to medicate again I need food." Sarah hadn't signed up for this when they headed out today. "On second thought, I'll go. What's the worst that can happen?"

Sarah stood with her hands on her hips, her brows knitted. "Oh, I don't know. You fall and need stitches? You vomit in the nearest trash can…or not?"

Cam snickered. "Well, there is that." She made eye contact through the haze of pain. "You've been more than attentive. I'm supposed to be working for you, not the other way around."

"Did you plan this little episode to make me your nursemaid?" Sarah waved dramatically.

"No, but…"

"Cam."

"Yeah?"

"Shut up." Sarah picked a couple of bills out of the pile she held and dropped the rest on the stand.

Once she was out the door, Cam chuckled through the pounding thud at the back of her head. "Yep. She's a spitfire."

❖

Sarah couldn't conceive the level of pain Cam was in. Headaches were rare, but she hated even minor ones. What did it feel like to have one bad enough to make someone sick to their stomach, to not be able to handle light or motion? She didn't want to think about it.

Lucky for her, the kitchen was still open and she ordered a couple of sandwiches to go. The vending machines were well stocked and she got a variety, not knowing what Cam liked. She gathered their goods and headed back to the room.

"I didn't know what..." Sarah took one look at Cam and quickly shut the door before setting everything down on the small table. "Just what in hell are you doing?"

Cam sat in the easy chair, her head resting in her hands. One leg was bare, her pants pooled around the other. Her shirt was unbuttoned, revealing a sports bra.

"Trying to go to the restroom?" Cam mumbled.

Even in her current state, Cam's voice held some levity. She couldn't help the small grin she was glad Cam couldn't see. "How's that working for you?"

"Not very well."

Sarah knelt and finished removing Cam's pants, pressing them flat and draping them over the back of the desk chair. She did everything she could to focus on the material and not the hard muscles of Cam's thighs. "Do you want to stand?"

"That's the goal," Cam said, finally looking up and sporting a grin of her own.

She managed to get Cam into the bathroom, leaving the door ajar should she need her. On her instructions, Sarah rummaged in Cam's bag and pulled out a light pair of sweat pants and a soft, well-worn T-shirt. She leaned against the doorframe.

"I found them."

Cam opened the door all the way and took the clothes, assuring Sarah she could get them on by herself. A few minutes later, Cam reappeared. Her face was drawn and there were dark circles under her eyes, but she no longer looked to be in such excruciating pain. She made it to the table under her own power and dropped onto a chair. Sarah watched her take the lid off a cup and dump a creamer into it, not bothering to stir. She blew across the surface, then took a tentative sip.

"Not bad," Cam said.

She studied her a little longer before speaking. "Glad it meets your approval." She nodded to the cup. "You drink a lot of coffee."

Cam winced. "Sometimes it helps keep them at bay." She lightly tapped her temple. "Other times it helps counter the effects of the meds."

She sat across from her, then reached into one bag and pulled out a diet soda, popping the top and slurping the foam. "I ordered a couple of sandwiches." Two huge wax paper wrapped sandwiches came from another bag before Sarah dumped the contents of a third in the remaining space.

"Wow."

"Yeah, about that. I'm a list kinda gal. Otherwise I go willy-nilly and grab everything I see."

Cam was tempted to touch her, suddenly aware of where they were and how close Sarah was.

"I'm much better now. After we eat we can head out so you can get home. I'm sure you have better things to do than play nurse."

Sarah's face fell and she looked hurt. "No." Sarah started to unwrap a sandwich. "I mean, I don't mind." She shrugged. "I took care of my mom when she was going through radiation." The sandwich flopped down on the paper with a thud. Sarah picked around the edges. "Cancer sucks."

The weight of Sarah's statement tore her heart. Here she was complaining about a headache. While the pain was intense at times, she wouldn't die from it. *She must think I'm a crybaby.*

"I'm sorry you and your mom had to go through that."

"It's okay. She's not in pain anymore and she's with Dad. They're happy together again." Sarah swiped at her eye and blinked.

Cam started to wrap up her sandwich. "Let's get you home."

"Don't be ridiculous. You're in no shape to drive, and I'm not driving that beast in the dark, so you're stuck with me for the night." Her eyebrows moved up and down suggestively.

Cam laughed in spite of her body's reaction. She'd been having less than honorable thoughts about Sarah, and she hoped Sarah hadn't actually caught on. To hide her unease, Cam snagged a bag of chips, opened it, and picked one out before shoving it in her mouth.

"Okay, but don't say I didn't give you an out."

Sarah sat back. "Duly noted."

She glanced at the clock on the stand. The LED numbers flashed seven eighteen.

"Shit."

Sarah bit into the sandwich, then tipped her head in question.

"I need to call Maggie."

"Do you have a curfew?" Sarah asked after swallowing.

Cam felt her stomach drop in a much different way. Maggie wasn't her idea of a mother, although she did dote on her. If anyone was even close to being a mother figure, it was Liv, but even she had encouraged Cam to be her own person.

"Maggie's a good friend. She'll worry."

"Totally none of my business." Sarah looked chagrined. "It could explain why she doesn't like me though."

"What could?"

"I get the distinct feeling she'd rather I didn't contact you so much. Maybe she's jealous."

"Of you?" The more she thought about Maggie's recent behavior, the less crazy it sounded. It really was past time for that talk. The distant ache in her head notched up. She needed to stay calm and keep the tension out of her shoulders.

"You don't have to be so defensive." Sarah's smile was gentle. "It was just an observation, and I could be wrong."

Cam took a breath. Sarah was right. "Sorry. I'll just text her." Even though she felt somewhat human, she still had to move slowly. After a few careful steps to retrieve her phone, she sent off the message then silenced it, knowing Maggie more than likely would have questions. Ones she didn't want to answer.

"What?" Cam asked as she struggled to sit up and get as far away as she could.

"You had a bad dream. You were shouting."

Cam cringed. She had no idea what she'd said, but the edges of her dream were still vivid. Her stepfather was after her. He would make her do things she didn't want to do, then he would fuck her. His wife had turned her back, glad his attention was elsewhere. Cam had to know how much she'd revealed to Sarah.

"What did I say?"

"I think you were trying to get away from someone. After you yelled you said, 'Please, please' like you were begging to be left alone."

"Oh." Maybe she could worm her way out of telling Sarah the truth. She hadn't told anyone besides Liv about the sexual abuse she'd suffered. With any luck, Sarah wouldn't ask for more.

"Was it just a dream?"

She laughed to cover her nerves and hoped it sounded convincing. "I was tormented as a kid. I was a bit chunky." Both statements were true, even if they had nothing to do with the nightmare. "Just a memory of one of many days." She didn't really want to think about those times. She'd had a feeling this case would open old wounds.

"Why now?"

Cam's brain was sluggish, but revealing the truth terrified her, and she was glad to be able to come up with a plausible reason for her nightmare. "It happens when I'm stressed. I'm sorry you're stuck here, with me, and having to deal with all my issues."

"I'm not. I'm glad you aren't alone." Sarah went to the small refrigerator and produced two bottles of water, handing one to her. "Do you think you can go back to sleep now?"

After finishing off half the water, Cam shrugged. It was only a little after two. Way too early to get on the road. "I'm going to try."

CHAPTER TEN

S arah stood next to her car. They'd gotten on the road right after breakfast, and it was still early. She should be grateful. There were only a few times she'd shared a hotel room with a virtual stranger, and they'd all been for meaningless sex. It wasn't like Cam would have had the ability to do anything, even if the thought had crossed Sarah's mind. *Stop*. That's not what she wanted. Not at all.

"I can't thank you enough for all you've done. I hope I haven't ruined your weekend plans," Cam said.

Sarah snorted. It had been more than a year since she'd had "plans" for anything besides work, taking care of her parents, and her art. She supposed now that her schedule had thinned out there would be time for socializing. At the moment, it seemed like too much effort to even think about it.

"Not hardly."

Cam tipped her head in question.

"I was a bit preoccupied the last year or so. There wasn't much time for anything else. I haven't quite gotten around to having a life again yet."

Cam nodded as though she understood. "Life sometimes gets in the way of life."

Exactly. Too bad Cam exhibited such a cocky attitude when she was working. She was much different in casual settings. Perhaps it had been the migraine that knocked her down a peg and made her more pleasant to be around. Or seeing how vulnerable she was after her night terror. She still didn't think Cam had been totally honest about what that was about, but it wasn't really any of her business. Still, she felt like she knew her a little better.

"I should get going. The housework and grocery shopping aren't going to get done if I don't do it." Cam's eyes flashed a darker shade, shifting to another hue. This wasn't the first time Sarah saw something akin to melancholy. Anguish? Or maybe it was nothing at all and she was once again allowing her loneliness to fill in the gaps. She had to stop wondering about Cam. She'd gotten to see another side of her. A very attractive side, but she wasn't in any frame of mind to think about relationships, hers or Cam's. The last month had been full of emotional bruises and financial worries. How could she contemplate opening herself up to another possible heartache if someone she loved left or got sick? And she had to work all the hours she could find thanks to the debts she had to pay. It wasn't like she had time for anything more than a no-strings night with someone here or there. One thing was for sure, Sarah didn't know Cam well enough to let her inside. Besides, she didn't even know if Cam was single, and she certainly wasn't going down that road, no matter how attractive Cam was.

"I'll let you know when I have more information." As if to ward off Sarah's constant demands about the case she added, "Patience and time. That's what will get you closer."

Sarah had let her impatience show through on a number of occasions, and it wasn't necessary. She had to let Cam do her job and remember she wasn't her only client. She tossed her bag on the threadbare passenger seat of her car.

"Take care of yourself, Cam. I've waited all these years. A few more weeks, or months, won't change things."

The elevator ding reminded her to put one foot in front of the other. She'd accepted the metal box as a necessary evil in the high-rise, and unless she was desperate for exercise, she'd forego the ten flights. She still wasn't sure what had happened in the last twenty-four hours. She and Sarah had grown closer, that much she did know. The question still loomed why she'd been able to drop her tougher veneer and let Sarah see her at her weakest. The most disturbing part was when she'd dreamt of her abuse. She never wanted anyone to know about those dark times. That was a big part of why she didn't do relationships and rarely spent the night with anyone. There were doors she would do whatever she had to do to keep closed.

Cam was still deep in thought when Maggie's voice startled her.

"Well, look who's come home." Maggie stood with her hands on her hips and her lips pursed.

She wasn't in any mood to listen to Maggie berate her about her "less than professional action" by going to a hotel with a client. Little did she know they'd shared a room.

"Is the coffee on?" Cam asked as she headed for her office. It was time she and Maggie had that long overdue talk.

"Of course."

"Good. Fix us both a cup and bring them to my office, please." Cam rarely asked her to wait on her, but she needed the time to think about her approach. Maggie was a great assistant and she knew how to handle any task Cam threw at her. She didn't want to lose her, but she also didn't want Maggie to think she was running the show.

Maggie set Cam's mug in front of her as she sat in one of the chairs facing her desk. "I take it this isn't going to be a social visit." She blew across the steaming liquid before taking a sip.

"You're right. I want to know what's bugging you about this case and, in particular, Sarah Peters."

"No beating around the bush then," Maggie said as she stared into the mug in her hands.

"Have you ever known me to?"

"Not when it comes to work." Maggie settled back, staring at Cam. "I'm afraid this case is going to dredge up things from your past. Things you aren't going to want to think about."

Cam hadn't expected that explanation. She'd never shared details of her sordid past, although Maggie knew she'd been bounced around foster homes for most of her life. Some secrets were meant to stay secret.

"I appreciate your concern, Mags, but don't you think that's my decision?"

"Of course I do. I just can't help worrying about the recent uptick in headaches and the possible correlation with this case. Maybe it's just coincidence, but what if it's not?"

Maggie's rationalization wasn't farfetched. It still didn't explain her attitude toward Sarah. "If what you're saying is true, why are you taking it out on Ms. Peters? She can't help the situation she's in, and I can't blame her for wanting to find someone to call family. Can you?"

"It's not her, although I think she's looking for a little more than a professional relationship with you. Why can't you give the case to Kevin?"

Cam's ire rose. Whether or not Sarah was motivated for reasons other than finding her sibling as a rationale for putting in personal appearances at the office shouldn't be any concern of Maggie's. Perhaps Sarah's initial impression of Cam's ability to do the job was still in play, but she hoped not.

"I've never mixed business with pleasure, and I have no intention of crossing that line now. But if I did, I'd appreciate you keeping your opinions to yourself as to the wisdom of such action."

Maggie leaned forward. "Cam, I—"

She raised her hand, silencing the argument. "No, Maggie. The discussion is over. I decide how to handle every case, professional or otherwise." The hurt in Maggie's eyes caused her to soften her stance. "I know you're concerned, but I can't have you treating a client less than courteously. Ms. Peters told me she doesn't think you like her. I can only surmise something you said or did gave her that impression. And that's not the professional vibe we've always presented. I don't expect any less."

Maggie glanced down. "I may have been less than patient with her. I'm sorry. I'll apologize the next time we speak."

Cam leaned across the desk. "That would be good. I appreciate everything you do around here to keep the office running smooth,

Mags. I never want to have a reason to second-guess what happens out there." She tipped her chin, indicating the reception area. "That's where some of the real magic happens." She winked, and Maggie laughed.

"Such a charmer. No wonder the Peters woman has taken a shine to you." She raised her hand before Cam could give another warning. "I know what you're going to say. I'll keep my opinion to myself. Before I go, I do need to know one thing."

Cam sat back. *This ought to be good.*

"On a scale from one to ten, with ten being the worst, how bad was it?"

Maggie didn't need to clarify. "Eleven." Cam expected to hear motherly advice about going to the doctor. She was surprised when Maggie left without saying another word, quietly closing the door behind her.

The envelope from Dover sat on the kitchen table staring back at Sarah. It had been more than two weeks since the trip to the city of her birth, and she'd begun to think it wouldn't ever reach her. She wanted to open it and see her mother's name, although in truth, it wouldn't change anything about her parents. The people who raised her had loved her unconditionally. The only thing the birth certificate could provide was a trail for Cam to possibly find more information. Hell, maybe she wasn't meant to find her brother. She'd be no worse off than she was now, no matter how much Sarah wanted family. If that meant creating her own, then so be it. Lesbian couples everywhere were having children and making lasting memories in their own family units. She wasn't too old to start one of her own. Still, it would be nice to have a blood relative. Find roots.

She slid the letter opener along the edge, freeing the contents. The first paper was a copy of the payment Cam had given the clerk. The second was the certificate.

Baby girl Jones, born to Judy Jones and Paul White. March 15, 1989. Dover, Delaware.

Did that mean they weren't married? Was *Jones* Judy's mother's maiden name? As a person without experience, she didn't see much to go on. She wasn't sure what she'd expected, but her mind was racing at warp speed, and she wondered if that was how Cam felt when she was on a case. The feeling could become addictive if she wasn't afraid her heart would explode before long. It took a few minutes for her to calm down.

"That's why I hired you, Camdyn Stark," she said to the empty room. She had to trust her gut and her gut had told her she had hired the right person. The more she saw Cam outside the office setting, the more convinced she was something in Cam's past made her keep her pretentious shield in place.

Sarah picked up her phone and stared at Cam's contact numbers, wondering if she should call the office. She didn't want to talk to the snarky receptionist. The woman's attitude annoyed her. She wasn't sure what she'd done, if anything, to set her off. Maybe that was just her way. If so, Cam should consider replacing her. Her interactions with clients weren't conducive to running a business.

A text was her best solution. She'd send Cam a message, letting her respond when she had time. Sarah had gone back to work a couple of days ago. The job had helped keep her mind occupied and recover some of the small contingency account she'd stowed away for lean times, like now. It was enough to get her through two months. Anything more than that and she'd be in arrears with her parents' medical bill payments and eating on the skinny. Not expecting a reply from Cam, she went to the pantry and pulled out ingredients to make soup. If she made enough, she'd have dinner for the next few nights. Along with a grilled cheese sandwich it was the perfect meal. Inexpensive stick-to-her-ribs food.

Beans and chicken stock simmered in the pot. Sarah added cut-up celery, carrots, and potatoes. After they were soft, she'd add diced tomatoes, some cooked sausage, and a can of corn. It wasn't the best she'd ever made, but it would fill her up. She cut thick slices of Italian bread and spread a thin layer of butter on one side. She wasn't fond of orange cheese, but it was cheaper. She was just about to heat up the pan when her cell phone vibrated across the table.

The thought of ignoring it was tempting, but there were only a few people who had her number. It might be a call related to another job or art project. She stared at the number and bit her lip. Cam.

"Hello?"

"Hi, Sarah. It's Cam."

"Yes?"

"I got your text about your birth certificate. I'd like to take a look at it as soon as possible."

"Uh, sure. When?"

"Is now a good time?"

She looked at her simmering pot and the prepared sandwich. "I can't leave right now."

"I don't mind coming to get it if that's more convenient."

Cam was being accommodating and she should at least agree to letting her earn some of the fee she was charging. Sarah was trying to stretch what gas she had until her next pay check.

"That's fine."

"Great. I'll see you in about twenty minutes."

"Okay." Sarah hesitated. Her parents had taught her to take nothing for granted and to be kind whenever the opportunity presented. She didn't think Cam was lonely, but looks could be deceiving. "Cam? Have you eaten dinner?"

"I'll grab something later."

"If you don't mind simple, why don't you plan on having dinner here?"

"I don't want to impose. I could come after you've eaten."

"Don't be silly. I have plenty. It's just homemade soup and grilled cheese." Sarah hadn't really thought about spending more time alone with Cam, but she didn't need to. Cam was coming on professional business. She was going to eat anyway, and a meal was always more pleasant when there was someone to share it with.

"Sounds delicious. Thanks for the invitation. I'll be there in a little while."

❖

Sarah wiped her hands on her apron, then opened the door. Cam stood at the threshold with two bottles of wine, a white and a red. There was a folder tucked under her arm.

"Hi."

"I wasn't sure which was appropriate for grilled cheese, so I covered the bases."

She stepped back to let her in. "You didn't have to do that."

"I may seem crude at times, but I know common etiquette." Cam set the bottles on the sideboard, then glanced around. "Cute place."

Not sure why she felt awkward having company in her own home, she forced a smile. "Thanks. It's not much but it's home."

"I think it's perfect." Cam stared at her for what seemed like ages, then rubbed her hands together. "What can I do to help?"

She didn't want Cam in the small kitchen with her. They'd be too close. Closer than even the hotel room. With the table already set, there wasn't much to do, so she took two goblets down from the cabinet and set them on the tiny island. "You can open the wine. The corkscrew's in that top drawer."

"No problem. Red or white?"

Sarah placed two sandwiches on the griddle. "I vote for red."

"Red it is."

While the first side toasted, Sarah ladled the soup into small crocks. After flipping the bread, she put croutons and some shredded cheese on top of each bowl and set them under the broiler.

"What else?" Cam leaned on the counter, watching her every move.

"Here." She handed Cam the sandwich plates before setting a bowl of chopped chives and cilantro on the island, then opened the oven door and removed the crocks. The cheese was bubbly and golden, just the way she liked it. One at a time, she put a bowl on the mat at each place setting, then brought the herbs to the table. "That's it." She took a seat across from Cam as she poured wine.

Cam picked up her goblet and held it out. "Thanks for the spread." She waited until Sarah touched her glass, then sipped. She nodded. "Pleasant."

"I'm sorry?"

"The wine. It has a pleasant bouquet."

"Oh, yes." Sarah wasn't well versed in wine, another reason she'd let Cam order when they'd had dinner together. If she drank at all, she usually indulged in an ice-cold beer.

"So is the company. Pleasant, I mean." Cam looked over her glass.

Sarah looked down as she felt heat rise in her cheeks. She met Cam's gaze. "We should probably eat while it's still warm." Cam's expression was unreadable, but she thought she saw a twitch at the corner of her mouth. A mouth that looked very tempting.

"Let's." Cam dug through the cheese to the contents in the bowl, then withdrew a heaping spoonful of steaming vegetables. She blew across it several times before closing her lips around it. "Mmm, this is great," she mumbled around the mouthful.

She'd been spellbound watching Cam's mouth and almost missed the compliment. "It's nothing special. I just threw together a bunch of stuff."

"That's usually the best kind." Cam sipped wine and ate more. "So, did you look at the certificate?"

Sarah kept chewing, giving her time to prepare for what might be ahead. "Yes."

Cam watched her with an intensity she realized was a frequent behavior and most likely due to her profession, not attraction. Her heart sank a bit at the sobering thought.

"And?"

"Just the names you wanted, but it had my mother listed as Judy Jones." She shrugged. She still had a hard time processing all the family history she hadn't been aware of. She remembered Cam saying Mary Jones was too common to give her any solid trail, and she couldn't help thinking the same for the names she had now. At least now Cam was sure she had the correct first name. Maybe she should have left well enough alone. *Mom and Dad…Why didn't you tell me sooner? Or not at all.* Cam's voice penetrated her thoughts.

"Sarah?"

She looked up.

"I'll take the certificate and dig a bit deeper." Cam's expression was one of empathy.

Sarah appreciated Cam not asking anything else of her. She wasn't sure she had more to give.

CHAPTER ELEVEN

Cam folded her hands on top of the file. "I can't find any contact information or public hospital records related to Judy Jones other than a woman by that name giving birth to twins, so at least we know we've got the right person and hospital. Your brother was born twenty-eight minutes after you, at five forty-two a.m. So far, your father's name hasn't revealed any leads either, but White isn't uncommon."

Sarah stared into her coffee cup. After a few minutes, she looked up. "So where do you go from here?"

Cam had prepared for the inevitable. "I'm not sure there's anywhere else *to* go. I'll investigate a bit deeper in to your father's name, but that too, will be a shot in the dark. Because ultimately, your birth parents aren't the key here. They were out of the picture by the time you two were adopted, so without your brother's name now, or some idea of who adopted him, there's nowhere to look. And obviously we can't get a copy of his records without him being present."

Sarah's face turned red. Cam could almost see the steam coming from her ears. "If you can't do the job why did you take my money?" She stood and held out her hand. "I'd like it back. Please."

Cam guessed Sarah was itching to wiggle her fingers, making her demand clear. As much as she wanted to be angry, she couldn't. She admired Sarah for having balls. She fought against the grin tugging to raise the corners of her mouth.

"Can't." She could tell by the way Sarah shifted her weight she wanted to stomp her foot, and she looked so damn adorable. Cam cleared her throat to mask the chuckle. "You signed a contract. It clearly states no refunds." She sat back, secretly enjoying the shocked look on Sarah's face. That was until she saw the pool of tears forming in her ice-blue eyes. "And for that reason alone, I always do my best. If you were paying attention, I said it would be 'almost impossible.' Not that I couldn't get the job done. I just need you to be aware of what we're up against and not get your expectations too high."

Sarah dropped back in the chair, relief etched in her features. She took a breath, then another before looking back up. Her composure had returned. "I'm sure we can come to some equitable agreement. I know there's not a lot, but at least you have *some* information. Right?"

Her standard response was to not pull any punches; however, she wasn't willing to dash Sarah's hopes just yet. There was a possibility, even though it was slim, she might be able to pull a rabbit out of her hat and find a lead. *If only it were that easy.* She wasn't holding her breath, and neither should Sarah.

"I'll do my best." She'd said those same words to dozens of clients. This time, without knowing exactly why, she wanted to give Sarah a reason to bring back the spark of hope she'd seen earlier. And the fire. Especially the fire. Cam didn't want to admit the connection of abandonment motivated her even more. "I'm not giving up, but I've spent hours going through records and I'm not sure how much more time I can spend."

Sarah looked deep in thought. The crease between her brows and her steady scrutiny made Cam feel like she was a bug under a microscope. The uncomfortable silence continued for several long minutes before Sarah spoke.

"Does that mean you want more money?"

Sighing, Cam leaned forward. "Like I said, I don't know if there's more to find."

Sarah's lips thinned. "How many hours did you spend looking?"

She sat back. This was the spunky woman she remembered from their first meeting, and Sarah wasn't going to take no for an answer. Cam wasn't sure she wanted her to. She liked her tenacity. She hadn't wanted to tell Sarah she was already in arrears, but Sarah was leaving her little choice. "Considering my usual rate, more than you've paid for." A look of shame turned Sarah's young features old. She regretted making the comment. "That's not the point, Sarah. I can't make a promise I'll be able to find more, and if I do, it could be costly. Are you prepared for that scenario?"

"What about the adoption agency? There had to have been one, right?"

Cam heard hope in Sarah's voice and she hated dashing it. "I tried, Sarah. I found the agency the hospital used back then."

"You didn't tell me." Sarah blinked and she wondered if she was getting pissed again.

"Because there wasn't anything to tell. The only way they will release those records is if the adoptee produces an original birth certificate and files a petition with the court."

"Then that's what we'll do."

She leaned forward. Sarah had to not only listen but *hear* what she was saying. "I've already filed one. They said the backlog is at least six months and could be as long as a year."

Sarah stared at her lap a long time. "I'll do whatever I have to do if it will help find him. You have no idea how it feels to be living without any family, without anyone in the world."

You have no idea how wrong you are. Cam pulled the file closer, scribbled a note, and then tucked it in the folder before tossing it on the top tray. "I'll call you if I find anything new."

"Thank you." Sarah sounded despondent.

Sarah left, shutting the door softly behind her. Cam stared at it, wishing she would come back. Sarah didn't know she'd touched on a sore spot. How could she? But the bigger question was why did Cam care? She'd gotten into the business because there were times law enforcement's hands were tied and there wasn't anything they could legally do to help alleviate a family's grief over the sudden disappearance of a loved one. Or the couple who seemed to have it all, only to find out all was not as it seemed. Gambling debts could knock out a family's financial resources without the other partner's knowledge until it was too late. Not to mention a thousand other scenarios she'd run across. Her obsession to find her own birth mother had been the ultimate reason she was in this predicament with Sarah, wanting to provide her the thread Cam had never found.

But she'd never taken on a case where she cared enough to want more time with a client, though she and Sarah remained in a professional relationship. Personal relationships were painful. She'd seen enough in her life to know that, even with the one or two friendships she'd cultivated while on the street. She hadn't had the stomach for seeing them suffer from failed couplings. But she was older now, and she'd learned to cope with the constant ups and downs of life. Hadn't she? Or had she just managed to hide them beneath her work, lose herself in the distance of client relations, and let the other half...the half with partnerships and marriages, and relationships that actually worked, pass her by? She thought she was stronger than that, but every emotion that involved Sarah gave her a reason to step back instead of forward. Proof that any thought of a future with Sarah in it caused a kaleidoscope of conflicting emotions. She'd had more than her share of those for a lifetime.

Perhaps it was Sarah's desperation to be connected again. She'd lived with love her entire life and then it was stripped away. Cam didn't understand her mother and father keeping such an important fact secret. It was downright cruel, and a shining example of how even the best relationship could screw you over. And though Sarah *was* special, she wasn't going there.

Then she remembered the tears in Sarah's eyes. "Fuck." She pulled the Peters folder in front of her. As much as she didn't want to admit it, the truth was she *did* care what Sarah thought about her. The yellow legal sheets with her notes were clipped to the front cover. She'd start there. If she found the elusive brother, Sarah Peters would be out of the picture for good, and she wouldn't have to look into her expectant, amazingly blue eyes any more. *It's for the best.*

She just had to keep telling herself.

❖

Sarah stared at the screen on her laptop. The meeting with Cam hadn't gone as she'd hoped, and finding out she likely owed Cam money didn't sit well. Curiosity won out and she began searching for the "standard" fee for private investigators. The range she found left her sagging. Cam's retainer was probably on the lower end of what others charged. *So, I do owe you money.* With that bit of information, she felt rather foolish for challenging Cam. But she didn't believe that was the reason Cam's demeanor had changed following Sarah's blurted statement about not having family. She hadn't meant to hurt Cam's feelings, but somehow she had without knowing why. From what little she knew, Cam was a woman who had always gotten what she wanted and still did. But now Sarah wasn't so sure that was true.

On a whim, she typed in Camdyn Stark. The search hit on her agency, citing high profile cases. Cam looked smug; pleased to be the center of attention and soaking up the limelight. What was unnerving was the lack of any public record older than her business. Guessing Cam was in her mid thirties, there ought to have been something. School records, high school sports…something.

Twenty minutes later, she gave up. Searching the internet was exhausting. What Cam did for a living wasn't easy. Perhaps she'd rushed to judgment by her all-consuming need to connect with her brother. That didn't explain the lack of a childhood for Cam in this age of technology. Who was she really? Wayward thoughts filled her mind. What if she'd hired a criminal? *Oh my God! That's it! I'll bet Camdyn Stark has a sordid past.* A life of crime that…*Stop.* Her runaway imagination was getting the better of her. There was no way she'd be licensed to carry a gun if she were an ex-con. Or would she? And did it matter if she was doing the job Sarah had hired her to do?

"Ugh." Sarah shut her laptop and went to make her lunch. She was being ridiculous. Lots of people had varied histories that they weren't proud of. Maybe Cam had a troubled youth and now that she had her act together, she preferred to leave her past behind. Maybe she'd ask Cam about her family the next time they were together to satisfy her curiosity about Cam's mystique. Of course, that was assuming she'd actually have a chance to see her again. Though, at the moment and thanks to how things had been left between them, she wasn't sure of anything.

❖

The microwave dinged and Cam pulled the plastic off the rest of her meal before shoving it back in for another ninety seconds.

As brief as it was, she'd reread what little info there was in the entire file after Sarah left the office. She'd been thinking about what other direction she could take when the lightning flash struck. It was a precursor to the migraine she'd been staving off for days. She got home before the crippling pain sent her to her knees. She managed to take her meds and fall onto her bed, and she was grateful for the blackout curtains she'd bought a while ago. The medication knocked her out, and when she woke up three hours later her headache was gone, leaving only the residual ache and tiredness as usual. The price she paid for indulging in medication was nausea, made worse by having not eaten since breakfast.

She set the steaming tray on the counter and poured a glass of iced tea. It was cold and refreshing. The article on her laptop covered adoptions in the nineties. She hadn't had much luck with the mother's name, but there might be something with the father. There was only one other case on her plate at the moment, and tailing a suspected cheating spouse only kept her interest so long. Cam had given the late-night surveillance to Kevin. He was eager to find dirt on the woman and bring something back for a big payoff.

The information scrolling in front of her made for a dry read. Apparently, there wasn't much in the way of mandates for record keeping for social service adoptions in Delaware, as the requirements varied state to state, and even less so in closed adoptions. The only other name in any of the Kent hospital records was the children's caseworker. Unfortunately, on a cursory internet search, she'd discovered the woman had died two years ago. *Another dead end.*

"Big help," she mumbled. Cam tossed the chicken bones in the trash and rinsed the tray for recycling. The bottle of wine in the refrigerator called to her. Thinking better of it, she rinsed her glass and set it in the dishwasher, deciding on a cup of coffee instead. The caffeine would help dispel the last of the leftover grogginess, and she remembered how Sarah had teased her about her caffeine intake. Coffee in hand, she plopped on the couch and made another list of a few possible resources to start with tomorrow. She would contact the State Regulatory Agency and try to locate someone who would be willing to help. She went back to the picture of Sarah as a baby and the woman holding her. Who was she? It was a long shot, but she pulled up the obituary picture of the caseworker. It was of a much younger woman, rather than the sixty-eight-year-old in the obit. She enlarged it, then made a few adjustments before she held Sarah's picture up for comparison. Cam looked back and forth, taking in the details of the two women's eyes, their hair, their lips and nose. Though she wasn't an expert in forensics, she was fairly certain the two pictures depicted the same person. One mystery solved, but not the one that counted.

Cam tossed the file on the coffee table, then stretched out to relax. The minute her eyes were closed she saw bright blue ones staring back at her. Sarah's subdued departure left Cam feeling like she'd let her down, even though there was nothing to indicate she'd done so in how she'd handled the case so far.

As she edged closer to sleep, she had visions of the past few weeks. Sarah in the office, at the hotel, and sitting across from her during the meals they'd shared. Those times, she'd been focused on Sarah's expressive face. She tried to imagine her behind a welder's mask, but instead Cam's mind produced a vivid picture of Sarah in the throes of passion as she straddled Cam's hips. She startled awake, looking for any sign it hadn't been just a fantasy. *Damn.* Cam sat up and her slick center left no doubt it had felt very real. Those were the kind of images people conjured when they were infatuated. She wasn't infatuated with Sarah, and Sarah certainly wasn't interested in her. It was the only thing about this case she was sure of, or so she kept telling herself.

CHAPTER TWELVE

Cam tapped her fingers impatiently. She hated wasting time on hold, but it was a part of investigating that was unavoidable. She glanced at the phoenix tattoo on her right forearm she'd gotten after her degree. It was there to remind her how strong she was. Liv had helped her realize that. *God, I miss you.* She wasn't sure why she was thinking about her friend, mentor, former lover. At the time she'd decided on the mythical creature she'd thought she'd come a long way, and she had, but she wasn't so sure anymore. Between the migraines, nightmares, and conflicting feelings about Sarah, she was on a slippery slope again. *I have to keep focused on my job, that's all.* She'd risen from the ashes once, but Cam didn't know if she could do it again. Maybe she needed to see Liv and reaffirm she was where she needed to be…and that she was okay. The tightness in her chest lessened. The annoying music in her ear stopped.

"Ms. Stark, I have two details for you. Paul White's DOB is March 26, 1964. I also have his Social. I can give you the last four digits." The woman on the phone gave her the numbers. "I hope it helps. Sorry I don't have anything on the woman."

"Not a problem. I'm sure this will help. Thanks for your time." Cam stared at the paper. This was the first real information she'd had for the Peters case. The former dead-end road just got an extension. However, there remained the question of money. While one part of her brain insisted it was time to ask for more, another part wanted to spend whatever amount of time and energy it took to find Sarah's brother whether Sarah could afford it or not.

"You're not running a charity here, Stark." She scrolled through the contacts on her business phone until Sarah's name appeared. She hesitated, hovering over the phone icon, unsure what she wanted to do. A text would be less awkward. It was also a coward's way of confronting an issue, and that was one thing Cam had never been.

The phone rang several times and Cam thought she'd get to leave a message until Sarah's expectant voice came through.

"Hello?"

She sighed internally. "Hi, Sarah. I've made a few discoveries. The first is that the picture of the woman holding you was of the hospital social worker."

"Then you can talk to her."

"I would, but she's deceased."

"How do you deal with the letdowns?"

Cam heard her plop down somewhere with a grunt. "I don't have a choice, but I do have a date of birth and a partial Social on Paul."

It took Sarah a couple of beats to answer. "That's good, right?"

"It is, but there's a little matter we have to settle first."

"I know. I'm sorry I gave you a hard time the other day. You deserve to be paid for the work you're doing. I get that."

Cam was pleasantly surprised she didn't have to argue over money. "Thanks. If you let me know what figure we're talking, I can tell you the hours I have to work with."

"Uh. What would one thousand buy me?"

Cam rubbed her hand over her face. "It would bring us just about even."

"Oh." Sarah sounded disheartened. Cam heard the rustle of papers and waited. "How about two?"

"I can work with that." She wrote some quick figures on the scratch pad. "I could start with half that if it would make you more comfortable." She thought about how things had been left between them when Cam had been abrupt after Sarah had struck a chord with the family comment. She was better than that person. It had taken a while to learn not every comment made was a personal attack.

"Is that your way of telling me if you don't use it all I won't be getting a refund?" Sarah's teasing tone made her smile.

"Well, that depends." *What the hell am I doing?*

"On?"

She squeezed her eyes shut and took a breath. "On if you'd consider grabbing a bite to eat while we discuss what else I find."

"You mean 'if' you find something," Sarah said.

Cam could feel her mouth stretch. "Not if, Ms. Peters. When. Definitely when. I always do my utmost for my clients." She hoped Sarah could tell from the tone of her voice that the formal address was a tease, though she meant it when she said she always gave her best.

"I think I can manage a meal even with the outrageous fees I'm paying my PI."

"I would have never guessed you needed one, but I'm sure you've hired the best." *My PI.* Cam liked the sound of that.

❖

"Mr. White, my name is Camdyn Stark. I'm a private investigator and I was wondering if I might have a few minutes of your time?" She'd gotten incredibly lucky with finding an address for Sarah's birth father. Even luckier it was only a few hours east of her office and she'd taken a chance he'd be home. The man staring back at her didn't share any of Sarah's facial features, but there was no mistaking they had the same ice-blue eyes. Sarah hadn't mentioned an interest in finding her birth parents, and she assumed it was because Sarah might harbor anger over being given up. She hoped Sarah would let go of any ill feelings and pursue every avenue for family, even though her own discovery had ended in more heartache. Though Cam's contract was clear about who she'd been hired to find, she'd give Sarah his address.

A bit wary, the man kept his hand on the door. "What's this about?"

"Do you remember having fathered a set of twins, Mr. White?"

The man grasped the doorframe tightly while shadows danced across his eyes, the same way they did when Sarah became quiet.

His reaction told her she'd found the correct individual and Cam's persistence had paid off. She reached out to him. "Mr. White, can we go inside? I think it would be best if you were sitting down."

After a minute, he nodded, though he said nothing. She followed him into a small but neat home. The furniture was older but clean.

"You got ID?"

She flipped out her wallet, producing her badge and license. Paul studied it for a minute. "Can I get you a drink, Ms. Stark?"

"It's Cam. Water would be good."

He wavered before smiling. "I hope you don't mind, but I'm going for something stronger."

"Not at all." She took the opportunity to glance at the pictures on the small mantel above a tiny fireplace. They were all family from what she could tell. Paul and who she assumed was his wife in one. A young boy holding a trophy. His features resembled Paul as he stood behind him. An older boy with a darker complexion, dirty blond hair, and blue eyes. He looked pissed at the world. He didn't look like Paul but had similar eye color. The next one froze her in place. It was a younger version of Sarah laughing, her eyes sparkling. She held the two pictures side by side. While their coloring was marked opposites, their facial structure and features were the same. She snapped a few photos with her phone. She had a picture of Sarah's brother.

"They grew up to be good-looking, like their mom."

Cam gently placed them back on the mantel. "But she has your eyes."

Paul handed her a glass of water with ice. His tumbler barely contained enough amber liquid to see and she admired his restraint. "The only good thing I gave her." He sat down heavily in one of the two chairs. She took the other.

"You've been in touch with them?" She knew he hadn't with Sarah, but perhaps he had with the boy.

He sipped before answering. "No. I hired someone a long time ago. It was on a whim. I was in a bad place and thought…" He shook his head. "I didn't want to interfere in their lives. I just needed to know they were doing okay. I wasn't the one who wanted to give them up."

"I'm not here to judge you, Mr. White. I'm looking for your daughter's twin." Whatever reason the man had for looking for his children was none of her business.

Paul's eyes glistened. "Why does she want to know after all these years?"

Normally that was the kind of question Cam asked, but the man had a right to know. "Sarah's adoptive parents are recently deceased. She's found out about her twin and asked me to help her locate him." She didn't miss the pain transforming his already troubled face into the type of regret she'd seen on many occasions in her field. The deep regret that even time didn't heal. "Sarah might also want to find her birth parents, but I'm following the lead to her twin."

"Not surprised. Her mother—not my wife"—he nodded to the pictures—"said getting pregnant by me was the biggest mistake of her life." He finished the contents and set the glass down, then looked back at Cam. "It wasn't. I told her the biggest mistake was giving up the two beautiful children in the nursery. She only let me see them once." He began to cry softly, his hands over his face.

Many people had called her numerous names over the years, but callous had never been one. "Mr. White, would you like me to come back in a few days?" Sarah might be upset, but how she conducted the investigation was up to her, and she wasn't about to take Sarah's impatience out on this man. He still suffered from past mistakes, and she had no doubt his children's estrangement was a big one.

He took a minute, then cleared his throat. "It's okay. I had an inkling this day would come. What do you need?"

"Do you happen to know your son's adoptive name?"

Paul got up and pulled a small album off a bookshelf. He sat and reverently flipped through the pages. She caught glimpses of the two youngsters in the photos she'd studied. He pulled a piece of paper out of a sleeve toward the middle. Paul held it between trembling fingers. "The person I hired, he stayed in touch over the years. Once in a while he'd send an envelope with a picture or two, including a location and date written on the back." He thought for a minute. "I wish I could remember his name. There was never a return address, and the postmarks were from all over the country. Maybe he was worried about being sued or some such thing. People are money hungry these days, looking for an easy way to make a buck instead of honest work. Whatever the reason, I wish I could thank him."

He handed Cam a rumpled square of paper and she studied it. "Brace Archer." She snapped a photo with her phone. It had an address but no phone number. Her pulse picked up speed. This was a definite lead. Better than even she had hoped for.

"That's the last one I got." He nodded to the open album. "These stopped coming a number of years ago. Maybe four or five." He tipped his head to one side and stared off. "Memory's a little cloudy these days." He took the paper and slid it back into the album.

She should be pushing for more, but she didn't want to offend him. He was her best link to discovery, and maybe Sarah would want to talk with him at some point. Blood was blood. "Have you spoken to their mother, Judy Jones?"

"Ha. That what she put down as her name?"

"Yes."

Paul shook his head but went on. "I tried a few times. She was a nasty cuss. Had high falutin' ideas that she was gonna be a star... make it big, and she couldn't do that with two screaming babies." Paul went quiet.

Cam thought she'd heard all she was going to.

"I'd never hated anyone in my life until she got rid of those little angels as fast as she could. Said she was leaving the hospital in a couple of days and didn't care if they had a home or not." Paul nodded to the picture of Brace. "From what I understand, he'd been sick when he was born. They said it was fetal alcohol syndrome. That damn woman was so self-centered she didn't care what she was doing to those babies."

Paul looked as though he had a nasty taste in his mouth, and Cam imagined the thing between him and Judy had been doomed before it even began.

"What was her real name?"

"Judith Anne Matthews. Hell, I slept with her on impulse, so I'm part to blame." He pressed the heels of his hands to his eyes. "If I'd had a legal leg to stand on, I would have taken them, made do however I could have. She denied I was the father. Said she'd never admit otherwise. I never understood why it mattered to her if I took my babies, except she likely did it out of spite." He took a breath and shook his head again, though it seemed more in defeat than disbelief. "Water under the dam. Anyway, I heard she died a while back." He sighed. "Regrets...you know what I mean?"

"I do." Cam had a few of her own. It was time to leave him be. She doubted there was anything else of consequence. When she stood, so did he. "Thank you, Mr. White. I appreciate your help." She extended her hand and he grasped it, hanging on as though it were a lifeline. Cam pulled out a business card. "If you think of anything you'd like Sarah to know, call me."

"If she asks, tell her I never wanted it this way. Tell her...I'd like to meet her." He glanced at the mantel. "Her brother, too."

Cam studied his face. Sarah would have done well to have him as a father. Hell, Cam would have probably been okay with a man of his character, too. She didn't want to dash his hopes, but she didn't want to lead him on either.

"If she asks." She gently squeezed, and he let go.

He looked down at the picture he was holding of Sarah from a few years ago. She could see tears pooling and wanted to comfort him, wondering if anyone had loved *her* that much. The door closed quietly behind her, but the click was deafening.

CHAPTER THIRTEEN

"Maggie, can you come in here?" Cam clicked off the intercom and pulled a pile of papers from the blue folder. Each page was stamped with the file number, one she knew by heart. The last piece held today's date. Paul had struggled at times, but he'd told her all he could. It was too bad about Judith Matthews, and his reaction to her name cleared up the issue of seeing her first name as Judy on documents. It wasn't like the current culture where businesses, including hospitals, asked for a photo ID. No matter. She'd gotten what she wanted, Sarah's brother's adoptive name, and on top of that, she'd spoken to Sarah's birth father. Paul might be someone else Sarah might consider contacting, but she could do that on her own. Even if Cam couldn't find the brother for some reason, she'd still found actual blood, and that was a damn good thing. The time for deep cyber sleuthing had arrived.

"What's up?" Maggie stood in front of her desk, a pad and pen at the ready.

"I've got a new lead on the Peters case. Can you do a quick search and see what you can find on Brace Archer, common spelling? Check the usual, including social media."

"On it," she said as she turned away.

"Thank you." She'd been hard on her staunchest supporter, and to her credit, Maggie's attitude had changed over the last few weeks. Cam wanted to make sure she knew she noticed. Sarah's hypothesis that Maggie was jealous in some way had been put to rest, and that made life a lot easier. Maggie was being a friend, someone who worried about her. It wasn't something Cam was used to, and it made the boss/employee relationship a little blurry, but she could live with it.

Maggie winked at her. "You know I can't say no to you even when I think otherwise." She tapped the pad. "Let me see what I can find."

Cam forwarded the pictures from her phone to her email, then saved each one before making hard copies. She stared at Brace, wondering what he'd been thinking when the boyhood picture had been taken. He looked like a typical brooding teen. Based on the date on the back, he should have been in college at the time, though he looked young. She was thankful Paul had written their ages and the date he received each photo. Brace didn't appear to share Sarah's disposition. Sarah was a deep thinker and feisty, but she was also kind and thoughtful. The night they'd shared a hotel room had proven that. Even though she'd been incapacitated, Cam remembered how sexy Sarah had looked fresh from the shower, with her wet, wavy hair and lack of makeup that she didn't need. If she'd been able to think, even a little, she'd have taken the opportunity to get to know Sarah on a more personal level and found out more about Sarah as an individual instead of a client.

While Maggie tracked down the easy stuff, she delved deeper into her databases. Thankfully, the Departments of Motor Vehicles from across the nation had joined forces and created a massive database, making it easier for other states to see traffic infractions and suspended license information regardless of the state of issuance. She typed in his name and date of birth, then watched while the system searched. It wasn't long before it pinged.

His original license had been issued in Philadelphia, which was the address Paul provided, and likely where he grew up. And a renewal two years later in Miami. She opened another resource and discovered he'd gone to Broward College in Florida, earning an associate degree in criminal justice. Three years later, he showed up in New York. She tapped her pen on the pad in front of her. Something felt off. What had he done between college and coming to New York? Miami was a hotbed of grand theft, gang violence, and drugs. Maybe he'd done internships somewhere. She opened another screen and went to her LinkedIn account. Bingo. Brace Archer flashed in front of her. A few clicks later, and his résumé appeared. The years between his degree in 2002 and joining the Poughkeepsie Police Force in 2005 were still missing. The void didn't point to a negative connotation. She had some missing years of her own and they were going to remain that way. Maybe he hadn't bothered updating his résumé with work that didn't seem relevant.

What Cam did want to know was how he'd survived on his own with no visible income, and she verified her hunch by searching his name plus employment history, again finding nothing as far as Social Security deductions or taxable income. Of course, he might have worked under the table, which would prove to be another dead end. She rubbed her eyes and rolled her neck. Digging could be tedious, and coffee was in order. She went to the small break room and rinsed her day-old remnants away. The refrigerator hummed and she grimaced, wondering if the takeout she'd shoved in there sometime earlier in the week was growing mold. She opened the door and peered in to find the shelves clean and a neat stack of grab and go snacks lined up on the top one. Satisfied no one would die of botulism, she turned to find Maggie in the doorway, a paper shopping bag in her hand.

"You need more than junk food. Maybe half your problem with migraines is your existence on caffeine and crap." Maggie gestured for her to take a seat at the table. "And how about water or juice for a change?"

She wanted to defend her eating habits, but how could she? Never mind about the five pounds she'd lost in the last month. At some point her body was going to revolt more than it already was, and she had no one to blame but herself. After staring at her abandoned mug, she grabbed a water from the fridge before taking a seat.

"I remember a time when you didn't come across like a drill sergeant." She cracked the seal and took a swig, wrinkling her nose. Coffee would be better.

"Perhaps because there was a time when you actually gave a shit about your health." Maggie emptied a variety of containers on the table. "Salads, pasta, and a small slice of cheesecake to go with that coffee I know you'll eventually have."

She knew better than to argue. Maggie had hit all the high points. She was an emotional mess and running on empty most of the time. Nights were the worst. She'd lay awake thinking about Sarah and how much she enjoyed spending time with her and how the whole idea of getting personally involved was weighing on her. Cam was trying her best to maintain distance, and just when she thought she managed to do so, she'd find a reason to see Sarah. Which reminded her she needed to send a text and set up a dinner date. No, not a date. Getting together to discuss what she'd learned from Paul. A client meeting, with food.

"Earth to Cam. What *are* you stewing over?" Maggie had removed the food covers and was staring at her.

Cam felt herself blink several times to clear her head. "Nothing. The case. Did you find out anything?" She scooped some eggplant parm onto her plate and a small helping of Caesar salad, ignoring the scolding look from Maggie.

While there were still blanks to be filled, Cam had confirmed his current address. He was, at least technically, in Poughkeepsie. Which was great since she never liked the heat of the South and had hoped she wouldn't have to travel anywhere near Miami. While it was out of the norm in the function of a PI to introduce herself to the person she was trying to find, that's exactly what she intended to do with Brace, but not until she had more information. No one had ever been concerned enough about Cam to keep her out of harm's way, but she intended to be that person for Sarah, especially now that Sarah didn't have anyone to look out for her. Once she was confident he was honorable and no threat to Sarah's well-being, all she had to do was pass the information she'd gathered on to Sarah and she was done. *Finito*. Certainly, she couldn't be faulted for making sure Sarah wasn't being set up for another disappointment. *That's the responsible thing to do.* Cam wondered why she was chancing her career for the sake of a client. She'd never gone over the line from professional to personal involvement before. Well, not while she was still employed by the person. But when it came to Sarah, she was willing to ignore the confines of common practice.

❖

Sarah cracked open the electrolyte drink, downing half before unwrapping her sandwich of leftover chicken, lettuce, tomato, and cheese. Her day on the high-rise would end in a few hours, but she hoped the supervisor would ask for volunteers for overtime. She had to make all she could to build up her reserves. Winter would rear its ugly head soon enough, and construction would slow down, if not halt altogether. She pulled out her phone and checked her messages. Lisa, of course, telling her to stop being a ghost and come see her. A couple of bill reminders from her bank. *Oh yeah.* And Cam. She swallowed hard, then opened the message.

Wondering if you would be free for dinner Saturday night. I've got some updates on your case. I could pick you up at 7.

Her stomach tightened. Had she talked to her birth father or mother? Could Cam have found her brother? She stared at the message, hoping for more.

Saturday is good.

It didn't take long for the phone to alert her to an incoming message.

See you then.

Sarah had a million questions, but they would all have to wait. It was obvious whatever Cam had to tell her, she wanted to do it in person. *Maybe that means she doesn't have any news and wants to break it to me gently.* She'd drive herself crazy with wonder. She just had to finish out the next few days, then she'd have answers.

Sarah looked off in the distance as she ate and wondered if her brother was out there somewhere in her line of sight. She'd resisted contacting Cam though it had damn near killed her. The not knowing what was going on every minute was absurd, and she'd managed to keep it at bay only because she'd been too exhausted to think and had fallen into bed each night shortly after eating. The weekend was coming, and she was looking forward to strolling through a couple of nearby modern art galleries. She needed to get her name out there somehow, and networking was her best option. Lisa had offered to go with her to lend moral support, but she wanted to prove to herself she had what it took to make it in the art world, as fickle a place as it was. Perhaps she'd bring along her modest portfolio in hopes of striking up a conversation with a another gallery owner since they tended to peruse works by artists other than the ones they displayed. She had nothing to lose by trying.

Sarah opened a wet towelette and cleaned her face and hands before running the soft cloth over her neck and forearms. A soft breeze dried the moisture in an instant, making her skin tingle. Cam made her tingle, too. How many times was she going to have to reign in her wayward thoughts? Cam would find her brother and that would end their relationship. Sarah's gut twisted. Her growing attraction was likely a factor in wanting to contact Cam, but she knew she should just leave her alone and let her do her job. Even though Sarah was more than ready to start her own life, Cam wasn't going to be part of it. *Then why do I keep finding reasons to keep her in it?*

Between Cam and Maggie, they'd uncovered details about Brace's adoptive parents. They lived in the upscale area of Scarsdale and owned a large home, nearly the size of a mansion. No doubt they had money and moved in affluent circles. So why was he a police officer when he could have pursued any career avenue he wanted? Cam would have liked to believe he'd done it out of a sense of duty to his community. A higher calling, so to speak. But there was something sinister and threatening in his expression. Cam shook her head. Maybe that was just her grasping at straws and fabricating parallels from her past in order to delay Sarah's departure. She needed to consider other motives for what she considered an unfriendly demeanor.

"He's egotistical and so full of himself I almost barfed." Maggie pointed to the screen. From the pictures on his social media site, Brace Archer was, indeed, a male chauvinist. There were a lot of women who chatted him up and he smirked into the lens several times a day, showing a big smile. His comments had to do with women's anatomy and ability to serve, rather than anything worth reading. And none of it did anything to hide the darkness in his eyes. Whether it was cruelty or just a general malice for life, Cam wasn't sure.

The thought of Brace and Sarah in a room together brought a foreboding chill up her spine. He looked like he could be easily provoked into a rage, and Cam was all too familiar with what male rage could lead to. It was the same look she'd first seen in the picture on Paul's mantel.

She'd do whatever she had to do to keep Sarah from being disappointed by Brace if she could help it, whether it was her place to do it or not. She hoped he wasn't as big an asshole as he looked, although at least if he was blatant about it, Sarah would find out right away and not become too attached.

"I agree." Cam had two more databases to search. Then she'd decide on the next step of her investigation, if there was one. "Not the wholesome, all-American young man I expected."

"Sarah's nothing like him," Maggie said.

She looked over her shoulder and Maggie laughed. "You don't have to look so surprised. I told you my behavior had nothing to do with Ms. Peters and everything to do with you. I've apologized to her, and I promise I'm on my best behavior." She gently tapped Cam's shoulder and moved around the desk. "I'll leave you to it. Let me know if you need anything else."

"Could you put on some coffee before you leave?"

Maggie scowled.

Cam ignored her as she rapidly clicked through a succession of screens. When Maggie hadn't moved, she made eye contact. "I ate lunch, now I want coffee." *And it will keep any migraine at bay.* The telltale sign of pressure behind her eyes let her know something was headed her way. She didn't share that pearl with Maggie.

❖

"Sarah."

Mark Johnson handed her an envelope and she moved off to the side. Some jobs paid better than others, but work was work and she'd taken the first available job that was offered. As she tore into it, she held her breath, hoping it would be enough to pay a few bills and buy some groceries. The gross amount was good, but once all the deductions were taken out, her mood soured. It would barely be enough to get by. Still, she was grateful for the work. Once her boss was done handing out checks, she approached him.

"Mr. Johnson?"

He turned to face her and smiled. "Yes, Sarah?"

"Do you know if there's any overtime on another job?" Sarah tried to keep her voice even, not wanting him to know how desperate she was for the extra money.

His forehead wrinkled. "Haven't you put in a full week already?"

She glanced around, making sure none of her coworkers were in hearing distance. "Yes, but the extra helps to pay off my mother's medical bills." She hated admitting she was struggling to make ends meet, but she knew honesty was the best way to get someone on your side.

He studied her for a long minute, then nodded. "I'll call around and text you if I find something."

Sarah looked down at the envelope in her hand. *Maybe I should get a roommate.* If someone else shared in the expense of the utilities and general upkeep of the house, she'd have a much easier time. Then she could spend her free hours on her art rather than working overtime. Her pieces might even sell with more time to promote them. Mark cleared his throat, rousing her from her deep thoughts. She raised her face and met his kind look.

"Thank you."

Sarah got in her car and prayed it would start. Lately, the vehicle sounded as though it was in need of a tune-up, but that was an expense she didn't have in her budget. After a few tense seconds, the engine turned over. She patted the dash and mumbled, "That's a good girl." It didn't escape her that it had been a very long time since she'd had as much attention.

❖

"Good afternoon." Cam looked at her notes again, even though she knew what she'd written by heart. "Could I speak to Officer Archer, please?"

"Who's calling?"

Cam heard voices in the background and considered if she should have made the trip, rather than try to find out more over the phone. "My name is Camdyn Stark. I'm a private investigator."

She listened as the officer called out, "Anyone seen Archer?" The cacophony of noise was deafening, and she wondered how anyone got anything done in an environment like that. She preferred her quiet setting, where she could concentrate on the details of whatever case she was working.

"Hold on a minute."

A litany of crime prevention tips began playing in her ear. Never leave the keys in your car. Always lock your doors. Be aware of your surroundings. Blah, blah. Though she appreciated the sentiment, Cam was in no mood for the android voice droning in her head. Relief loosened her jaw when the phone clicked.

"He's not here. Wanna leave a message?"

"Any idea when Officer Archer will be there? It's not critical, but it is important that I speak with him."

"Your guess is as good as mine. He's probably pounding pavement. No telling if he'll even show today."

Cam knew how it went, especially since Archer was working in the narcotics division. He might be on a stakeout, meaning he could be away for hours...or days. "Can I leave my number and a message to call me?"

"Yeah."

Cam gave her info and hung up. Something was niggling at her brain, and she felt uneasy. It wasn't a good sign. She reached for the phone.

"Yeah, boss?" Maggie asked.

"I'm going to pay a visit to the station where Archer works."

"Isn't that a little out of the ordinary? You've got the basics."

Cam looked at the papers spread in front of her. "My gut's telling me he isn't what he seems. So yeah, it might be just a hunch, but I'm going."

There was only a moment of hesitation. "You're the boss."

Cam looked at the receiver. Maggie was being agreeable, and when it came to going above and beyond the norm, she usually had an opinion. One Cam would have called her on in this case. She was more than aware she was stretching her professional duty and couldn't remember another instance when she'd ridden the edge of impropriety. Everything that involved Sarah was anything but normal, and neither was her need to protect her. Sarah was already emotionally invested in her brother, and for Sarah's sake she hoped her instincts were wrong.

CHAPTER FOURTEEN

C am stood waiting for the officer behind the bulletproof barrier to end his phone conversation. They'd made eye contact and he'd held up a finger between head nods and scribbling on the pad in front of him. She had all she could to keep from pacing. It wasn't like her to be so impatient, but the feeling of dread had steadily built on the drive. She had no idea what it meant, but she wasn't about to ignore her instincts. They'd managed to keep her out of the ground so far.

"What can I do for you?"

She glanced at the name on his badge, then cleared her throat and showed her identification. "Camdyn Stark. I called earlier to talk with Officer Archer. Would he happen to be around, Officer Graves?"

He studied the open wallet before glancing at a roster sheet and flipping through several pages, then looked back up. "He checked in a little while ago. Narc division's on the second floor." He was about to reach under the counter for what Cam knew was the door release before he hesitated.

"You carrying?" He looked her in the eye. She didn't miss his quick assessment of the form-fitting button-down shirt she was wearing.

"No, sir."

He nodded and a loud electronic buzz sounded. The metal detector was silent as she stepped through. Cam adjusted the folder in her hand and made her way down the short corridor to the elevators. The drone of voices with the occasional shout echoed along the flat gray walls. They really needed to hire an interior decorator. Their job was already depressing enough.

She took a deep breath before spotting the sign for the staircase. She took the stairs two at a time to avoid one more death trap box. It wouldn't be fair to have an attitude before even meeting him if she got the chance. She needed to keep her personal feelings about Sarah in check. She was on a fact-finding mission.

She glanced at the folder in her hand. She hadn't brought any identifying information on Sarah, except for a recent photo she'd requested that Sarah supply the last time they were together. The close-up showed off Sarah's striking beauty, making the most of her startling blue eyes and blond hair. The lighter streaks were most likely due to exposure to the sun rather than from bleach. She became momentarily lost before regaining her footing.

Cam read the signs on the doors as she walked along. Interrogation One. Interrogation Two. Men's. Women's. The farther she went, the darker the hallway. When she reached the end, the door facing her was the one she wanted. She squared her shoulders and put on what she hoped was her "all business" look. Opening the door, she heard the murmurs and rapid tapping of keys. No one noticed her. A bit troubling for a police division, but then, they probably had a lot more to worry about with the gang activity and random shootings that centered around drugs. She picked out an officer who looked affable and cleared her throat.

"Excuse me. Would you happen to know where I might find Officer Archer?"

He leaned forward, looking toward an empty desk off to the right. He sat back. "He's not here." She didn't miss the contempt in his voice and wondered if she'd found a way to get a little more information than she could from public records. She stuck out her hand and smiled.

"Camdyn Stark, PI. Do you happen to know when he'll return?"

"Barnes," he said as he stood and took her hand. Barnes glanced around. There were a half dozen other officers in the room, all preoccupied on the phone or the screens they were staring at, or talking to each other. "Not likely. He's…" Barnes appeared to be chewing on his words, but it was obvious something about Archer was either bugging him or pissing him off. He shrugged. "He's not here often and rarely returns once he's left."

She hung on to his words, hoping to convey a serious level of interest in what he wasn't saying. Maybe she could convince him to tell her why if she was careful. "Is that how everyone works in the division?"

He snorted. "Hardly." He glanced around again, suddenly seeming nervous.

She leaned in and kept her voice low. "Would you like to get a cup of real coffee? I know I would, and I'm not familiar with the area."

Barnes glanced at his watch. "What the hell," he said as he stood and grabbed his jacket off the chair. "Close enough for lunch."

It was barely after eleven, but she imagined he'd been there since early morning. Most officers she knew didn't sleep that great and would rather work than toss and turn. Once outside, they walked side by side in silence until Barnes slowed and pointed to a nondescript cafe. "Doesn't look like much, but they have good coffee and even better specials." He opened the door and waved her in.

While the outside had appeared less than welcoming, the inside was bright and clean. The din of busy workers and patrons was a nice change from the greasy spoon diners she imagined most on the force frequented.

"We can order and get our drinks. They'll bring our food to the table." He perused the menu, settling on the chicken salad on rye with a side of fries. Chicken salad sounded good, but she opted for the coleslaw instead of fries. Maggie would be proud.

After fixing their coffees at the sidebar, Barnes pointed to a table at the back. Cam could tell he was worried. Maybe if his coworkers saw him they'd give him a hard time for chatting it up with a PI. Then she remembered the only one who knew her profession was the officer at the front desk, and he hadn't been there when they'd walked out the front door. The coffee was strong but smooth.

"You're right. The coffee is good."

Barnes smiled. "Coffee and cops. The standard cliché." He took a gulp before fixing a hard stare on her. "What do you want with Archer?"

"I don't want anything. There's someone who'd very much like to meet him."

Something akin to panic, or maybe anger, made his jaw bunch. "Who's that?"

"I'm not at liberty to say." She stirred her coffee absently, trying to figure out what it was she did want to say. "But if there's something about Archer I should know, something that matters to my investigation and my client's safety, I'd very much like to hear it."

Barnes looked in his coffee as though trying to decide how to answer her. He looked like he wanted to bolt, or kill someone, and she questioned why. She'd gone with her instinct when she offered him an escape so he wouldn't be overheard, believing he wanted to talk, and she was happy to be the one he talked to.

"If, and that's a big if right now, I'm going to tell you, I need more."

She'd expected as much, and hoped he'd still be willing to share, otherwise why were they there?

"Off the record? I was hired to find Officer Archer, although at the time, I didn't know his name or what he did for a living." Cam had always prided herself with keeping her clients' identities secret, but under the circumstances she wasn't going to get Barnes's cooperation without giving him something. "It turns out he has a twin sister who's looking for him."

Their food arrived, giving Barnes time to process the news. He looked down at his plate, and when he glanced back up, there was something in his eyes she couldn't read.

"She's better off not finding him." He picked up his sandwich and took a bite.

"Why is that, Officer Barnes?"

He swallowed, then washed it down with coffee. "Jimmy." He looked around again as the deli began to fill up and leaned forward.

"He's scum hiding behind a badge." His disgust was apparent as he pushed away the remainder of his lunch. "He dishonors the force. A mockery of his sworn duty." His face turned red, and Cam knew it was the anger raging inside causing it.

"My client isn't going to be satisfied by vague answers, Offi—Jimmy. I'll have to keep asking."

"It would be safer for both of you if you didn't do that. If you walked away and told her you couldn't find him."

Cam had a talent for getting to the truth, a skill she'd honed since becoming a PI. She loved watching the person she posed questions to think of all the outcomes, or consequences of their answers. Often a person wanted to be rid of the secrets they were hiding, and she provided an outlet. Not to say it always worked. She'd encountered her fair share of uncooperative people. How they thought sooner or later she wouldn't find what she was looking for never failed to amaze her. She was a damn good investigator. Yes, her ego got big once in a while, but she could live with it considering how often it resulted in success.

"I'm not afraid of finding out the truth." Cam pushed away her own plate.

"You should be. He's dangerous to be around. And not just him. His runners are lowlife scum, too."

She wanted to be sure she hadn't misinterpreted what Barnes was telling her. "He's dealing?"

Barnes drained his cup and caught the eye of one of the waitstaff. She came over and refilled both cups before hustling back behind the counter. "Wonder boy is as dirty as they come."

Shit. Sometimes being right wasn't all it was cracked up to be. She picked up her coffee and sat back to listen.

Chapter Fifteen

Cam spun her pencil on her desk and thought about what she'd learned from Officer Barnes. When she asked why he thought Archer was involved in drugs, he'd shared his personal opinion of the typical rich kid syndrome. Brace had bragged about never having to work for anything as long as he did exactly as his parents said. They wanted him to go to college and get a business degree. He wanted to roam the streets, hang out, do as he pleased. He'd caved under their threat of closing his bank account. He earned a two-year degree in a Florida college and stayed in Miami for a while. Barnes said Archer didn't elaborate, and he came to his own conclusion that Brace had been learning the business of selling drugs. Brace had said that when he joined the force, there was little his parents could do to stop him, and they accepted his chosen profession, even though he'd done it just to get under their skin. They'd wanted a businessman, not a blue-collar worker. Clearly, he'd done it out of spite and for all the wrong reasons. She dreaded having to share the news with Sarah.

"Hi, Sarah."

"Hey. Everything okay?"

"Just checking we're still on for tonight and that seven still works." It was a solid reason for calling, though she'd done it because she yearned to hear Sarah's voice.

"I'm looking forward to it. Unless something's come up on your end?"

Cam didn't miss the anxiety in Sarah's voice. "No. I'm good, but I was wondering if we could order in at my place instead of going out. It's been a long day."

"Sure." Cam gave her the address. "See you then."

Sarah hadn't hesitated, and Cam questioned the real reason she wanted to be alone with her. The food arrived while Sarah still stood at the front door, and Cam was grateful for the distraction. Sarah looked as beautiful as always. Her hair was held in a loose tie at the nape of her neck. She wore a pair of faded, ripped jeans and a form-fitting long-sleeve T-shirt. The color was a shade of blue that highlighted her eyes. *Focus. I can do this.* She opened the door wider and stepped back to let her in.

"Make yourself at home. I'll be right there." Cam paid for the food, closed the door, then took a breath before facing her. "I hope you like Chinese." She hefted the shopping bag onto the dining room table and shared what she hoped was a smile that didn't give away the butterflies in her stomach. She wasn't sure why she suddenly felt like this was a first date with a woman she'd been crushing on, but it did.

"It looks like you ordered enough for a dozen people." Sarah helped pull out containers.

Their hands brushed as they both reached inside. The resulting buzz shot through Cam with the intensity of an electric shock.

"Are you expecting more people?"

Sarah's soft, teasing voice did nothing to halt her building desire. Cam shook her head. "No. Just us." Once everything was out on the table she had to agree. There was way too much food. "I just ordered a bunch of different stuff because I wasn't sure what you liked."

"You could have asked." Sarah chuckled. "I brought a six-pack of beer."

Cam hadn't noticed anything except Sarah. Not her signature carryall or the grocery bag she reached for.

Sarah took out two bottles, twisted off the caps, and set one by each plate.

Cam put her hands on her hips. "What, and spoil the fun of having a little of everything? No way." She took the remaining bottles and slid them in the fridge, grateful for the opportunity to regroup. After taking her seat, she lifted her bottle and tipped it in Sarah's direction. "To feast or not to feast."

Sarah clinked her bottle. "To feast!"

"Dig in," Cam said. She watched as Sarah opened containers. She wrinkled her nose at one or two, which transformed her face from beautiful to adorable, and once again Cam was swept away. She marveled at the smooth skin of Sarah's throat and farther down to the hint of cleavage visible at the V-neck opening.

After her plate was filled, Sarah glanced up at Cam. "Aren't you eating?"

Damn it. So much for not being distracted. "Uh-huh, but don't wait for me. Eat while it's hot." Cam concentrated on the containers in an attempt to rein in her unprofessional thoughts. Her movements felt mechanical. It was hard to focus while Sarah moaned over her food. Cam's sex tightened in response.

"This is delicious," Sarah said around a mouthful of General Tso's chicken. She looked up, then smiled. "I rarely eat out or order in. This is a treat." She moaned again. "Sorry," she mumbled before swallowing. "I'm acting like I haven't eaten in days." She put her fork down and picked up her drink.

If Cam wasn't mistaken, Sarah looked embarrassed. She hated thinking Sarah was uncomfortable with her. It was the last thing she wanted. Regardless, she had to find out if there was a reason she seemed ravenous. "Have you?"

Sarah's brows knit in confusion.

"Eaten?"

Her cheeks flamed before Sarah dropped her gaze to the half-eaten plate of food. "I eat. No worries there." She met Cam's stare. "I may have forgotten today."

"What kept you so busy?"

"I...uh..." Sarah stumbled and studied her plate before looking up. "I'm a bit behind on bills, so I spent the day at my shop, and I forgot to eat. If I can sell a piece or two it will help." She glanced at her plate again. "But I'm not starving."

Cam grasped Sarah's hand. "I'm sure you'll work it out." She slid her hand away. The flesh beneath her palm had been soft and firm at the same time, like Sarah. The sad part was she hadn't realized Sarah's financial situation was as bleak, or bleaker, than she thought, and she regretted having mentioned the need for more money.

"Then you better eat up because there's a decadent dessert for later, and I can't possibly eat all this by myself."

"Good, because I'm still hungry and this is really good." Sarah looked at her from beneath her eyelashes and smiled before picking up her fork.

Was Sarah flirting with her? The tingle that shot down her spine in a most pleasant way landed with a thud in her crotch, doing nothing to help her keep her wits about her. She wasn't sure if Sarah had meant to be seductive, but that's how it felt.

After another beer, they sat back with satisfied grins. She'd learned a bit about Sarah's childhood along with several grade school antics.

"I'd like to see your workshop sometime."

"Why?"

Cam was the one who did the questioning. Sarah flipping the tables on her was unexpected. She shrugged, unprepared to answer. She thought up an excuse. "I've never known an artist." Not a lie, but the reason was lame. *Should I just tell her I want to spend more time with her?* She wasn't ready for rejection. Sarah watched her as she twirled the bottle clutched in her hands.

"Okay."

Cam let out a breath.

Sarah leaned in. "I know next to nothing about you in general, and I've never known a PI, so that makes us even." Her brow moved upward.

Cam laughed. "I guess it does." She felt like she owed Sarah the courtesy of hearing a little about herself, so she told her a bit about Liv, though she left out exactly how they'd met.

"Olivia sounds like a wonderful person. I'm so glad you can trust her." Sarah's face turned pensive.

"Who do you trust, Sarah?"

Sarah opened her mouth several times, but nothing came out before she shook her head and picked up her plate. "I'll do the dishes."

Cam let it go as she closed up containers and placed them back in the shopping bag. All except the shrimp lo mein and the garlic chicken, which Sarah had avoided like the plague, and she slid everything into the fridge with plans on sending it home with Sarah. While she worked, her mind wandered back to their earlier conversation. As much as Cam was physically attracted to her, it was more than Sarah's beauty. She and Sarah had a common thread—they'd both been given up. Maybe it was for totally different reasons, but the central theme was the same. They had been unwanted, though Sarah might have never made the connection since she'd always been loved. Cam fought the angst inside, where her younger self still had a voice, telling her to do everything in her power to make sure Sarah never felt a similar pain. Liv had been her savior, and Cam hoped she could do half as well for Sarah. The only remaining question was how.

The most logical thing to do was to decline Cam's invitation and keep their relationship purely platonic. Then she'd decided the hell with logic and here she was. Sarah watched as Cam poured steaming coffee into a mug, and a slow smile appeared as the aroma filled the air. Until that moment, she hadn't realized how much she missed being around her. She had the perfect opportunity to stare at Cam's high, firm-looking ass and narrow waist. She wasn't pretty in a traditional sense, but she was alluring and sensuous in many ways. Her long dark hair and matching eyelashes highlighted her hazel eyes. Her voice was deeper than her appearance would suggest without being masculine. She talked with passion about her work, and when she became serious on a particular subject, her eyes flamed with intensity. Her fingers were slender and sure. Sarah envisioned how they would feel on her skin, and her breath froze. *No, no.* She couldn't go there. Not with Cam. Not with…

"I can't remember if you take sugar, but I have several kinds." Cam placed a bowl of packets on the table.

She jumped, startled from indulging any further in her overactive imagination. It took her a few beats to catch up. "Sugar?

A little." She accepted the mug from Cam's outstretched hand, then reached for a packet of brown sugar.

"Where'd you go?"

Sarah's cheeks heated and she shrugged, hoping the subject would be dropped. She should have known better.

"Sarah, you don't have to be secretive." Cam sat and added a splash of cream to her coffee.

"Is that because you'd put your investigative powers to work on me?" Sarah asked.

Cam shook her head. "I'd never try to force you to tell me something you didn't want to, but if something's bothering you, I hope you know you can trust me with whatever it is."

The sincerity in her voice made Sarah second-guess her decision of keeping their relationship purely professional.

"Why are you single?" *Oh fuck.* She couldn't believe she'd just blurted out what she'd been wondering since they'd met.

"I..." Cam faltered.

Sarah laughed. "See? It's not that easy to spill your guts."

Cam smiled into her mug as she took a sip. "Touché."

"You don't have to answer. It's none of my business." She needed to focus anywhere except on Cam's gentle expression staring back at her.

Cam let out a long breath before touching Sarah's hand again. "Sarah, I don't tell many people about my life, or my past. It's dangerous to let anyone have an upper hand in my line of work."

"I get that." Sarah waved her hand dismissively. "Besides, I don't think that's the reason you invited me here."

Cam cringed inwardly. Even though her excuse was the truth, it was just that, an excuse for not opening up to Sarah. It was the same line she gave to any woman who got too curious. The sad part was she *wanted* to open up to her. And unless she was losing her touch, she would bet money Sarah was attracted to her, too. But she couldn't cross that line. Not now. Maybe not ever.

"I met with your biological father, Paul. I caught him off guard, but he said he thought the day would come when someone would approach him about his past."

Sarah stared ahead. "Do you believe that?"

"I do. He…" Cam thought about how much she should reveal about Paul's emotional state. "He never wanted to give up either of you. It was all your birth mother's doing."

Sarah's head came up. "And what does she have to say about that?" she asked.

She tried to keep her voice neutral. "She wasn't there. She's deceased, and they were never married."

"Oh." Sarah's looked away. She took her time and drank from her mug.

Cam reached for Sarah but stopped short of touching her, though she ached for physical contact. "Paul seems genuinely interested in meeting you."

Sarah's lips thinned. "Then why didn't he try to find *me*?"

Here goes. "He did. Find you, I mean. The same way you hired me to find your brother. I think he was afraid you'd hate him for what happened, but that's something you'd have to ask him yourself." Cam wasn't sure if Sarah's silence was a good thing. "But that's not the real reason I asked you here."

A few long minutes later, Sarah broke the quiet. "What was it then?"

As much as she was glad to drop the focus from herself, she was dreading what she was going to tell Sarah. The news from Jimmy Barnes hadn't given her any reassurance that Brace had redeeming qualities. From what she'd learned he was a cop gone bad, and she didn't want Sarah anywhere near him. In fact, if she had her way, she wouldn't tell Sarah anything at all about her long-lost twin. She'd never breached the ethical line and she was uncomfortable she had even considered it. But it wasn't up to her.

"I have a really bad feeling in my gut about some of the trails I've been following, and it's never let me down before."

Sarah's eyes hardened. "So, what are you saying?"

"I know how much finding your brother means to you."

"No, I don't think you do, but go on."

"I just don't want whatever I find to be worse than the not knowing. Maybe we shouldn't spend more time or money on this."

She looked away. Her professional side was at war with her personal one. The one that cared for Sarah so much she would jeopardize her ethics. "Maybe you could let it go for now."

The look on Sarah's face left no doubt she was pissed at the idea of giving up. "I knew it." Sarah slammed the table with her fist. "All that talk about being the best and always finding who you were looking for was just a crock of shit." Sarah stood and grabbed her satchel, slinging it over her shoulder so hard she almost strangled herself. "Well, guess what, Stark? I don't have any more fucking money to hire someone else, so you're it."

"Sarah, that's not—"

The door slammed so hard Cam thought she heard the wood crack. She knew she should go after her. Should have tried to make Sarah see she *was* doing her job. Maybe a little too well. Considering the lack of information she'd shared, maybe Sarah was right. But it's not like she'd had the chance. Well, that wasn't totally true. Cam had been hedging all evening. Maybe she'd had no intention of telling Sarah any of what she'd learned and was just stringing her along hoping she'd drop the idea of finding her brother altogether so Cam could pursue her in a less than professional manner. But she really did believe that if Brace came into Sarah's life, he'd bring a world of trouble with him.

"Jesus Christ, Stark. You've really fucked this one up."

Cam robotically picked up the dining room then stood staring out the kitchen window. Defeat hadn't ever been in her DNA. Sure, she'd been lost as a teenager, but she'd come through the other side. Those long-ago feelings rushed to the forefront as she paced around the house mumbling to herself for the better part of an hour before picking up her cell. There had only ever been one person who could talk her out of the funk she was spiraling into, and she prayed Liv would answer the phone.

❖

The next day, Cam listened to the steady heartbeat beneath her head, finding the same comfort she'd always found in Liv's embrace.

Their relationship would probably baffle most people's perception of what was "normal." She was okay with that. Liv had never asked for anything for herself, though Cam hoped she provided something that Liv needed, too. She owed so much to the woman who had given her a second chance, and then a third when she'd fucked up shortly after agreeing to Liv's terms. Liv had been the mother's love she never knew, the father's direction she'd never had, and the kindness and understanding she'd been convinced she'd never find anywhere else.

"What has you so tangled up inside?" Liv stroked her back.

The rough pads of her fingertips reminded Cam hard work was honest work. Liv was nothing but honest in everything she did. She had cared for Cam when she thought no one could, or would, telling Cam "even a blade of grass deserves to be cared for."

Cam's anger at herself had melted into sobs of despair after Liv had pulled her in for the hug she admitted she needed. She sighed against the warm, firm flesh under her cheek. "A client."

"Uh-huh."

Liv continued to soothe her, and the motion made the last vestiges of her resolve to not bring up Sarah melt away. Liv had a way of helping her bare her soul, and Cam believed it was the one thing that had saved her from herself.

"Sarah's...different."

Liv lifted her chin so she could see Cam's face, as though searching for what she wasn't saying. "Different in what way?

"I think she's getting...inside," Cam whispered as she shivered. The wall she'd constructed around her heart had weakened. It had never happened before, and she didn't know what to do.

"Everyone lets someone in at some point in their life. I'd say you're finally ready, but it's scaring the hell out of you."

She chuckled. Liv knew her better than anyone. "Maybe." It was hard to admit, even to Liv. In many ways she was still a loner, and it came down to a matter of trust. With Liv, the trust between them had grown over time at her own pace. With Sarah, it felt more like a wrecking ball, smashing against her barriers every time they were together. If she let Sarah close she was going to want to know everything about her. It could be the reason she'd remained single for so long. But they were childish fears and she needed to let go of them if she were to have a meaningful shot at something deeper.

"Maybe." Cam slowly moved out of Liv's embrace, and sat cross-legged on the sofa, like she used to when she'd first come to live with her. "I can't deny she's the first woman I've even considered letting get close." Then she remembered how things had ended between them, and her heart seized. She lowered her head, closing her eyes against the sting.

Liv faced her, leaning against the opposite corner. "What happened?"

Cam gave her the abbreviated version of everything that had transpired. Liv interrupted her a few times for clarification, and now Cam could see she was mulling over everything she'd told her.

"You have a shine for Sarah, and you think if you give her what she's paying you for, she'll end up in danger, and you won't have an opportunity to pursue her in a romantic capacity."

She opened her mouth, then snapped it shut. There wasn't any way around what Liv had so easily figured out in a very short amount of time. And really, was there a good reason to deny the facts?

"Even after all this time you can't think I'd lost my ability to read you, do you?" Liv laughed.

Cam had to agree with how ridiculous it sounded. "No." She smiled.

"So, what do you want to do about it?" Liv disappeared into the kitchen, giving her time to think. She returned with bottles of beer, handing one to Cam.

"You make it sound so simple and it's anything but."

Liv took a drink. "You always were a deep thinker."

Cam grimaced. "Is that a bad thing?"

Their gazes met. "It can be when it's keeping you from taking a chance on love." Liv nudged her knee with her foot. "Stubborn cuss."

She laughed. "Hey. I should be offended."

"But you aren't because you know it's true."

They discussed the pros and cons of different scenarios because Liv understood that was how she functioned. Logically.

Methodically. Which was why Sarah threw her into a tailspin. Nothing about their situation was logical.

A short time later, she was standing at the door. A large bag of food and a few photos Liv had printed, framed, and carefully wrapped sat on the floor next to her feet. Liv pulled her in for a fierce hug.

"Stop being so damn stubborn and let Sarah in." She kissed her cheek and pushed her roughly away. "You keep in touch, you hear me?"

Cam studied Liv's weathered face. There was something new there and it wasn't anything she'd ever seen before, but it disappeared when Liv looked at her again.

"Why do I feel like this is good-bye?" She fought against the unshed tears burning in her eyes. What was Liv doing? What in her actions told Cam things between them had shifted? Was Liv severing ties with her so she would let Sarah take her place? Panic churned inside her head, making her stomach queasy.

Liv shook her head. "That's never gonna happen. What *is* going to happen is you're going to take that step forward you should have taken ages ago." She trailed her hand along Cam's cheek and Cam leaned into it. "Maybe I should have pushed you harder." Liv shared a lopsided smile. "Ah, well, we've all made mistakes, but it's not one I regret." Liv gathered the photos and handed them to her. "Now you get out there and do what you do. Be careful."

"I will." She bent to pick up the bag, but for some reason her feet wouldn't move. "Liv…"

Liv didn't give her an opportunity to finish. "Make sure you bring Sarah by. I need to meet the woman who finally got in here." She tapped the area over Cam's heart.

"You know I will, if it ever happens." Liv seemed sure about Cam's future. She wished she shared her certainty.

CHAPTER SIXTEEN

Sarah sat on the couch flipping channels but not seeing anything. It had been almost a week since she'd left Cam's place and she hadn't heard from her. She chewed her bottom lip, worrying her rash reaction had been a huge mistake. It wasn't only about the money—well, part of her reaction *was* about the money, but it was just as much about her and Cam. *Was* there something between them? She got up and poured a glass of wine from the near empty bottle she'd opened the night they'd argued. She brought the glass to her lips and closed her eyes hoping she'd find solace, but what she saw was the look on Cam's face the second before she'd stormed out.

She carried her glass back to the couch and plopped down, nearly sloshing the wine over the rim. Pinching the bridge of her nose only gave her momentary relief from the pressure that had started a few hours ago. Thank God she didn't get migraines. This was just a tension headache and would be gone if she took a couple of aspirin. The type of pain Cam had displayed the night in the hotel had been bad enough to debilitate her, and she got the feeling Cam rarely let anything stop her.

Sarah picked up her cell for the hundredth time and stared at the screen. It was an ongoing debate in her head whether she should call Cam and apologize or leave well enough alone. She scrolled through her contacts and stopped at the familiar number before sighing and tossing the phone face down on the table. The next thing she knew, she could hear a tiny voice, and it sounded like they were saying her name. She picked up the phone and gasped, her hand covering her mouth as she read who was on the other line.

"Hello? Hello? Sarah?"

Sarah cringed before placing the cell phone against her ear. She hadn't meant to dial Cam's number. Or had she?

"Cam?"

"Yeah. I've been yelling to you for a while. You okay?" Cam asked.

"I'm fine." Sarah braced herself and pushed on. "Since I have you on the phone, I need to apologize for blowing up like I did." She waited, thinking Cam might not let her off the hook for her bad behavior.

"Apology accepted, but I have a confession. I haven't been totally honest with you and I'd like to. Be honest, I mean." Cam sounded flustered.

"Are you going to piss me off again?" Sarah hoped Cam could hear she was teasing and was relieved when she heard Cam chuckle.

"I'll try not to."

"Good. Do you want to come over?"

"Now?" Cam sounded surprised.

She looked at the clock. It was after ten in the evening. Being Friday, she didn't have to get up in the morning and she hoped the same was true for Cam. "I've got nowhere to be, but if it's not good..."

"I'll be there in twenty."

The line went dead and Sarah smiled. That was before she realized she looked a wreck and the house was a mess. She hadn't done much the last few days except work and mope. She ran to her bedroom, picking up discarded clothes along the way. She didn't have time for a shower, but at least she could brush her hair and put on something without holes all over it. *Why am I even worried?*

Twenty-five minutes later, the doorbell rang, and she shook her shoulders to help dispel the dread that had built since the phone call. She was ready for whatever Cam wanted to tell her. At least, that's what she kept mumbling as she went to answer the door.

❖

The quiet street added to her anxiety. Cam had never been one to back down, but each second that ticked by challenged her nerves, and she wondered if it was too late to change her mind. She pressed the small circle and heard the chime inside.

"Hi. Come in."

Cam had wanted to bring alcohol. Something, anything, to help her relax so she could tell Sarah the truth. She owed her that much. Instead, she'd brought some of the cookies Liv had packed up for her, and she shoved the container at Sarah.

"What's this?"

Cam shrugged. Still nervous. Still unsure what she was going to say. "Cookies."

"Are you trying to sweeten me up?" Sarah laughed, a light sound that loosened the knot in Cam's stomach a bit.

"You don't need sweetening up, you already are." Embarrassment coursed through her. *Christ.* Could she be any lamer? This wasn't how she'd wanted to start baring her soul. Now that it was out, there wasn't anything she could do to take it back.

"Aww." Sarah studied her for a long time before reaching out. "Come on. Let's not stand here all awkward. What can I get you to drink?"

"Whiskey. Straight up?" Cam said it like a joke, but she wouldn't turn it down if Sarah offered some.

"Sorry, no such animal in the house. I have beer, wine, tea, coffee, and milk." Sarah pointed to the cookies, smiling.

She shoved her hands in her pockets. "Coffee would be great." Cam had been living on the stuff and she wondered when the ulcer she was sure the acid was causing would let itself be known.

"Coming right up."

While Sarah was busy at the counter, she studied Sarah's backside. She was wearing silky-looking lounge pants that hugged the cheeks of her ass, and the smooth dark blue T-shirt revealed she wasn't wearing a bra. The resulting flare of heat in her lower belly wasn't unpleasant, but her timing sucked. Sarah turned, and Cam averted her eyes to the container she'd brought as though it was the most interesting thing in the kitchen, which it wasn't. Not by a long shot.

"It will be a few minutes. I hope you don't mind decaf. It's a little late for high test."

"That's fine. I probably don't need any more caffeine." She forced a small smile.

"Why don't we sit. I'm sure you didn't come all this way for coffee."

Cam moved to the couch and Sarah sat next to her. She wished she hadn't. Being so close was going to make it all the more difficult to confess what was going on. *Just get on with it already.* She inhaled deeply, then let it out in a whoosh. *Here goes.*

"I've found him." She winced. So much for preplanning. "Your brother." Sarah's eyes got huge, but she stayed quiet. "He's a cop."

"That's fantastic." Sarah's excitement was palpable. Until she must have noticed something in Cam's expression that said otherwise. "Why do I have the feeling you aren't as happy by the discovery as I am?"

"It's complicated. I haven't actually met him."

"Do you usually?" Sarah asked.

"Not unless a client requests it."

"Which I haven't." Sarah ducked her head to see her eyes.

"No." She was finding it even more difficult to explain the why behind her behavior to Sarah, then she remembered Liv's words. Thankfully, Sarah let it go and moved on.

"Okay. So, when do *I* get to meet him?" The coffee pot beeped. "Wait. Let me get that. I don't want to miss any of the details."

Cam chewed her cheek. Sarah was expecting her to have answers. Her struggle continued as she decided if she should do her job and not worry about what happened once she relayed everything about Brace Archer. But her stomach gurgled, warning her that nothing good would come from their meeting. Hell, she wasn't even sure if she wanted to tell Sarah his name, though she knew ethically she had to, and that made her gut twist even more.

Sarah brought a tray to the coffee table and handed Cam a steaming mug. She took her time fixing it to just the right color. Out of the corner of her eye, she could see Sarah watching her. She finally met her intense stare.

"Here's the thing. He isn't a very good cop." Well, that part was true. Maybe if she didn't press too much, Cam could actually keep most of the details from Sarah.

"I don't care if he's good at his job. I just want to know him. What's his name? Where does he live?"

She weighed her options. Surely Sarah would become angry again if she withheld information she'd paid for, and rightly so. Maybe she could reason with her and convince Sarah to let her find out more before she made contact. *Yeah, right.*

"I don't know if he's good at *being* a cop, I just know…"

"For Christ's sake, Cam, just fucking tell me."

The now familiar fire in Sarah's eyes made Cam want to see if it carried over into the bedroom. This wasn't the time to fantasize about what most likely would never happen once their conversation was over.

"He's dirty." There. She'd said it.

"You mean ill-kempt?"

Cam stood and began pacing. This conversation was proving even more difficult than she thought. She stopped moving and faced Sarah.

"No. I mean he's dealing drugs under the cover of his badge."

Sarah sat back, a look of comprehension crossing her face. "You can't be serious."

"I'm afraid I am."

Sarah looked down at the contents of her mug before fixing Cam with a hopeful expression. "Maybe your source isn't reliable?"

"I wish that was the case, but I spoke with another officer in his department. He was adamant."

"There has to be a logical explanation. Maybe this officer has a vendetta or something against my brother."

Cam sat next to her. "I don't think so. Your brother doesn't appear to have too many friends on the force."

Sarah took up pacing over the worn rug that ran the length of the living room. She stopped abruptly. "This is rather convenient."

"I'm not sure what you mean."

"You haven't wanted to find him from the beginning, have you? Why, Cam? Why can't you just do what I hired you to do?"

"Sarah, please. Let me dig a little deeper. Make a few more inquiries and see where they lead. Then you can make an informed decision about whether you want to meet him or know anything else."

"To what end? So you can tell me to forget I have a sibling and I can go on feeling alone?"

"You wouldn't be alone if you contacted Mr. White."

"Did you investigate him, too?" Sarah's gaze bored into hers. She wasn't going to let this go without a fight, if ever.

"Not yet..."

"Then spill it, Stark," Sarah said with her hands on her hips in defiance.

"I'm concerned about what he might do if his secret got out."

"Well, it's not much of a secret if his buddies know it, so what's the harm of me meeting him?" Sarah ran her hand through her hair. The tussled look made her even more appealing. "What difference does it even make to you anyway? And why would he assume I even knew about the drugs, if that's true? I'm not asking to be his business partner." She collapsed onto the couch.

Cam took her hand in both of hers. "I know it might seem illogical, but I think you're better off with all the information I can give you. I want you to be safe." Cam rubbed the back of Sarah's hand. "Please. Let me do more digging." She hoped her plea for more time would work because she couldn't stand the thought of anyone going after Sarah. Sarah wasn't the one who should pay for her snooping. Cam would deal with whatever fate had in store for her.

Sarah looked at their joined hands. Cam's impassioned plea awoke her hopes Cam had feelings for her beyond the scope of a client. She dared to think about the attraction between them, and there wasn't anything cocky about the way Cam begged her for more time. As she stared, she recognized worry in Cam's eyes, and that made her hesitate. Cam didn't appear to be the type to worry about much, and if she was this concerned about her meeting her brother, maybe she shouldn't be so gung ho either. Still, this was her twin they were talking about. And even though she hadn't specifically asked, Cam had her birth father's information. If he wanted to know her, surely her brother would want to know about her, too. She couldn't fathom anyone who wouldn't want that kind of information. Still, she'd waited this long...

"How long?"

"What?" Cam's surprise registered in her voice, and Sarah tried to not laugh.

"How long do you want me to wait?"

"Two weeks. No...three. Give me three weeks, then I'll tell you everything I have on your brother. I won't hold anything back, and you can do what you want with the information. Just...let me make sure you have everything you need to make your decision, okay? And then you can get pissed and break my door again if you want to."

Sarah was close to giggling. It seemed for the first time since she'd met Cam she had the upper hand, and she had to admit she rather liked it.

"Fine. If you really want a face-to-face with him first, I won't ask you not to."

Cam finally released her hand and sat back; her relief clear as her expression relaxed. "Good." She ran her hands through her long, dark strands as if to settle herself. "Thank you."

"I'm not doing this for you. I'm doing it for me. If you're worried about what you've discovered so far, I should be, too. You know how important finding him is, but I guess a few more weeks won't kill me." Cam frowned. Maybe that wasn't the best choice of words. "In the meantime, I'll think about meeting my birth father."

Cam brightened. "Great," she said, but continued to fidget.

"What now?" Sarah was beginning to lose her patience.

"I'll run his name in the morning, just to be sure he doesn't have a record or anything." Cam shyly smiled.

She almost hated to admit she was okay with Cam being cautious. "Let me heat up your coffee and I'll share whatever's in that container." Sarah tipped her head toward the tray.

"Sure." Cam handed her the mug.

She was disappointed at the delay, but there was a heavy weight on her chest that had nothing to do with Cam and everything that had to do with her brother.

CHAPTER SEVENTEEN

Cam stopped her rapid-fire typing. She was transcribing handwritten notes into the Peters file, and the part regarding her conversation with Officer Barnes brought her up short. She hadn't remembered him saying the word "ruthless," but there it was, and since she'd gone back to her car and immediately made notes on what they'd discussed, Cam believed he'd said it. Gooseflesh rose along her exposed arms.

"You bastard." Cam pointed to the screen. This was why she didn't want Sarah anywhere near Brace Archer. He obviously didn't give a shit about his parents finding out about the drugs, or if he did, maybe he thought Daddy's money could get him out of any situation. She would bet her reputation on their not knowing what their son was up to. Cam considered using them as leverage until she stopped and thought it over. No. Brace didn't look like the type to take well to a warning, and it would likely just piss him off. No telling what he would do then. Cam had to tread lightly. She wasn't the only one involved, and Sarah had put her faith in Cam. She had to gather everything she could so Sarah could come to the same conclusion she had—Brace Archer was dangerous.

She'd only begun to scratch the surface of what she was sure was a closet full of skeletons belonging to Archer. Uncovering them would require poking the bear. With a big stick. She'd have to try to get more from Barnes, but in the meantime she'd let Archer know she was investigating him on his sister's behalf. Of course, she wasn't about to reveal any details about her client, and doubted he'd have the wherewithal to even begin to look for Sarah. She was counting on it. The news of Sarah's existence would either cause him to get reckless or, if her current information was bogus, he'd be as excited as Sarah was at the prospect of having a sibling. Cam believed that was the least likely scenario. However, she did enjoy a challenge and got off on the hunt. She wasn't a fool who took unnecessary chances, but there were cases out there that deserved to be solved, and those were the ones that made her blood race, especially when those being hunted deserved to be taken down.

This one had turned personal, though. *Sarah* had become personal. She probably didn't feel the same about Cam, no matter how much she'd been floored by her agreeing to wait for a complete picture of Brace. That alone spoke volumes, and although Sarah hadn't apologized for storming out of the office, Cam had the impression she regretted it.

Her next step was a face-to-face with the hard to locate Brace Archer. She'd lucked out with Barnes and had even convinced him to text her the next time Brace was in the office. There was no guarantee he'd still be there when she arrived, but it was worth a shot. Jimmy told her Brace gave a song and dance to his lieutenant, saying he was doing undercover work, infiltrating gangs and getting close to the people higher up the ranks of dealers. Brace showed up in the office enough to keep the lieutenant satisfied, though a few of his fellow officers believed Brace's excuses were nothing but a crock of shit.

Cam had prepared a list of questions for him, including why he had decided to become an officer, though she may or may not ask that one, depending on his initial reaction. Most officers wearing the uniform strived for a promotion to detective, or at least sergeant. Barnes had confirmed the real reason Brace hadn't taken the promotion test was his desire to be virtually anonymous on the street. He could remain a low-ranking cop able to move among the unsavory individuals who sold his drugs without having to give much back, except for the promise of keeping them out of jail.

She'd called in a favor from one of her informants who could hack most "secure" systems, asking her to pull up Brace Archer's arrests record over the last five years. Interestingly, even though he was a lead in the narcotics division, all his recent arrests were of street level mules and minor players. He probably took down people who crossed him, doing just enough to stay under the radar of the upper echelon's scrutiny in the department.

She finished her notes and checked the clock in the corner of her screen. Where had the time gone? She had missed lunch and was headed for the same with dinner. After saving the file, Cam gathered her notes and stuffed her bag. She hadn't been paying much attention to the one other case she had, and she knew that had to change. Sarah had taken precedence over everything else and she felt a little guilty for shirking her responsibilities. *I'll get back on track soon.* Cam wasn't sure who she was trying to convince.

Two days later, the steady click of her camera meant she'd have some good information for her client. The cheating wife was laughing as she and an unknown male walked to a motel room on the first floor, giving her a clear view of them both. The license on the dark blue sedan she'd arrived in matched the one the husband had provided, along with a recent photo of the supposed happy wife whose smile didn't reach her eyes. There might be a very good reason why she'd strayed, but it was rare for Cam's conscience to suffer when dropping the dirt on a subject she investigated. This was her job, and she was being paid to provide answers to her clients.

It wasn't the same with Sarah Peters. Since they'd come to their agreement, Cam had little additional news about Brace's extracurricular activities. However, she had found several accounts linked to an individual named Archie Brace. The similarity in names sent up red flares, and after a little more digging, she found an old cell number that used to belong to Brace attached to one of the accounts. Sloppy on his part, but it was probably before he'd gotten better at covering his tracks.

After the couple disappeared inside their room, she set her camera aside and jotted some notes in her tablet. She thought about ignoring the buzz of her phone, thinking it was probably Maggie asking if she'd eaten today. She swiped the screen and froze. It was from Barnes. Archer was in the office at his computer typing reports. It would be her best shot at catching him. She turned the key before securing her seat belt, praying this was the break she'd been waiting for, and at the same time she hoped her fear of Brace being a possible threat to Sarah was unfounded. Experience told her she knew better.

❖

Sarah slid her dark goggles up on her head. She set down the grinder before picking up her thermos and drank the tart lemonade she'd made that morning. Once she was sure the metal had cooled, she ran her hand over the joint to check for smoothness. The commissioned piece would serve as both a focal point and a statement for the local architecture company that had hired her. They'd given the green light with respect to the type and subject matter of her sculpture, trusting she would be able to capture the essence of the company's creed on design. She hoped she'd done them justice, knowing if she hit the mark there would be a lot of free publicity. Her name would be displayed on a plaque at the base of the piece which would be prominently placed in the firm's lobby. The announcement would introduce her skills to the world. She was ready for the recognition others said she deserved from pursuing her passion.

The three-dimensional cubes, stacked at gravity defying angles, would be mounted in a base of marble granite, the colors of which would be reflected on the polished finish of the cubes. According to the specifications she sent, they would rotate counterclockwise, giving the impression they were boring into the base. It was an optical illusion she'd been working with on her computer for months. At least it would be the buffer in her budget she'd been hoping for. It wouldn't be a huge amount, and she probably should have asked for more for the piece, but being a virtual unknown, she considered the equivalent in publicity and thought it fair. By the time she paid for materials the residual would get her through several months of no construction work without worry. Winter was coming and the competition for bidding on jobs would become tougher. Her skills were well known in the industry, but she didn't have a family of mouths to feed. Sometimes employers picked those workers first, knowing they'd show up every day else their paycheck would suffer. Little did anyone know she was in the same predicament.

It felt good to have someone believe in her as much as her parents had. Her personal well-being had always been of utmost importance to their happiness. Too bad they hadn't thought the same true when it came to not letting her know about her twin. Sarah shook her head. She couldn't change the past. She imagined Cam would lead her to a new chapter in her life, and things would be different. But what did that mean? Was she hoping Cam wanted to explore the unmistakable connection between them? And what *was* that connection? There was no doubt it was there. Why else would Cam find reasons for them to share meals and get together as often as they did, even when she had very little to communicate? She could just as easily send Sarah the information in an email, or with a phone call. Why did she always insist on a more personal interaction? Maybe insist wasn't the right word. After all, she'd never turned down an invitation to spend time with Cam. Sarah had to admit she was lonely. The sudden change in her life from a carefree daughter to caregiver for her father, then her mother, had left her little time to indulge in satisfying her own pleasures. Now she had time to spend on her art, yet she was filled with restless energy and a longing for human company instead of cold metal.

She hoped the future would be less solitary than the one she'd led up to now. She really needed to get out more and mingle with people her own age, but almost everyone she knew had families of their own, or worked so many hours there wasn't a lot left for socializing. She could commiserate.

Sarah pulled her glasses down and picked up her grinder. A few more hours and it would be finished. What would she do then? She didn't have any more orders and she was running out of material. She'd have to go to the junkyard soon and scour the construction site for debris. It wouldn't be the first time. Someday she'd be able to order what she needed. Someday.

❖

Cam had been damn lucky. She'd broken almost every speed limit she'd gone through to get to the station before Archer left. She smoothed her clothes and fluffed her hair. She hated using her sex to get what she needed, but sometimes it was the only weapon the moron she was talking to understood. She'd deal with her mental fallout later. It would just be one more regret in a long list she'd have to think about on her deathbed.

She slid her ID through the shallow slot. "Hello, I'm Camdyn Stark and I'm looking to speak with Officer Brace Archer, if he's available." If she could have crossed her toes, she would have.

The officer behind the desk looked over her ID, then picked up the phone. "Hang on." There were a few seconds of silence before he spoke again. "Murphy here. Is Archer still around?" He grunted something unintelligible, then hung up. He pushed her ID back through.

"You're in luck." He handed her a visitor pass to clip on her lapel. She was grateful she'd gotten in without one the last time in case Archer got suspicious someone had tipped her off. "You carrying?"

"No."

When she got to the narcotics division door, she went in and scanned the area. Barnes was there, but she ignored him. Instead, she walked confidently to the captain's office and knocked on the casing. The name on the door was labeled Larson, and she hoped it was his name, rather than another division. He looked up from his desk.

"Can I help you?" he asked without grumbling. Cam took it as a good sign.

"Yes. I was hoping to speak with Officer Brace Archer?" She remained in the doorway since he hadn't asked her to have a seat.

"What do you want with Archer?" He eyed her suspiciously.

"It's a private matter, sir."

That garnered the standard grunt, and she barely contained a smile.

"Archer." The boom of his voice echoed through the doorway, making her flinch. He must have noticed. "Sorry."

She nodded but didn't say anything. It wasn't long before a man with dirty blond hair and a big build showed up at the door.

"Yeah, Captain?"

"This woman…" He hesitated.

"Camdyn Stark." Cam stuck out her hand. She didn't miss Archer glancing at the sergeant before reluctantly shaking it.

"Ms. Stark wants to speak with you."

Archer opened his mouth, but Larson cut him off before he said anything. "In your cube."

Archer nodded. "This way." He pointed to the desk that had been empty the last time she was there.

It was devoid of the chaotic stacks of paper invading many of the other officers' space, and she wondered how much time he spent doing police work compared to running his drug business. Barnes had told her he was into the heavy stuff. Heroin, coke, and meth. The kind that got people killed.

Archer gestured to the one chair facing his desk as he sat down, leaning forward. She was sure he wanted to intimidate her. Little did he know she'd grown up with harsher tactics and she'd survived. Now she was the one who used intimidation when it was necessary to get information.

"What do you want to talk about?" His nostrils flared and he looked over her shoulder at the door, like he was in a hurry to leave.

Cam sat back, crossed her legs, and smiled. If he thought he was going to strike fear in her, he needn't bother. "I'm a private investigator." She paused long enough to let it sink in. Archer looked around again, likely to see if anyone was close enough to hear them. "I've been hired to locate you, so here I am." She kept her smile in place.

Archer's jaw tightened. "By who?"

"Your twin sister."

"I don't have a sister. Someone's wasting your time." He leaned back as though unconcerned by the news, but the white knuckles as he grasped the armrests spoke volumes.

Cam opened her brief and produced the one sheet of paper containing the information she was willing to give him. There was nothing on it that identified Sarah.

"Is your date of birth March fifteenth, nineteen eighty-nine?" He nodded. "Born at Kent General in Dover, Delaware?"

Archer's face started to turn red. "That doesn't prove anything." His voice rose.

Cam ignored the warning bells of impending danger and leaned in. "Why are you upset? Aren't you happy about having a sister?"

"Why the hell would I be happy about it? My family is fine just the way it is. I don't know who put you up to this, but it's bullshit." His voice carried across the space, and Larson walked toward them.

"Everything okay here?" Larson looked between her and Archer.

Archer stood, fixing Cam with a hard stare. "Yeah. Ms. Stark was just leaving."

Cam slid the paper onto his desk and placed her card on top. "If you change your mind, call me." She made a motion to shake his hand, but Archer's balled fists were clenched at his sides. Cam pivoted to the captain instead. "Thank you."

She focused on maintaining slow, deliberate strides as she headed to the exit. She'd be damned if she'd give Archer the satisfaction of thinking he could scare her. He had no idea how many tentacles her investigation could grow, and she was far from finished. Or maybe he did know and was afraid news of his drug operation would get out if someone started poking around in his life. In the meantime, all she had to do was keep Sarah away from him. *Easy.* She sighed and rested her head against the steering wheel when she got in the car. Sarah would most likely prove more difficult to handle than Archer.

CHAPTER EIGHTEEN

If it's not to give me information on how to reach my brother, then what do you want to tell me?"

Sarah had been excited when Cam called and suggested they meet. She'd had second thoughts about Cam seeing her workshop, but she needed to finish before she got paid, and time was a luxury she didn't have. Cam leaned against the Range Rover's grille, her arms folded and a cocky smile plastered on her face. The smile that made her so damn attractive was also the one that infuriated Sarah at the same time.

She'd told herself that she didn't want to be one-on-one with Cam any more than she had to, that it was too complicated, but she had once again jumped on the opportunity to spend time with Cam.

"He's not the friendly type."

"What the hell does that mean?"

"It means he wasn't happy with finding out he had a sister and denied your existence."

Sarah swiped at the hair that had fallen into her eyes. "I wasn't so sure of his existence either. That's why I hired you. You can't judge him based on how he reacted to that kind of news. I didn't take it so well at first either." She waited for Cam to come up with a rebuttal, but instead she sighed and motioned toward the building.

"Are you going to show me your workshop?"

"No." She turned to head inside, but Cam was at her heels.

"Sarah, wait."

"For what, Cam? For you to keep up the charade of reasons I shouldn't see my brother?" Her throat constricted as her anger grew. "To what end? Why won't you just do what I hired you to do?"

Cam's eye color changed from muted hazel to a forest green-gray. Something dark passed through them, and she wondered what they looked like when she was having sex. Her blood heated, and her body screamed for release. *Christ.*

"You're going to get hurt by him, Sarah." Cam lifted her hand as though she were going to touch her before she stopped in midair and her hand fell to her side.

"You can't judge a person on one meeting. I have a right to form my own opinion. I hired you to find him, and I've cut you a lot of slack. Now you're pissing me off." Sarah turned away, her lips pressed together. Cam's fingers closed on her wrist.

"I don't want to argue with you." Cam stared into her eyes, and she wondered what she saw. "Will you let me inside?"

Panic stilled the breath in her chest. What was Cam asking? "Cam, I…"

"I want to see your art. I want to see where you work that isn't hundreds of feet off the ground." Cam's intensity remained, but her features had softened.

Sarah hid her disappointment. She'd thought…well, she wasn't sure what she'd thought, but Cam's interest in her art wasn't at the top of the list. She'd been foolish to think otherwise. She and Cam would never be good in a relationship. They were polar opposites.

Cam wondered if it was a mistake to push Sarah, but she wasn't ready to let go of their tentative connection. She'd missed her, and that was the reason she'd called. She hated admitting there were so many things that could go wrong, but what she wasn't wrong about was her growing need to protect her. Sarah was challenging her and she was so damn cute doing it, Cam wanted to kiss those pouty lips.

"Do you know how much you piss me off?"

She rubbed the tender flesh beneath her thumb. "Yeah, I do."

"And you're not the least bit sorry, are you?"

She raised their joined hands to her lips. "A little, but not enough to let you step into a hotbed of uncertainties." A truer statement hadn't come out her mouth in a long time. Sarah had that effect on her. Of getting her to confess to things she ordinarily kept hidden.

"God, you're frustrating." The corner of Sarah's mouth twitched, but to her credit she didn't smile, though her gaze traveled between Cam's lips and her eyes several times before she glanced at their joined hands and gave a little tug. "Come into my lair." She waved with her free hand. "It's where the magic happens."

I doubt that's where the real magic happens.

Sarah led her through an old dented door into a garage that didn't look much better. The single section of fluorescent bulbs hardly gave off enough light to see the entire space. One wall held a pegboard of various tools and a narrow bench cluttered with scraps of metal, iron, and copper. A couple of outlets were mounted on the front. A torch sat in a corner near the overhead garage door, and a grinder of some sort sat on a rickety crate near the center. Three shiny metal cube frames, each one at least four feet square, stood at precarious angles on top of each other, defying gravity. The bottom one sat in a vise-like contraption. Cam stepped forward, mesmerized by the gleaming metal. She extended her hand, then stopped.

"Can I touch it?"

Sarah nodded. "It's cool by now. I'll have to polish it again before delivery, so it's fine."

She slid her fingertips over the edge and then on to the welded areas. The chrome-like metal was cooler than she would have guessed, and the joints were smooth as glass. Each section contained narrow reflections like small mirrors, and she was fascinated by how Sarah had brought the piece to life.

"This is amazing, Sarah. I had no idea." Cam walked around the sculpture, marveling at the contours and edges. The symmetry and the lines. Sarah had talent. There was no reason she should be struggling financially. People should be clamoring at her door.

Sarah stepped beside her and looked at it with obvious reverence. "I love this part of my training." She traced one of the polished edges of the middle cube. "It would be a dream come true to do this full-time." Her hand fell away.

Cam hadn't missed the melancholy in Sarah's tone. "You should be. You've got a lot of talent."

Sarah shared a wry smile. "Hard to do when so few know about it." She looked back at her work. "Besides, I didn't have much time before…" Sarah sucked in a breath. "When I was taking care of my parents. They came first."

She stepped closer. "I think you haven't put yourself first for a very long time." Cam was close enough to breathe in the lavender scent of Sarah's hair, filling her lungs with it. She wanted to hold her. To help her make her dreams come true. To make her happy.

"I…" Sarah shook her head. "It doesn't matter now."

Unlike Cam, whose original intention had been to help other people, but whose work had started to become so routine she mostly did it for the money, Sarah had sacrificed herself for others, and she couldn't help thinking Sarah was unquestionably the nobler of the two of them.

Cam stepped in front of her and looked at the eyes she saw even in her dreams. "Everything matters, Sarah." She tried to keep the emotion out of her voice.

Sarah swayed for a second before she cleared her throat and stepped back.

"I have more work to do."

If Cam could have saved the moment…saved whatever they'd just shared, she would have, but it was too late. She nodded. "I'll leave you to it then."

"Cam?"

She squeezed her eyes and gathered her thoughts before facing Sarah. "Yeah?"

"About my brother? What you said? Are you sure I shouldn't meet him yet?"

"Normally I would say go for it, but not with Brace."

"And why not? Spell it out for me."

Cam closed the space between them, her vision filled with the shape of Sarah's lips before meeting her questioning eyes. "Because I don't want anyone to hurt you." She brushed the back of her fingertips down the side of Sarah's face before stopping at her jaw to gently cup it.

"Why does that matter?"

"I'd never forgive myself if I didn't give you everything I could possibly find on Brace and you got hurt because I'd gotten careless. I couldn't handle it."

Sarah stilled, as though holding her breath. She stared into Cam's soul, as though wanting to be inside where her thoughts ran amok. Now it was Cam's turn to not breathe. Could she? Dare she let Sarah know how much she was attracted to her, partly because her life had been so different yet similar to her own? What if the chasm proved too wide for them to navigate?

She fought against the urge to pull Sarah into an embrace. "Isn't that enough?" It was proving harder than she thought.

"Cam, I…" Sarah responded by moving her fingers to take Cam's hand. Her eyes glazed with the heat of desire. "We have to think about what's going on between us."

She wasn't the only one with feelings. The quickening of her body wasn't unwelcome, but the timing was all wrong. It took her a moment to recognize it as fear. She was afraid she wouldn't have a chance to get to spend more time with her. Afraid she was even considering letting Sarah see a side of her she hadn't let anyone know. No matter how many times she'd heard "it wasn't your fault" she would always carry the shame of not having fought harder. Maybe that was why she was adamant about not being silent with regard to Brace. She'd fight for Sarah because Sarah didn't see the threat. Cam always had. "Why?" she asked.

"Because I don't know what to do with it." Sarah stepped back, blinking. "I think you should go."

Going was the last thing Cam wanted to do. What did that say about her? Was this *her* life-altering turning point? She stayed put, frozen to the spot by indecision.

Sarah might be telling her to go, but her eyes revealed something else entirely. All she had to do was figure out what.

"Cam…"

Before Sarah could protest more, Cam closed the distance between them once again. She stared into Sarah's eyes for an eternity before taking in the details of her mouth. And that's when she kissed her. Her lips were incredibly soft, as though Sarah was afraid of bruising her, like she was as fragile as butterfly wings. Her breath quickened in acknowledgement of the desire she'd been fighting and the resulting flood in her briefs brought a moan deep in her throat. She lightly placed her hand on Sarah's hip, her heat searing her palm like a hot piece of iron, branding her. Then Sarah pressed her hand to Cam's chest, and though it felt like she was forcing herself to, she tenderly pushed Cam away. The breath she took was shaky at best. Her body tingled with anticipation of what lay ahead.

"I know you feel it, too. The pull. The need. The desire."

Sarah flushed. "That's not the point." Her eyes darted everywhere but at Cam.

"The point," Cam said, "is I can't stop how I feel. About you. About Brace."

Sarah took a step and turned away. Her silence lasted an eternity. "I don't know what to believe anymore. I'm not sure if you've ever told me the truth. Did you put off telling me about him just so you could spend more time with me?"

She faced her then, and Cam's heart seized at the sadness in the shimmering pools staring back at her.

"If you stay away from Brace until I know more, I promise I'll tell you everything about the case right now. And about me, if you want to know." Cam's pulse beat in her neck so hard she could feel it in her toes. She was scared to death to let the nightmares free, and she'd most likely end up being unable to sleep. It was a small price to pay for keeping Sarah safe one more day.

Sarah's eyes cleared and she cocked an eyebrow. "You don't have a past."

Cam sucked air. "What?"

"You aren't the only one with an inquisitive nature."

Cam saw the twitch of Sarah's lips before she smiled. "You searched? About me?"

Sarah came closer. "What have you been hiding?" Sarah asked. "*Who* have you been hiding from?"

Cam's world closed in, and for the first time since she'd been abused, she saw how perfect her life was now. She'd been through hell, but that was long ago when she had no control over her life, and even with her past, Sarah was here and interested in the person she'd hidden away. Sarah wanted to know *her* in every sense of the word. Everything she'd ever wanted in a woman…a relationship… was at her fingertips. How could she not have seen?

"Myself. Relationships. On purpose at first. Then it became habit." She hesitated. Sarah's body swayed in her direction.

"Do I have to ask again?"

She couldn't say anything without touching Sarah. Though terrified at the prospect of falling so hard she'd never recover, Cam took both Sarah's hands in hers, praying Sarah wouldn't run in the other direction. "No. I'll tell you everything, but not here." True confessions would either break her or set her free. Whatever Sarah decided, Cam was willing to take the risk. For once in her life she didn't think she could handle another mistake. This time she wasn't thinking about just herself.

❖

"Let's go."

Cam's eyes widened.

"You don't have to act so surprised." The reaction led her to believe she'd been just firm enough, just stubborn enough, to get Cam's attention. She hadn't meant to be stubborn, but she'd gotten Cam to concede, at least a bit, so it was worth it. She had to be able to trust her as a person before she could trust her with her heart.

"You always surprise me when you give in and I get my way," Cam said, her voice so low it was barely a whisper.

A witty retort died on her lips. Cam was the one doing the surprising. Every time Sarah thought she had her figured out, she went and did something so unexpected Sarah had to retreat and reconsider. Reevaluate. Throw away her previous misconceptions.

She was attracted to this side of Cam. The quiet, unsure, vulnerable Cam who had captured *her* attention. Her mysterious, nonexistent past would be cleared up, though she wasn't sure she wanted to hear it. What if Cam told her things she couldn't deal with, and any possible future between them ended before it had truly begun?

Sarah gathered her things while Cam went to her car to answer a text from earlier. The fire in Cam's eyes conveyed so much more than her words, and Sarah wasn't sure who had more to confess. Until tonight, she hadn't let on how Cam affected her. How every time they were together she imagined what it would be like to have a partner to come home to. What did she want from Cam? Just as important, what did Cam want from her? There was only one way to find out.

Sarah pushed away the negative thoughts. Intelligent, sexy Cam was concerned for her well-being and they hadn't even slept together yet. *Yet* being the key operative. But then, there were so many questions unanswered, so many issues to consider. If she could set them aside, if there was a way to trust that Cam was the person Sarah thought she might be…maybe there was a chance after all.

Cam glanced in the rearview mirror making sure Sarah hadn't changed her mind. She wondered what had possessed her to offer a confessional, tell-all session. There was no doubt she'd wanted to keep Sarah safely away from her brother, and to do that she had to tell Sarah all she'd learned about Brace. It would take more than a gentle warning to make an impact on Sarah. But that didn't explain her agreeing to tell *her* story, as well. She shook her head. It was time she stopped lying to herself most of all. She wanted to be honest with Sarah, and the one thing she'd been intimidated by, telling Sarah about her childhood, was the one thing holding her back.

The drive to her house gave her a chance to compartmentalize the anger and the shame she still felt, though she avoided the topic in her everyday life. Liv had given her hundreds of reasons not to hang on to all the negative energy that came with holding grudges and dredging up the black and bleak memories that, one by one, constructed a wall around her heart. It kept people from knowing her, and thus, knowing her secrets.

Cam pulled into the driveway and Sarah slowed to a stop behind her. She tried to remain calm. Sarah was watching her, letting her set the pace. God, she was falling for her. Hard. *Let's hope I get to tell her someday.*

CHAPTER NINETEEN

Sarah watched Cam as she sat in her car. The nervousness she'd observed earlier made her question what was really going on, and she gave her a few minutes to gather her thoughts. She'd push only if she had to. This was Cam's story to tell, and Sarah wanted to learn all she could. Cam finally got out and she joined her on the walkway.

"I'm not sure what I have in the fridge, but I'm sure I can rustle up something edible." Cam smiled awkwardly.

She was trying to put on that facade of the self-assured, cocky PI, but Sarah could see through it now. "Whatever. I'm good." Cam unlocked the front door and ushered her in. It was still neat and clean, and likely she was seldom home. Cam dropped her keys and wallet on the hallway table. She didn't make eye contact.

"Come to the kitchen and keep me company?"

Sarah slid onto a stool and waited for directions on how she could help, her thoughts jumbled. It hadn't been all that long ago she didn't want anything to do with Cam and her smug demeanor, remembering how she'd all but rolled her eyes at Sarah during their first meeting, yet here she was, pining after her. Wishing hard for something just for her. She couldn't remember a time when she'd done that.

Cam rummaged in the fridge. "Ah-ha." She began to stack items on the counter. Eggs, veggies, cheese, and cream. "Omelet?"

Time to lighten the moment. "I'm impressed. A player and a chef." The second the words left her mouth Sarah regretted them. "I didn't mean that the way it sounded."

Cam's head hung at first, then she looked directly at Sarah, and she felt the tenuous connection between them slide a little.

"No. You're right, in a way." After looking away, Cam began chopping broccoli and spinach. "I was…have been, a bit of a player. As for cooking, there's never been anyone to cook for aside from Liv."

"Tell me more about Liv." Sarah understood they were friends, that Liv was a mentor of some kind, but didn't know much more.

"Liv," Cam said as her expression softened. "Is the woman who saved my life."

Sarah gestured to the egg carton to see if she could help, but Cam waved her off. "How?"

Cam sighed "It's complicated and hard to explain."

"Try." Sarah wasn't going to let her off easy.

"I met Liv when I was nineteen. She was older and a lot wiser than I could ever hope to be." Cam broke the eggs methodically and Sarah focused on her movements. One at a time, they tumbled into the bowl. "I was reckless. Living a dangerous life. Unprotected sex all the time with strangers. No idea when I'd eat again or where I'd sleep. Liv took me in. She understood me."

Cam stared ahead and Sarah wondered if she were reliving that time in her life.

"Liv showed me how unconditional love should feel."

Sarah held Cam's gaze with hers. Her own breathing stilled. How had Cam not felt love until then? She watched Cam's emotional shield drop. "How did it feel? To be loved unconditionally that way?"

Cam turned back to the stove. "Safe. Comfortable. Without worry. Satisfying."

Sarah had known she'd been loved for as long as she could remember. There wasn't ever a time she didn't think her parents would do everything they could to help her grow and learn and become her own person. Cam had obviously not had the same charmed childhood she remembered.

"What else?" Sarah spread out the silverware while Cam finished the food.

Cam slid an omelet onto each plate and brought them to the bar. "She taught me I'm enough." A tear slid down Cam's cheek, staining her perfectly smooth skin.

Sarah reached for Cam, taking her hands and holding on. The movement felt natural. Right. "You didn't know?"

"I'd never been told."

Sarah's heart broke.

Cam held Sarah's hands. They were strong. A bit large for her tiny frame, but feminine, too. There were many contradictions to Sarah, and each one fascinated her, teasing her senses and making her want to know more. One thing was certain, Sarah wasn't someone who would back down, and she was prepared to answer any questions she might have. The time for hiding was over, at least with Sarah. She'd never known this kind of connection with anyone, not to mention a love interest. Is that what Sarah was? A love interest? The look on Sarah's face revealed how hard she was concentrating on each word Cam spoke. When had anyone other than Liv shown any real interest in her or her life, other than for sex?

"You're more than enough, Cam." Sarah's fingers trailed along her jaw. "I wouldn't be here if I thought otherwise."

The air left her lungs. "I...I'm not sure where to start." Of all the times she'd used her cocky bravado to push people away or get answers, she was at a loss when it came to opening up.

Sarah let go and picked up her fork. "This looks delicious. Let's eat while it's still warm."

Cam nodded, deep in thought. They ate in anticipatory silence. Sarah was being patient, but Cam's mind raced in a million different directions and she had no clue how to stop it. They exchanged a few meaningless words about the weather and food, then she set their plates in the sink and held on to the edge, needing to find the strength to go on. Somehow, she'd get through the sordid details.

Sarah led her to the couch, pulling her down with her. "How about you begin by telling me about your life. You start wherever you're comfortable. I'm sure I'll have questions, but I'll try to wait."

Where did she want to begin her life story? As a child, she'd been judged as worthless by the people who should have been building her self-esteem and she hadn't found it until her twenties. She might be damaged, but she was still a good person and a contributing member of society. Those were the things she needed to remember. She squared her shoulders and searched for the beginning. Her beginning, as far back as she could go. Sarah looked at her with so much compassion, she knew she'd chosen the right person to tell her tale to.

"I searched for someone a long time ago. I wanted to know how I'd ended up where I did—a child of the welfare system. What I found…let's say I would have been better off not knowing." She didn't want to talk about her mother. No one, not even Liv, knew what she'd found. Sometimes it *was* better to leave well enough alone.

"Family?" Sarah asked.

Bile rose in her throat. She thought she'd put this ghost to rest. "Yes." She met Sarah's compassionate eyes. "My mother." She went back in time to when she'd wanted to know everything and why it had been so important to her. To when she'd become obsessed with hope. She imagined Sarah was feeling much the same way, and Cam didn't want Sarah's fate to be the same. Cam's had been nothing but a disappointment.

"My mother gave me up." Cam couldn't imagine starting anywhere else. That one action had propelled her into a perpetual nightmare. "I never knew her, and for a long time I didn't want to, but as I grew older…" Cam looked away, unsure she could put to words what she was feeling. She cleared her throat and focused on Sarah. "I was old enough to ask questions and look for relatives I'd never known. Then I found her obituary and the name of her sister. It took me months, but I tracked her down."

"Oh, Cam, that's…" Sarah got excited, but she must have seen her anything but happy expression, because she stopped. "What happened?"

"Lucy, my aunt, told me my mother was a drug addict. Said she couldn't remember how often she'd been arrested, then she spit on the ground. She said the cop who had arrested her the last time saw an opportunity. He told her he'd get her drugs in exchange for sex. I saw a picture of her. She was young and pretty. A couple of months later she was pregnant, and the cop didn't want anything more to do with her. With no income, no drugs, and pregnant, my mother moved in with my aunt. Once I was born, they contacted the cop, thinking he'd want to see his daughter, but that's not what happened." She took a couple of breaths before continuing.

"He told them if they ever contacted him again, he'd make sure my mother paid the price of letting herself get pregnant. Lucy said Jill, my mom, made up her mind to turn me over to the state right after I was born, then she didn't have to worry about me."

"How did you feel?"

Cam pulled at her shirt, feeling confined. "I developed an aversion to family and cops, and when I stopped long enough to think about everything that had happened to me, I remember hating her."

Sarah raised her eyebrows but nodded sympathetically.

"I know. Strong words, but she gave me to a system that didn't give a fuck what happened to the kids in it, as long as the people that took them in got paid for their 'services.' Nothing else mattered. *I* didn't matter." Cam hadn't cried over those memories in forever. The hot sting in her eyes told her they were close. "Life was hell."

"How old were you?"

She closed her eyes. How old had she been when she started rebelling against just about everything? "I was eight when a foster parent first touched me. He convinced me if I told anyone I'd be sent to a very bad place, and he said that he wasn't going to hurt me." She could still hear the door to her bedroom close in the dark, and she knew he was coming for her. Reflexively, her eyes closed against the memory. Against the pain. "In the beginning, he kept his word. He touched my crotch, but he wasn't rough, and even though I knew it was wrong, it didn't hurt." Cam felt her face heat as she shrugged, no longer able to look at the shock and pain she'd recognized in Sarah's expression.

"Cam, you didn't do anything wrong. You were a child."

The conviction in Sarah's voice gave her the courage to keep going. "I do know, but it doesn't make me feel less responsible." Cam needed to move, to stall the memories building inside her. "I need something to drink. Want one?"

"Are you going to try to get me drunk?" Sarah teased her.

"You might want to be. It's not a happy story," Cam said before heading to the kitchen.

Cam handed Sarah a beer and put some distance between them on the couch. She liked their physical closeness, but it made the telling all the more difficult, and she wanted to be done with it. She hoped Sarah understood her need for space.

"A couple of months later, he went from touching to rubbing himself against me. I think the only reason he didn't fuck me was because he wasn't sure if I'd end up pregnant." Cam tipped the bottle and drank. "I knew it was bad. I knew he shouldn't be doing that to me, but I believed him when he said they'd take me away. What would I do then? I mean, if the next place was worse?" Cam twirled her bottle. "Can we take a break? Watch a little TV or something?"

"Of course." It hadn't even occurred to Sarah that Cam had been part of the same system that had given her such a wonderful upbringing. She'd been lucky to have been adopted by a loving couple who adored her. Cam hadn't been as fortunate. She couldn't imagine how she would have dealt with sexual abuse. How could a child not be afraid or not think she'd done something to bring it on herself and that she deserved it? Sarah wanted to cry, but Cam didn't need her tears, she needed her strength and her patience.

Cam gave her the remote and flopped back against the couch.

As she flicked through the channels, Sarah wondered if Cam's professional persona was a ruse for self-preservation. The tension in the air hung thick, as though it was something she could see. She found a mindless show that had the possibility of making them laugh. After adjusting the volume, she slid the remote onto the coffee table, picked up her beer, and moved closer to Cam. Maybe it was a bad idea, but she had to let Cam know she was there for her. Sarah extended her hand and left it palm up in the space between them. It wasn't long before Cam's slid into hers, sealing the silent understanding between them. Perhaps Cam wouldn't tell her more tonight, and maybe not for a long time. But something had solidified between them, and for now, that was good enough.

"Cam?"

"Yeah?" Cam stared at the antics on the TV.

Sarah was aware she wasn't seeing what was on the screen. She was focused inward. "No matter what happened to the girl, the woman survived and thrived."

Cam shared a tentative smile. "Thank you. Sometimes I forget that part."

Sarah understood about forgetting the good things. She'd done much the same along the way. She'd forgotten how much love and devotion her parents had given her, and no matter what they'd kept from her, letting her know how important she was to them wasn't one. Cam rested her head on the back of the couch and closed her eyes. Sarah imagined confessing was taking a toll on her psyche. Their bond of trust was still tentative, still somewhat unsure.

"Was keeping me from going to see Brace the real reason you've told me about your childhood? Because you understand what having a dirty cop in your life can mean?"

"Not the only reason." Cam took a shuddery breath. "When the investigation is over, I'd like you to still be in my life."

Sarah's heart rate sped up. She had much the same thoughts these days. She didn't want to feel as empty as she had the last month. Even if Brace was a part of her life, he couldn't take the place of a partner. A partner to laugh and love and make a home with and…if she dared to hope…a family. Cam could be her family. Maybe she'd even contact Paul and he could be a part, too.

Cam squeezed Sarah's hand and hoped she had the courage to finish what she'd started. The telling hadn't been pleasant, but it was bearable because of Sarah's patience and understanding. She didn't see sympathy reflected in her eyes. Instead there was empathy, something Cam could deal with. She stared at the screen, not hearing or seeing anything. The show in her head began to play again. She took it as a sign to go on. She slid her hand away. Touching was too intimate for what she was going to say.

"Instead of telling anyone, I got angry. I became one of those children who acted out. A nasty and mean-spirited child. The one you look at and know all along something deep inside is broken...or neglected...and all you want to do is fix it." Cam's breath caught in her chest, just like then. "The county took me away. It should have been a blessing, but the next place was anything but."

Sarah folded her legs under her on the couch and sat kitty-corner from her. She could almost feel Sarah wanting to touch her. Be near her. Instead, she looked on with her full attention and waited for Cam's words to spill out. Cam wanted her, though. But if she succumbed, her reserve would crumble. She'd made a promise to tell Sarah everything and she intended to keep it.

"The next family had three other fosters. All boys. The father came into my room a week after I landed there. He was rough and didn't care if I got pregnant. Slapped me when I wouldn't answer him or refused to do what he wanted." The memories came upon her like the waves of a tsunami. All encompassing. Wiping out everything in their path. The sob that escaped her lips drew Sarah closer, and she soon fell into her embrace, not caring how weak she appeared or how forlorn she must seem.

"Let it go, Cam. Let it out and be done with it. You don't need to keep paying for what you had no control over." Sarah rubbed her back. Even in the middle of all the heartache she was likely feeling with her own recent loss, Sarah offered her a place of safety.

When she felt she could go on, she reluctantly pulled away. "But that's where you're wrong. I *should* have been able to tell someone at the agency and they should have believed me. I *did* tell my social worker. Do you know what she said? That I 'ought to be glad I had a roof over my head and a bed to sleep on.' I took that as meaning the sexual abuse was a small price to pay for what these strangers provided, which wasn't much. It was what they were being paid to do." Cam fought against the emotions swirling through her and kept the floodgates at bay. It had been more than a decade since she'd told her story.

Sarah got up, taking the empty bottles with her. A few minutes later, she returned with two more. It had taken her longer than it should have, and Cam didn't miss the redness in her eyes as she smiled and handed Cam a beer. She pulled Sarah down next to her and squeezed her hand.

"Hey. Don't cry for me."

Sarah shook her head. "I'm not. I'm crying because all these years I never once gave a thought to the children who weren't as lucky as I was, and I'm so sorry you were one of them."

Cam didn't have anything to add. She drank her beer, wondering how many others were suffering right now, and what she could do to change it. She'd gotten so good at ignoring her formative years and the life she'd turned her back on, she no longer considered it a part of her until now. Sarah was helping her face the demons head-on.

"When did Liv come into your life? I know you said you were nineteen. But how did she find you? She seems important to you and I'd like to know about her, too."

There were worse things to tell about the next family she was placed with. But Sarah didn't have to know all the gory details to have a sense of why she was the way she was, and why the former Cam didn't exist anymore. But talking about Liv was something different…their relationship was sacred, special. It was hers, and she didn't share the details of their connection with anyone. No one could take that from her or make it change, and she wanted to be sure Sarah understood Liv would always be in her life.

"Like I said, I met Liv in a bar when I was nineteen. I'd been living more or less on the streets for a year, having unprotected sex, doing drugs…I was broken. Liv…she saw more in me than just some punk pimping herself. She took me in, taught me how to accept the help she offered. After a while, I started believing in myself, and seeing the good inside of me. To live like I wasn't broken. Eventually, I became the person she told me I could be if I left the past behind and walked forward into a different life." Cam smiled. The night they'd met had turned into one of her favorite memories. Meeting Sarah had become her second.

"I see you much the same way. The cocky bravado is sexy, but I knew there was more to you." Sarah's eyebrow arched.

Cam laughed out loud. "Is that how you see me?"

Sarah set down the bottle she'd been holding and got up on her knees, moving closer. "I see…" Sarah's index finger traced her jawline. "A beautiful, strong, independent woman who I wouldn't have met were it not for the life she had."

Cam swallowed hard as Sarah inched closer. She didn't want to move, afraid the moment would disappear. Afraid she'd wake from the pleasant dream to find Sarah wasn't real. Then Sarah touched her and she knew…Sarah was very real.

Sarah's lips parted. She took a quick intake of air before stilling completely as Sarah moved closer still. She hungered for Sarah to quench her thirst.

"Can I kiss you?"

Cam blinked, then nodded. She didn't remember ever having been asked.

The inches separating them were pure heat and sexual tension. Sarah brushed her lips over Cam's once. Twice. She moaned. The next time they touched, Sarah slid her fingers through the hair at the back of her neck, pulling her to her. Sarah traced her lips with the tip of her tongue. She opened to her probing, and Sarah gently explored her mouth. She could have gone on kissing Sarah forever just like she was, but there were more important things happening. Sarah smiled against her mouth and backed away.

"That was nice," Sarah said.

"Yes." She touched Sarah's cheek. The kiss confirmed their attraction and she didn't want to think about Sarah being in danger, especially if she weren't there to keep her safe. "I don't want anything to happen to you."

Sarah's forehead wrinkled in confusion. "What?"

"I know it's wrong…unethical even, but I don't want you anywhere near your brother."

"How did we jump from a hot kiss to my brother?" She tapped Cam's forehead. "Let's not worry about him right now. I want to hear about why there's nothing to be found on Camdyn Stark before the age of twenty-one."

If they were going to build on what they'd started, she knew Sarah wouldn't settle for anything but honesty. She prayed she'd be capable of giving her what she deserved.

CHAPTER TWENTY

C am took the next hour to finish telling her tale, explaining her relationship with Liv and how she'd reinvented herself. The one thing she didn't have to worry about anymore was her last foster father looking for her; he was the reason she'd fled to Florida. He'd been the only person from her past who might look for her, since he'd become a governor, then a senator. A sexual scandal would ruin his career, and she used to wonder if he'd find some deep well to drop her in if she resurfaced as her former self. At one point, she'd wanted to bring him down, but Liv had talked her out of it and she'd been right. Who would believe her when she'd been selling herself on the street not long before? Instead, she'd worked to put the past behind her and had taken a new name. She'd kept tabs on him for a while, but she hadn't had to worry. Three years after becoming a Nevada senator, he'd been caught in bed in Las Vegas with a couple of show girls, ending his career and his marriage. Cam had felt the last threat from her past fade away. She kept her new identity, liking it was of her own making, and she was proud of the person she'd become.

But none of it mattered as she studied Sarah. When she'd finished talking, Sarah had sat back, keeping space between them. She wasn't sure if it was a bad sign, but she was willing to wait it out. Finally, Sarah responded.

"Thank you for being honest. It couldn't have been easy."

"It was important to me for you to know who I am. What I am."

"And what is that?" Sarah tipped her head.

"I'm damaged goods, Sarah. I have issues stemming from my childhood and they occasionally raise their ugly head. I've worked hard to put it behind me, but still, I have an odd way of dealing with the ghosts of my past when they do come up." Cam had used women and work to create space from repressed memories and emotions, including anger. If Sarah got closer and then decided she couldn't handle the many sides of Cam, she'd be devastated. She hoped if she gave Sarah an out now, the pain of loss wouldn't be enough to crush her.

"We all have issues at one time or another. That doesn't mean you can't have a meaningful relationship, does it?"

Does it? It was a question she'd never had to answer till now. "I think with the right person, I can get beyond the doubts I've had about relationships in general. I guess, maybe, we'll find out together. Right?"

Sarah sat quietly, watching her intently, and though her nerves were frayed, she didn't look away. Cam wanted to bask in Sarah's intensity and her fiery spirit.

"Take me to your bedroom and I'll show you."

Fire shot through Cam's body. Sarah's entreaty caught her off guard, something she hadn't experienced since she was a youngster. She didn't even try to deny her body's craving to be near Sarah without clothes. Without barriers between them. The lies were no longer hidden, but how deeply she was attracted to Sarah hadn't been fully revealed either. She wasn't sure she could play true confessions any more tonight. Hopefully, there would be days, weeks, and months ahead for the two of them, and if Sarah asked for more, she'd share what remained hidden. She'd do anything to have a future with Sarah.

Sarah stood, and she took her hand to lead her down the hallway. She couldn't remember if she'd made her bed, though she had changed the sheets yesterday. Cam had never been shy in the bedroom, but for some reason she was suddenly uncertain. Maybe this wasn't such a good idea after all.

❖

Sarah still tasted Cam's kiss. The sweet undertone reminded her of a familiar flavor, though she couldn't name it. Then she'd surprised herself by telling Cam to take her to bed. She couldn't dwell on the future when all she wanted to do was live in the here and now—to be in the moment. To hell with conventional wisdom. How often did hesitation lead to missed opportunities? She was tired of playing it safe, of putting her desires on hold. She wanted to *live*. The truth was her body craved more of Cam, and unless she was sorely mistaken, Cam wanted her, too.

As she stepped into Cam's bedroom she didn't bother looking around. Cam's décor didn't interest her—Cam did. She pushed away all the distracting details of what she'd learned and concentrated on Cam. Cam looked both aroused and scared. She smoothed her hands over Cam's broad shoulders and down her slender arms. She moved her fingers to the top button on Cam's shirt and stopped, waiting for permission to go further.

"I want you."

"I want you, too."

"That's good, because I want you to enjoy everything we do, but you are in control. Please tell me to stop if you need to." She gently kissed the corner of Cam's mouth. "Whenever you want, you can tell me no, and I *will* hear you." Cam trembled, a nod her only response. It was all Sarah needed. She undid one button at a time until the shirt hung loosely off Cam's shoulders, revealing a strip of tan flesh between her sports bra and her navel. The belt at her waist was another obstacle, and she yanked hard enough for the two ends to fall apart. Sarah ran her thumbs inside the material, pressing them flat against Cam's abdomen, and watched her pupils contract. Unable to decide what she wanted first—to see Cam's breasts or reveal her in stages—she opted for slow and opened the button, then pulled down the zipper on her pants. Cam stilled her hands.

Sarah leaned in and nipped the exposed flesh of Cam's chest.

Cam groaned. "Wait."

"Too fast?"

"No, I want a turn." Cam's hot mouth move to her ear. "I really need to feel your skin, like now."

She swayed against Cam and would have told her yes if she'd been able to find the words. After taking a step back, she held her arms up, suggesting Cam make the next move. Cam's eyes burned with desire and made her pulse soar. Sarah was in deep. It had been a very long time since she'd slept with anyone she was more than mildly attracted to. Sarah had a feeling Cam was going to rock her world, and she had every intention of returning the favor.

Cam grasped the hem of her shirt and slowly lifted the silky material to below her breasts, revealing her heaving stomach. Cam went to one knee, loosely holding the folds in place, and skimmed her tongue along the outer edge of Sarah's belly button before dipping inside. Her muscles tightened in response. She hoped Cam wouldn't make her wait for more, but Cam seemed in no hurry, and she became enthralled by the gentleness, but it wasn't long before it was replaced by frustration.

"Enough." She grasped Cam's biceps and helped her stand. "Finish what you started."

"I'm pretty anxious myself." Cam grinned, her eyes hooded in desire.

Sarah poked her playfully. "What are you waiting for?"

Cam pulled the material over Sarah's arms, stopping at her hands, and wrapping it around her wrists in a move that surprised her with its suddenness, but she recovered quickly, and Cam backed Sarah across the short distance. "Is this what you want?" She lifted Sarah, placing her on the bed, and crawled up beside her.

"Yes."

Cam held Sarah's hands over her head and kissed the tender flesh below her ear. Nipped at her chin. Licked the hollow of her throat. Moisture pooled between her thighs. She was beyond turned on and fought the conflicting emotions of being both tender and rough, driven by her body's longing to take Sarah over the edge. Cam no longer believed Sarah had spent time with her only for updates. Maybe there'd been some innuendo that should have clued her in, but she'd been off her game ever since they'd met.

This...pleasing a woman...*this* she knew how to do, and she relied on her instincts to guide her. She lost herself in Sarah's captivating eyes. The interplay between them brought out a level of excitement so intense it left her breathless. She stared at the stiff nipples poking through the smooth material of Sarah's black silk bra. She traced the waistband of her matching panties with her fingertips, then moved to the covered slit at the center. The dampness beneath them was hot, and Cam wondered how long she could go on without removing the last barriers between them. Sarah appeared more than ready. So was she.

"You're so hot." She let go of Sarah's hands and straddled her, sitting high on her thighs. "So beautiful." Cam slid her hands over Sarah's hips and up to the edge of her bra, her thumbs tracing the underside of Sarah's breasts. "I thought so the day we met."

A short laugh escaped. "I was rather...demanding." She'd freed her hands and reached inside Cam's shirt, running her hands over her hard nipples, eliciting a moan.

"Mmm."

Sarah had thought Cam would be more comfortable if she were the one in control, but Cam brought out the tiger in her, and she wanted to make Cam want her as much as she wanted Cam. She sat up and pulled Cam closer until their lips met. Slow and seductive morphed into steamy in seconds. *God, we aren't even naked.* The rapid beat of her heart matched the thrumming of her clit.

"Can I see all of you?" Sarah bit her lip. She hadn't known anyone who had been through what Cam had, and she wanted to tread lightly.

"You don't have to worry about me having a flashback." Cam pecked at her lips, then moved off the bed and slid the pants from her hips, then the shirt from her shoulders.

Her body reminded Sarah of a swimmer's. Lean and long with muscles in all the right places. She stopped herself from reaching to touch the ridges along her abdomen, almost giggling at the random thought of Cam doing push-ups on top of the women she bedded.

"More, please."

Cam slid the boi shorts down her firm looking thighs, displaying tight dark curls that had been neatly trimmed back from her glistening lips. Sarah's resolve melted and she reached for her, sliding her fingers along the track of wetness. Cam's head dropped back, and those same thighs trembled.

"Sarah," Cam whispered.

"Come here."

Relief showed on Cam's beautiful face as she climbed beside her. She brushed the back of her hand along Sarah's panty line, then down the outside of her leg. She held her breath. The last time it had taken this long to get her clothes off for sex she'd been so drunk neither Sarah nor her lover could figure out the buttons and zippers. She and Cam weren't drunk on alcohol, but she was definitely drunk with the craving to be satisfied. She pushed Cam onto her back.

"You still have your bra on."

"So do you." The corners of Cam's mouth slowly formed into a sultry smile. "I could fix that."

Sarah leaned over, kissing her way over Cam's chest to her jaw before pressing her mouth to Cam's. She ran the tip of her tongue over her lips in a barely-there brush. When Cam's mouth opened, she slipped inside, exploring, tasting.

Cam's world tumbled into a thousand-piece puzzle. So much had happened in the last few hours her head spun. One minute she was spilling her guts, and the next she was standing in her bedroom with Sarah. Her heart galloped like a runaway stallion—which is how she felt when Sarah's voice commanded her and all she could do was obey.

Sarah's hot breath wafted over her nipple and it tightened painfully, but not in a bad way. "I'm going to come so fast when you touch me."

Christ. Cam hadn't even managed to get her naked yet, but her body tingled from head to toe with the excitement of their "first time." She'd been fantasizing about a moment like this for weeks. Her schoolgirl crush had turned into a full-time distraction, and if it weren't for Sarah being her client...this wasn't the time to think about *that* little detail...she would have already made a move. Sarah was playing seek and find in her mouth. She stifled a groan.

"This has to go." Cam slid a finger in her underwear, careful not to touch Sarah's center.

Sarah sat back and licked her swollen lips, smiling. She stood on the bed and hooked her thumbs in her panties, drawing them down before stepping out. She gathered the garment in her hand and tauntingly ran it along the inside of Cam's thighs. They were soaked and left a trail of moisture on her skin. Sarah blew a hot breath over her exposed center. A moan tore from her throat.

"Can you take your bra off now?" Sarah asked.

And like that, it was gone. Thrown over the side of the bed. She trembled under Sarah's heated stare. The color of her irises deepened to an azure sky.

"You take my breath away." Sarah removed her bra, guiding the straps slowly down her creamy shoulders.

Cam became lost in the confidence Sarah showed in her eyes. The trust she saw in them gave her the courage to find her voice. To share her body, mind, and spirit with Sarah.

"Lie on top of me, baby."

Sarah pressed her length against Cam, and she held Sarah close as she rolled them over. "You're so wet." Sarah's blond curls were soaked with liquid essence. She nuzzled Sarah's neck before turning her attention to the nearest breast, licking circles along the peak before filling her mouth. Sarah lightly raked her nails along Cam's sides.

"Please touch me."

Sarah's breathy plea broke the spell of losing herself in all things Sarah and the growing ache in her lower belly. She shifted her weight and smoothed her hand down Sarah's hip before moving to her heated center. She spread her folds, slid over Sarah's swollen clit, then entered her. Sarah gasped in pleasure. Cam coated her fingers and pressed another inside. Sarah was hot and tight. Cam loved how she filled her with strong strokes. Sarah wrapped her hand around the back of Cam's neck and pulled her down in a demanding kiss. The inner muscles tightened around her fingers and Cam pressed deeper, shortening her strokes until Sarah stilled beneath her.

"Come for me."

Sarah arched into her and cried out, her legs shaking with the intensity of her orgasm. It took all Cam's concentration to not climax. She didn't want to take the moment's pleasure away from Sarah. It was for her and her alone.

Sarah's muscles stopped contracting and she gathered Cam to her. The dampness on her shoulder jolted her out of her blissful state.

"Cam." She rubbed her back. "What's wrong?"

Cam kept her face hidden as she shook her head, but she didn't move.

"Baby, please?" Sarah lifted Cam's chin from her shoulder. Her eyes were red. Her cheeks were tear-stained.

"I'm scared."

Sarah was confused. She didn't think she'd implied she expected a commitment from Cam. She didn't picture Cam as the commitment type when they'd met, and she could understand if she reverted to keeping emotionally distant.

"You don't have to be. I'm not asking you to make any promises…"

"No. It's not that. I'm afraid if he finds you, he'll hurt you."

Sarah studied the worry wrinkling Cam's forehead and the terror in her eyes. "Honey, I'm sure that's how it seemed, but I don't think you have to be concerned."

Cam abruptly sat up. "You didn't see the look on his face, Sarah. I did. He looked like he wanted to kill. I *know* his type. And I think he's convinced he'd get away with it because he's a cop. He's not the kind of guy you want to get close to."

She'd never seen Cam lose her cool before, and the idea that maybe she wasn't exaggerating about Brace made her uneasy. Maybe she should listen to Cam and forget about Brace before she regretted it. No. That was crazy. Cam's paranoia was rubbing off on her.

"This isn't quite the way I thought our evening would go." She pulled the covers over her. The feeling of being exposed and vulnerable was new. It gave her a better understanding of why Cam kept her distance.

Cam sat on the edge of the bed, naked and clearly frustrated. She grazed her hand along Sarah's jaw and she couldn't help leaning into the tender touch. Cam smiled. "That makes two of us." Cam took her hands and pressed her lips to the palm of each, then held them. "I know you think I'm overreacting. Trust me, I'm not."

"I do trust you. I would have never asked to share your bed if I didn't." She looked at their joined hands. "I hired you because I don't like the thought of not having any family. I couldn't do it myself, and I still want…need…the information you've found so far. You of all people have to understand what it feels like to be without ties." The moment the words left her mouth she regretted them. The last thing she wanted to do was hurt Cam's feelings.

Cam picked up her shirt and yanked it on, her back to Sarah. She rummaged on the floor until she found her pants. "You're right. You hired me to do a job and I willingly took your money." Her voice was devoid of emotion. She ran her hands through her hair and turned around. "Just give me a few days. If I find evidence that proves he's a danger to people who get too close, I hope you'll reconsider."

"And if you're wrong?"

Cam huffed out a sigh. "I'll give you everything you need. You're the client here." She moved to the doorway and stopped, giving Sarah a lingering look that was sad. "Thank you for listening tonight."

❖

Sarah pulled into her driveway and touched her swollen lips, the taste of Cam still on them. Her eyes closed as she pictured the near perfect body that had hovered over her a short time ago. She hadn't gotten to touch Cam the way she'd wanted to and regretted the lost opportunity. Maybe there would be another time. Cam's fear of her brother hurting her had surprised Sarah, but not as much as Cam's tears had. She'd been startled when she'd broken down in front of her, something she didn't think many people ever got to see. *That has to mean something.*

Sighing, Sarah dropped her keys in the dish on the stand in the hallway. Why did life have to be so complicated? Hadn't she dealt with enough over the last few years to last a lifetime? Then she thought of the things Cam had told her about her childhood. The trials she'd been through were trivial compared to the horrors Cam had experienced. Tears blurred her vision. How could she be so self-centered? Yes, she'd sacrificed her social and personal life for her parents the last few years, but they hadn't expected it and it had been her decision. Cam hadn't had a choice. No wonder she'd been less than enthusiastic to take her case. It probably brought back memories she'd just as soon forget.

At least now she knew why there was no early information on Camdyn Stark. She hadn't existed until she was twenty. The woman named Liv had been instrumental in guiding Cam to a happy, meaningful future. But was Cam really happy? Or was it a facade she presented, like the first day Sarah had met her? Cam was complicated and far deeper than Sarah had given her credit for.

She hung her head. What had she been thinking when she'd asked Cam to take her to bed? The answer was simple. She'd wanted to show Cam she was all the things she feared she wasn't, but then she'd provided an emotional slap in the face with the crude comment about hiring her, and about her not having ties.

"Great. Just fucking great." Sarah shook her head. Left with the task of making sure Cam didn't think she was disposable, she needed a game plan. A way to show Cam she was interested in more than sex. Not like her fosters or the women she'd tricked with in her youth. *God. I hope Cam doesn't think I've taken advantage of her because she was in a vulnerable state.* That would be horrible. Could she have handled the situation any more awkwardly than she had?

She couldn't deny how good it had been to feel sexy and wanted. To see Cam's blatant desire in her eyes. She'd gone without those emotions for so long she'd almost forgotten how powerful an aphrodisiac the chemistry between two people could be, and she and Cam definitely had chemistry. She'd be damned if she'd let guilt override the physical and emotional pleasure she'd enjoyed. All she had to do was convince Cam she hadn't been opportunistic. That what they shared went beyond the physical. But she had no idea where they stood.

CHAPTER TWENTY-ONE

Cam sipped her beer, not really tasting it. Her stomach had been in a knot since last week when Sarah had stood beside her and they'd tumbled into bed.

"I need more. I need concrete proof." She said it out loud, but didn't really expect Jimmy Barnes to respond.

Sarah wanted answers, and she'd prayed what she'd shared was enough to convince Sarah, but it hadn't. She had no remorse about baring her soul, even if doing so kept Sarah safe for only a few more days. But her time was running out. She hadn't been very successful in finding solid versus circumstantial proof. She'd used her usual means to get information. Database searches, social media, tracking down friends—which aside from fellow officers, she hadn't been able to locate any, and that alone was odd. Why wasn't a rich kid from the suburbs surrounded by friends, even if they were the kind who hung out with him only because of the money? She'd messaged a few of the people on Brace's "friends" list, pretending to be doing a survey, but when she'd asked innocuous questions, their responses were similar. *I don't really know him. We've never actually hung out. His mood is unpredictable, so I keep my distance.*

Her street informants hadn't been any better. The only one who admitted he knew of a cop who was "heavy into selling" hadn't been willing to say more. All he said was, "That cop, he's not right. Crazier than the homeless guy who barks whenever anyone gets close." Cam knew the barker. He was harmless, but she had the distinct impression harmless wasn't a characteristic that would ever describe Brace.

She should have questioned more of his colleagues, but she'd been leery of tipping Brace off that she was digging deeper. She also didn't want to put Jimmy in a position any more awkward than he was already in. That didn't stop her from pushing him for a face-to-face meeting. He'd balked, of course. She'd had to rely on charm and a little coercion to convince him otherwise. After all, a fellow officer who knew of a dirty one on the force and didn't report it was just as guilty in her eyes, and she was sure the upper ranks of the department would agree. Jimmy must have felt guilty about that part, which was why he was sitting across from her.

"I don't know." He swirled the bottle in his hand and then threw the contents back in one long swallow. "Not only could it be my job, but if Archer finds out he'll go ballistic."

"So you'd rather keep turning a blind eye than get a bad seed off the force?" Cam would, at some point, file a formal complaint with the mayor. She rarely trusted internal chains of command, especially when the stakes were as high as this. Whatever she did, she'd make damn sure Sarah was safe from the long arm of the law—in this case, that meant Archer.

"He's not the only seed, you know. He's recruited some of the less successful officers to join him, and I sure as hell don't want him to have any reason to point a finger at me."

"I must be losing my touch. I would have sworn you weren't that easily intimidated. Clearly, I was mistaken." She stood and threw a twenty on the table.

"Jesus, Stark. I didn't say I wouldn't." Barnes gestured for her to sit back down.

"Then give me something I can use against this bastard."

"If I bring you proof how deep Archer's in, I need to know you won't say where you got your information." Barnes glanced around the dark bar. They'd driven forty minutes to the dingy dive to be sure no one would recognize them. At least the beer was cold.

"I never reveal my sources. I give you my word." Cam didn't have many scruples that she lived by, but giving her word was one she'd never failed to keep.

Barnes stared at her for a long time. She refused to show him how much Archer had spooked her when she'd talked to him. He pulled his hands down his face before glancing at the ceiling, as though making a deal with an unseen force.

"Okay. What do you need?"

For the first time in a while, Cam had hope the career she'd chosen would make a difference in people's lives. She would be the voice unafraid of exposing a bad cop and getting him off the force. Sarah, along with countless others, would be safer. She had to be brave enough to have her voice heard. This time she had to make sure of it. Unfortunately, the majority of those reasons had everything to do with the person she was investigating, and nothing to do with circumstances out of her client's control. This was one of those times she believed she could make a difference in her client's life in a good way. For the last few years, she hadn't been so sure there was honor in what she was doing. Sarah had given her a reason to do better than the status quo and restored her faith.

Sarah toe-walked the beam to the upright support, then lowered herself to a straddling position. After hammering in the bolts and tightening the nuts, she welded the metal, giving it more strength. She inspected her work, then stood up and moved to the next beam. She never thought about her elevation. Never looked down to see how far off the ground she was. There were a couple of men on the job with her who came across as fearless as they traversed the worksite, rarely using a safety line. Their trust in the unseen force that guided them amazed her. She'd never had that much faith in anything in her life, aside from her parents' love. No. That wasn't true. She had put her faith in Cam, trusting she would do her job and find her sibling, and she hadn't been disappointed. True to her word, Cam had located him, and a father she hadn't expected to find, but hadn't divulged much else. Sleeping with her might have been a mistake, but she couldn't deny how much her body had responded to Cam's touch. She smiled at the visceral memory…

Her concentration interrupted, the bolt slipped from her fingers and tumbled out of reach. She was twelve stories up. No one on the ground would hear her warning, and Sarah hoped everyone was adhering to the hard hat requirement.

Elsu called to her from above. "Sarah."

Sarah held her hard hat and looked at the beam above her. "Yeah, I know. Keep my head in the game."

He laughed and gave her the thumbs-up. He'd called her the "white version" of a sky walker, later explaining the history of steel workers. She hadn't taken offense at the reference because there'd been a twinkle in his eye and she knew he was teasing her. Steel workers watched each other's backs, and more than once she'd been glad to have their encouragement and support.

In her studio that night, Sarah looked at the near finished piece of iron and steel. It had taken her the better part of three months to get it in the shape she wanted. All that was left was grinding a few joints smooth and polishing parts to catch the lights that would be projected on it from different angles.

She chewed her bottom lip in worry. This was the last commissioned piece she'd contracted. While it would provide a healthy boost to her finances, once she paid off some bills, there'd be nothing left. Maybe she'd print up flyers at the library and hand them out, offering her welding know-how as a service she could provide. Something had to give. She couldn't keep working overtime and sculpting every evening, even if it was her passion. Sarah was running out of energy, and the little bit of down time she did have was so miniscule, she didn't have it in her to go out and have fun. *No time to think about that now.* She pulled her goggles from the top of her head, placed them snuggly over her eyes, and picked up the grinder. An hour later, she ran her hand over the still warm metal, feeling for burrs and imperfections. She poked her finger in one of the small openings, rotating it right and left. Erotic thoughts rushed through her and she groaned. She wanted it to be Cam, firm and hot, surrounding her finger. *Maybe I could call her and…* and say what? *I wasn't done fucking you. Can we have a redo?*

"Jesus." Sarah's laugh wasn't as happy as it might have been under different circumstances. Still, the phone on the bench called to her. It had been almost a week since she'd been with Cam. She'd promised to give her time, but she'd thought she'd have heard from her by now. Time to convince Sarah nothing good could come out of meeting her twin.

With the polishing done and her shop cleaned, Sarah's stomach growled. Eight forty. Where the hell had the time gone? There wasn't much in her fridge at home. Even if there was, she was too tired to cook. She thought about ignoring the empty pit, but she'd never sleep if she didn't have something substantial to fill it. The engine of her car sputtered to life and she drove down the main street to find a take-out place. None that she passed appealed to her. Sighing, she pulled into the only twenty-four-hour diner in town. At least she could get anything she wanted, and once she had the menu in her hand, she'd be able to decide on something.

The bell over the door jangled, and a few nearby patrons looked up. Sarah glanced around and her line of sight stopped on Cam. She was staring at her from a big booth in the corner. A smile started at one side of her mouth and traveled to the other. She waved her over. Sarah hesitated. True, a little while ago she'd been thinking about calling Cam, but this chance encounter hadn't been what she had in mind.

"Hi. What are you doing here?" It came out harsh and she winced. Cam either didn't notice or chose to ignore it.

"The same thing as you, I imagine. Maggie reminded me I hadn't eaten since breakfast." Cam pushed her papers to the side and shut her laptop. "Join me?"

Not sitting with her would make her appear rude, one thing Sarah tried never to be. That didn't stop her heart from beating faster and wayward thoughts of their last time together to come back in living color. *Christ.* They'd barely gotten undressed when she'd exploded in Cam's embrace. She hoped that wasn't the last memory she'd have of them together.

❖

Cam had been poring over the notes from Barnes. They had arrived yesterday by various means. Some via third-party email and some in a manila envelope addressed to her at the office. A number of the photos were a little blurry, most likely taken under less than ideal conditions, but with a bit of enhancement, she could see ninety percent of what was there.

She hadn't spoken to Sarah since the night they'd had sex. She hadn't been sure if Sarah regretted being with her in the biblical sense. She hoped not. Sarah stared at her. Whether in disbelief because they'd ended up at the same diner or because she'd been avoiding her on purpose, Cam wasn't sure. It didn't take long for Sarah's expression to change and the smile to reach her eyes.

"Sorry I was staring. I didn't expect to see you." Sarah stood awkwardly as though unsure if she should sit down.

"Likewise. But since we're both here, we should eat together." She wanted to find out how Sarah felt about her and the awkward way things had been left between them.

"I don't want to disturb you." Sarah pointed to the haphazard papers.

"I need a break. Besides, how could I concentrate when a beautiful woman is in the same diner as me?"

Sarah's cheeks turned a lovely shade of pink before she took off her jacket and slid in across from her. This booth was her favorite spot in the entire diner because no one could sneak in without her notice. Sarah joining her just added another reason.

Sarah looked up at her from under long, dark lashes. "I would have joined you without the compliment. Is that one of your favorite lines?"

Sometimes Cam wished she'd never admitted to being a player. But damn, she did like women. The one sharing her booth was not only sexy and beautiful, but there was a certain quality about Sarah that she couldn't name, though she didn't have to name it to make it true. They'd shared so much in the weeks between their first meeting, she knew Sarah wasn't one of her conquests. For the first time in her life, it wasn't about sex. She hungered for a real relationship.

"Only when it's the truth." Cam fell into the crystal blue of Sarah's eyes and lost track of what she was doing. In her mind, she pictured Sarah naked beneath her, her body glistening and flush before Cam had driven her over the edge and into a climax so beautiful to behold, she'd cried. It was only when Sarah's voice cut through the fog of her mush brain, that she snapped out of the fantasy she'd been riding.

"Cam? Are you all right?" Sarah shared a knowing look.

She glanced down at the menu the waitress had dropped off when she'd brought her coffee and hadn't touched since. "Have you eaten?" *Moron.* Of course she hadn't eaten. Why else would she be at the diner?

Sarah reached for the menu but didn't take it. "Have you?"

"No." The word came out as a squeak. She cleared her throat and tried again. "No. Maggie badgered me until I left the office and I came here."

"How long ago was that?" Sarah took the menu, opening it in front of her, then waited.

Cam looked at her watch. She hadn't realized how late it was. "Uh…a couple of hours." Maybe her watch was broken. After all, she'd had…she glanced into her mug…about half a cup of coffee that was now ice cold. The cream floated in a pool on the top.

Sarah twitched her finger back and forth. "Tsk-tsk. Whatever will Maggie say if she finds out you've ignored her?"

Laughing, Cam grabbed at Sarah's waving finger, but she yanked it out of her reach. A smile spread across her face before she joined in the laughter. The melodious sound filled the booth's intimate space. It would be easy to reach across the table and hold on to Sarah, but she didn't quite trust herself to behave. She didn't want to do anything to embarrass Sarah, in public or otherwise. When Sarah rested her hand on top of the menu, she covered it with hers and gently rubbed the soft flesh.

"Are you okay?"

"I'm not following?"

Here goes nothing. "With us. How we were at my place…" She didn't want to call it sex. For her it was much more. After confessing her past she'd felt so raw and exposed, she hadn't had anything left to hide. She'd shared herself, and her body, hoping she'd shown her feelings for Sarah as well. And she wanted more of the same.

"If you're asking if I have any regrets about being with you, you can stop wondering. It was a beautiful time. All of it." Sarah covered Cam's hand with her own.

Cam took in a quick breath. God. She had so many skeletons in the closet she swore she could hear the bones rattling. Why would Sarah want any part of the mess she dragged around behind her?

"And before you say anything else, Camdyn Stark, I'm only going to say this once. You, right here, right now, are the person I'm attracted to. Okay?"

Sarah's words touched her. Took her breath away. Gave her courage to stay open to the possibilities that lay ahead. For her. For Sarah. Maybe even for the two of them. She swallowed around the lump in her throat.

"Okay," she whispered.

Sarah squeezed her hand. "Great. Now can we eat? I'm wasting away here." She gestured to her body.

Cam couldn't resist. "We can't have that now, can we? Your body is perfect the way it is."

"Glad you think so. We have unfinished business to tend to at some point and I'd hate to disappoint you."

Heat shot through her. She tamped down her libido and opted for the real reason she wanted to spend more time with Sarah. Her heart was pure. If she were lucky, Sarah could help Cam open herself to living a full life. "You could never disappoint me, Sarah." There was a lot more she wanted to say. Words of gratitude and heartfelt joy for Sarah coming into her life. If she dared, she would also be grateful for a bright future. She shook her head. She was getting way ahead of herself.

"Let's eat, shall we?" Cam asked.

"I thought you'd never ask."

Chapter Twenty-two

S arah sat next to Cam on the couch. The heat between them was intense. The electricity of their attraction was akin to her welder's torch. The arc of bright light blinding—weakening her control, and she found it hard to keep her hands to herself. After they ate, Cam had suggested she come back to her house so she could tell her about the latest news. Maybe she was being stubborn, but she couldn't give up her hopes of having her brother in her life. There was always the possibility of Cam's information being wrong, though her gut told her Cam's instincts were a fairly accurate barometer when it came to knowing who was morally corrupt.

"Where did you get all of this?" Sarah held a stack of photos showing evidence from drug busts that had disappeared, entries in reports that had been altered, and a number of other documents that she couldn't make sense out of but guessed none of it was good.

"I can't tell you."

She sat back, hoping her expression conveyed her displeasure at Cam's avoidance.

"Sarah, you know I can't reveal my sources, for everyone's safety. Could you please trust me when I tell you it's reliable? The information isn't in question, but Brace's behavior certainly is." As if to explain, Cam picked up a sheet of paper with hard-slant writing. "See this? This is a police report about a bust that happened a few years ago. The score was close to a half kilo of crack. But when it was reweighed for trial, it was closer to a quarter. The sign-out sheet," Cam pointed to another piece of paper with a table grid on it, "states that your brother signed it out a couple of days after the initial logging."

"Is that unusual?" She had no idea how police procedure worked, but it made sense that any officer involved in an arrest would want to look at the evidence again.

"Not under normal circumstances."

"I take it there's something not normal here." She tapped the stack. A sour feeling churned the contents of her stomach, making her queasy.

"The original report is signed by your brother. So is the transfer of evidence log. But if you look really close you can see where someone's carefully altered the amount of drug confiscated."

Cam handed her a huge magnifying glass. It took her a while to focus, but once she did even she could see traces of uncovered pen marks under the new entry.

"That doesn't mean it was Brace who changed it."

"I compared the handwriting to the original report. It's his, Sarah, and that's not the only one that's been changed. My source believes once Brace established a network of street-level dealers he didn't even bother with reports. He took their drugs, made a deal with them, and sold it to the highest bidders."

Sarah shook her head. She didn't want to believe Brace was a criminal. A drug dealer no less. She expected him to be honorable and uphold the law, but if what Cam was telling her was true, he was far from it. Still, it wasn't in her heart to give up on him without even meeting and talking with him. It was foolish, and stubborn, and maybe even stupid. But she had to make Cam understand somehow.

"I know it looks incriminating, but I have to look in his eyes and see what's there. I need to see for myself, if only to be sure. Please?"

"Can't you just talk to your father and—"

"He isn't my father. He's a stranger."

"No more so than Brace."

Cam had a point. She'd reconsider her foolish pride and think about contacting Paul, but that didn't mean she would trade knowing one relative for another. "True, but Brace didn't have a choice."

Cam was silent while she gathered the papers into a neat stack. After putting them back in their envelope she looked up at her. "I can't persuade you otherwise?"

"I'm sorry. I'm sure by now you can understand how much I want this, so no."

Cam's lips pursed. "I'll write up my report and give it to you in a day or two. It should contain everything you need."

Cam appeared resigned, but the thing that bothered Sarah most was the sadness she saw. She preferred things to be relaxed between them. It didn't feel that way.

When Sarah went to the bathroom, Cam took the envelope and dropped it on her desk. She had no choice but to finish her investigation and write her findings. That should be the end of it, but she couldn't let Sarah walk away. Not before…

"Well, I guess I should go." Sarah shoved her hands in her back pockets and shared a tentative smile.

She picked up the wine glasses and went to Sarah, handing her one. "I think this deserves a toast. You've got a brother to bond with and another, a bonus relative, and I'm about to close another case." Cam should have been happy. Under other circumstances she would be, but this case had been anything but normal from the start, and she still had to decide what she wanted to do about Brace, though she didn't want to bring that up now. There was no question she needed to report him. But if Sarah ended up having the bastard in her life, bringing down Brace could make Sarah feel betrayed. Jesus. What a mess. The ring of their glasses touching sounded ominous. The wine was slightly heavy with dark undertones. It matched her mood.

"It's very good." Sarah regarded her as though wanting to say more, but she didn't.

Cam pointed to the couch. "Let's relax a bit while we enjoy it."
Sarah seemed hesitant. "Okay."

She snagged the bottle from the counter on her way. Even if Sarah didn't want more to drink, she was pretty sure she would. As she settled, she left a couple of feet between them, but it felt like a chasm had formed with Sarah out of reach.

Sarah cleared her throat. "What will you do?"

Sarah's voice startled Cam from her melancholy. "Do?"

"With all your free time, now that I'm not..." Sarah took a breath. "Now that you're down a case."

If Sarah only knew how much she was dreading the loss. She'd gladly give up any case for peace of mind and them having more time together. "I've got some unfinished business. Other cases to work on." Cam thought about the cases she'd dumped on Kevin so she could devote all her time on Sarah's. It hadn't been fair, though he hadn't complained.

"You're not the only one." Sarah's hand ran up her thigh. "There's another thing that feels unfinished."

Her sex tightened, and she stared where Sarah's hand rested. Her mind raced. Cam had hoped they would part amicably, but doubt had crept in. Sarah had what she'd hired Cam for and no longer needed her services. Now it seemed they weren't done after all.

Sarah stood and took Cam's hand. "Unless you'd rather not."

A loud click sounded when she swallowed. "No. Yes." She stood on wobbly legs. "I mean...shit."

Sarah laughed softly before a little grin formed. "That sounds a bit ambiguous."

Cam set her glass down, surprised she hadn't spilled any since her hand was shaking. "Jesus, Sarah. You make me come undone."

"Good." Sarah gave a tug. "So is that a yes, I want to?"

"Yes." Her voice squeaked.

"I know the way." Sarah pulled her along.

Cam willingly followed. She'd examine all the ways the situation between them had just become even more complicated later. Once in the bedroom, Cam stood still. Afraid to move. Afraid to breathe. She didn't want to break the spell Sarah wove around her with a look. A touch. She'd never been so off-kilter or upended by any woman like she was with Sarah. Everything she did sparked lightning through her, setting her nerves on fire. And her clit? Well, it had a life of its own at the moment. No matter how much Cam attempted to remain calm and collected, she was a live wire ready to sizzle.

Sarah reached for her. "We had a clothing issue last time." Sarah unzipped her jeans, then undid the button. She ran her hand around her waist, pulling her shirt free and opened the top two snaps. She leaned closer, her breath caressing Cam's exposed flesh. "Mmm, you smell so good. What is that?"

Her mind froze. Between the sultry look and Sarah's heat, nothing was working above her neck. She blurted out the first thing that came to her less than functioning mind. "Soap."

Sarah gave her a lopsided grin. "Is that so?"

"Uh-huh."

"What other great mysteries are you hiding?"

Sarah snaked her hand inside the front of her jeans and cupped her. A moan escaped her lips. When she squeezed her swollen flesh, Cam's knees buckled. She grabbed Sarah's shoulders to stay upright.

"My, my. I think I need to get you on the bed before you end up on the floor."

Cam was lost in Sarah's hooded gaze, and she waited as Sarah quickly finished undressing her and guided her onto the bed before discarding her own clothes. All except the navy blue lace thong she was wearing. She climbed on and straddled her. Sarah's breasts were perfectly shaped and begging for attention. If she had been in command of her own body, Cam would have sat up and taken the tip in her mouth. But as it was, all she could do was watch as Sarah took control.

Sarah leaned down and kissed her. Lightly at first, waiting for Cam to respond. Then she traced Cam's lips, teasing them open, and pressing her tongue inside. Cam was so engrossed in the feel of Sarah taking her, she started when Sarah pinched her nipple, waking her out of her stupor. Sarah broke away.

"Did I hurt you?"

Cam smoothed her hands over Sarah's lush hips. Her curves were so damn sexy she wished she could touch them whenever she wanted. "No. I'm just super sensitive right now." She smiled. "I was a little preoccupied."

"I noticed." Sarah moved a little farther down until their crotches touched and she began a slow grind. "I can feel how wet you are." She placed light kisses over her twitching stomach muscles.

She was going to explode if Sarah kept it up. She didn't want to. Not yet. But her body had other plans. She was hopelessly out of control. "I'm going to come if you don't stop."

Sarah paused and covered Cam's breasts with her palms, firmly massaging them. Her nipples rubbed against them. It was a surreal kind of torture.

"You don't want to come?"

"No. I mean yes. Ugh." Cam covered Sarah's hands with hers. "I can't think when you're touching me." Sara laughed. "Yes, I want to come, but not yet."

"I want you to come, too." Sarah flattened her hands on Cam's abdomen as she moved lower still, spreading her legs in the process, her eyes never leaving Cam's. "I want you…" Sarah settled between Cam's thighs. "To come in my mouth."

Cam gasped. The desire Sarah let Cam see made her vibrate from her head to her toes. She wanted to give every part of herself to Sarah. Her heart and soul. The thought thrilled and scared her at the same time. Sarah began kissing her inner thighs, first one side, then the other. Her fingers gently spread Cam's soaked folds before she lowered her mouth and took her in. Her hips reflexively rose to meet Sarah, and once again, Cam was lost in Sarah's touch.

So raw. That's how Sarah viewed Cam from her straddling position. Cam looked so exposed, so vulnerable. Sarah wanted to tell her how deeply Cam had touched her, and how alive she made her feel instead of just going through the motions of everyday life like she had been. She'd never felt the pendulum of emotions she experienced whenever she was in Cam's presence. Those moments when Cam's vulnerability brought her to near tears, and the others when she wanted to scream at her for assuming Sarah couldn't think for herself. Protect herself. Was it because Cam was experiencing her own conundrum in their precarious relationship? *Why is it we*

have to ponder the great mysteries of life at times like these? Sarah repositioned between Cam's muscled thighs, pressing them wider apart, opening her, and inhaled her musky scent. It made her dizzy with hunger.

She watched Cam watching her while looking over Cam's heaving abdomen. After kissing each thigh, she spread Cam's slick folds then slipped her tongue inside. Cam's head arched back, and she gathered fistfuls of bedding. Sarah smiled against the hot flesh. Moving in and out with her tongue, she slowly fucked Cam before swiping along the length of her. Cam's hips rose with every pass until Sarah placed her lips around her swollen clit and began to gently suck.

"So good." Cam moaned before snaking her fingers in Sarah's hair, holding her in place.

It wouldn't be long before Cam climaxed. She pressed a finger inside as she swirled her tongue over the tip of the nerve bundle. Her walls began to tighten around her. Cam stilled. A low groan rose in volume until her whole body shook with the strength of her orgasm while she called out Sarah's name again and again.

She eased out and lightly licked the swollen flesh until Cam's body calmed. Her own center throbbed, and the bedding beneath her was wet, evidence of how turned on she was from making love to Cam. Sarah crawled up Cam's damp body until their centers met. She placed sweet kisses along her breasts until her urge for more pushed her higher.

"Baby, open your eyes. Let me see you."

Cam fought her way through the fog of satiated bliss. Sarah was talking to her. Her first attempt to look at her ended in a flutter. On the next, she managed to keep her eyes open, at least a little bit.

"You wreck me."

Sarah bent close and passionately kissed her. "I hope in a good way."

She shared a weak laugh. "Oh, in a very good way."

Sarah stilled above her, chewing on her bottom lip.

Cam ran her hands over Sarah's hips. She knew that look.

"What's wrong?"

"Nothing's wrong," Sarah said. "I just…" She looked away, as if embarrassed. It was sweet and disturbing at the same time.

"Honey, you can tell me anything. I hope you know that. What is it?"

Sarah lay on her chest, drawing random circles around her breast. "I don't want to steal your thunder. It's selfish."

Cam used her index finger to tip Sarah's chin so she could see her eyes. "You aren't. What's selfish?"

Sarah pushed up and loudly sighed. "I need to come." She dropped her head in embarrassment.

Cam couldn't help laughing, and Sarah slapped her chest.

"It's not funny."

It took a minute before she could get her giggles under control. Cam pulled Sarah down and whispered in her ear. "Give me a minute to recover and I'll be more than happy to take care of you." She nibbled on Sarah's earlobe, making her shiver. After tracing her lips with the tip of her tongue, Sarah sat back up. The look on Sarah's face gave away she was more than ready to have her need satisfied. Sarah wiggled her way downward, leaving a wet trail along her body.

"Where are you going?"

"Right here."

Sarah put one leg over Cam's hip and raised Cam's other leg to her shoulder before repositioning. She began to slide her slick center against Cam's, creating friction. The friction changed to an intense grinding as Sarah sped up, kissing Cam's calf between strokes. Cam wouldn't have thought she'd be aroused again so soon. Apparently, she'd underestimated her body's ability to respond to Sarah.

"God. You feel so good." Cam touched Sarah's breast, kneading the softness beneath her fingers, enjoying how hard her nipple became against her palm. Sarah's eyes dilated, and the passion she saw in them only fueled the fire already burning in her body. The motion between them stopped. Sarah braced her hand on Cam's chest, and looked into Cam's very soul.

"Come with me."

It wasn't a question. It was a quiet statement, requiring that Cam succumb entirely to Sarah. To share a perfectly choreographed orgasm. She pressed her center upward against Sarah, holding on to her hip. Cam watched the firestorm in Sarah's eyes before they tumbled into a simultaneous climax. Her only thought was how perfect her life would be with Sarah's passion in it.

❖

Sarah blinked several times before her vision cleared. She looked around until the warmth of another body in her bed brought the night before into stark detail. Cam was still asleep, facing her with her arms outstretched as though reaching for her—or waiting for someone to fill them. Her breathing was slow and deep. Long black lashes lay against her pale cheeks. Her hair fanned out on the pillow in a tangle—the result of their active night together.

Cam had willingly shared her body and Sarah relished every moment. She couldn't imagine how Cam would interpret their night together. Hell, she wasn't even sure she wanted to analyze it. Their joining had been passionate and more than satisfying, substantiated by Sarah falling into contented sleep.

Maybe Cam wouldn't want more; she'd said she wasn't capable of commitment right at the beginning, and maybe Sarah needed to take her at her word. She wasn't sure if Cam had ever been with a long-term partner. Was she wrong to think about their future?

Sarah decided it was silly to read too much into Cam's actions, especially since she'd asked Sarah to stay the night, telling her it would be nice to wake in the morning with her in her arms. She couldn't say no. Not that she wanted to. If this was the best Cam could do at the moment, she'd make peace with it.

Cam mumbled something incomprehensible before she stretched, her fingers brushing Sarah's arm. Her eyes opened wide, then relaxed as realization dawned. "Hi."

"Good morning." She brushed wayward strands of hair off Cam's cheek.

"Come here. Please." Cam wiggled her fingers and spread her

arms.

Sarah's heartstrings tugged. Cam might not be able to express how she was feeling, but everything she saw in her eyes told her she wasn't alone in this. She scooted across the cooler sheets and settled along Cam's length. The sigh came uncensored.

Cam brushed her lips over Sarah's forehead. "I couldn't agree more."

"What else do you agree with?" Sarah felt Cam stiffen. "Are you going to bolt?"

Cam ducked her head to see her face. "No." She pulled Sarah closer, using her hand to press Sarah's softness to her firmer, leaner frame. "I'm not going anywhere."

Hope was a beautiful, if fragile, thing, and Sarah felt it bloom inside her for the first time in a very, very long time.

CHAPTER TWENTY-THREE

Cam glanced between her notes and the computer screen as she typed. She couldn't understand why Archer would take a chance selling when it was clear he didn't need the money. His parents were wealthy and he was likely earmarked to inherit everything. She would have liked to locate a will, but that kind of information was out of her reach. The best she could hope for was his parents were on to him. Maybe he'd pissed them off and his involvement in drugs was a revolt against the power they wielded. If they were smart and had a will drawn up with stipulations regarding his inheritance, they'd be smart to hide that kind of information from Brace. She wondered if they were afraid of their son and what he was capable of. Liv had done much the same to bury any connection between Cam's former name and her current one to keep her abusers as far away as possible. Anything could be accomplished, for a price.

Her phone alarm was a harbinger. She had one more meeting before the Peters case was officially done. She should have told Sarah there'd be more information if she'd give her a few additional days, but she knew stalling would make Sarah angry, though any reason to see that fiery reaction was almost worth the risk. Sarah's intensity was a big turn-on. Cam silenced her phone, saved her work, and gathered her bag.

After her GPS told her she'd arrived at her destination, she stood in a back alley with a jittery cop glaring at her.

Barnes looked behind him as he nervously puffed on a cigarette. "This is the last time."

She knew what he meant. It had been a monumental win for her to talk him into this meeting and even then, he only agreed if he could pick the location. They were on the outskirts of a seedy little town that no one would ever consciously choose to visit.

"Okay." She took the envelope and dropped it into her shoulder bag.

Barnes stomped out the butt, then shoved his hands into his pockets. "Good luck with everything." He acted like he wanted to shake her hand, but he took half a step back instead, then turned away.

"Hey," Cam called. Barnes stopped but didn't turn around. She glanced around, making sure they were still alone between the brick buildings, half hidden in shadows. "Do you think it's safe for his twin to meet him?" Maybe she'd read too much into the information she had because it served to keep Sarah around longer, and she wasn't sure she was looking at it objectively. For a long minute, she didn't think he was going to answer.

Barnes looked over his shoulder, his eyes dead serious. "No. Drugs are powerful motivators, and he's not someone whose conscience would deter him from using her any way he could."

She felt the same way, but Sarah was stubborn when it came to the topic and she knew she wouldn't get anywhere if she broached the subject again. Cam was in a constant state of conflict between her professional obligations and her personal desire to keep Sarah safe.

Later that day, Cam sat at her desk staring at the contents of intel on Brace Archer. She didn't have any remaining doubt how much of a criminal he was. This latest information intimated Brace had amassed a six-figure fortune that was spread out in a number of bank accounts, although none of the accounts had his name on them. There wasn't enough in any one of them to get the attention of the authorities. Cam considered the possibility he only kept them open for times he needed to dump cash somewhere in an emergency. He wasn't stupid, and there was probably a much larger account elsewhere, probably offshore. Others in the department had to know what he was up to, and not reporting it to the people in charge made them culpable. It had been easier and safer for the clean cops to say nothing. Unless the upper echelon was getting a cut of the action. That was another possibility Cam didn't want to consider. If she did, there'd be little help inside the force when she chose to report her findings. Then what? She'd have to think long and hard before she took action along those lines. It wasn't just her safety she had to worry about. Sarah would be on his radar too, and he might make a connection between her searching for him and his being ratted out. And if there were even more officers involved than Barnes thought there were, she might have to deal with people on the force giving her grief for any number of made-up offenses. Lucky for her she didn't live or work in Poughkeepsie, but word traveled fast.

When Sarah made it clear that her having her biological father in her life wasn't enough, that she still wanted a connection with Brace, Cam was forced to reevaluate the situation. There wasn't any guarantee she would be able to protect Sarah once she and Brace became known to one another. It scared the hell out of her. Maybe she should have simply refused to let Sarah inside and see how much Sarah's safety meant to her. No matter what happened, bad or good, Cam had a hand in the outcome. If she pulled away now, she'd be able to use the excuse that some of the onus was on Sarah. She swallowed hard. Convincing her heart would be harder than convincing her head, but her conscience screamed she had the perfect opportunity to take down a bad guy, and wasn't that partly why she was in this line of work? To root out the bad seeds? None of her options were without consequences. If she filed a report on Brace's illegal activities, Sarah would naturally blame Cam. It wouldn't be the first time she'd been in a situation where she had to do what was right, even if it was painful, but it was the first time her heart had played a part in her decision.

"Thanks for finishing this." Sarah looked at the laminated folder containing a sheaf of papers while she watched Cam fidget with the pile of documents she was stuffing back into an accordion folder. It was much thicker than a few weeks ago.

"You paid me to do a job, and I'm bound by duty to give it to you. What you do with it isn't my concern." Cam didn't look up. She looked everywhere except at Sarah.

Sarah leaned forward, trying to make eye contact. "Cam, I just want to meet him. There's no harm in that." She didn't want their personal relationship to be awkward, but she also wanted to meet Brace, whether Cam liked it or not.

Cam's lips pursed. "If you believe that, then I wish you the best."

She sat back. "What's that supposed to mean?"

"It means..." Cam looked up. Her eyes were hard. Unrevealing. "You can form your own opinion about the material I've provided." She gestured to the multi-page report. "I have no right to expect you to share my point of view. I realize it's jaded."

"Jaded?" Sarah was confused.

Cam let out a huff. "I'm concerned for your safety and you're not. It's wrong of me to let my personal feelings for you try to sway what you decide to do. I can't help being worried about you, because I don't think you understand the reality of the situation. But it's not my place to tell you what to do."

"Thank you." Sarah wasn't sure if she liked this side of Cam or not. It had been nice to feel cared for and worried over even if Cam's protectiveness had been irritating at times. "Anyway, you can see for yourself."

Cam's eyebrow lifted.

"You'll be there, right?"

Cam sat back, folding her hands on her desk. "No, I won't. This should be between the two of you. He's already not crazy about me, and my presence may make him hostile. You've got a better chance of him talking to you without me there. I've upheld my end of the contract."

Sarah hadn't thought it possible for Cam to create such intense anger in her any longer, but she was wrong. "Is that what I am now? A client with a contract? After what we shared?"

"To my understanding that's exactly what you want when you're in my office. And what we shared..." She shrugged but didn't say anything more.

"I see." She stood. "I'm glad you finally get it." Sarah picked up the report. "Thank you for this. I'm sure it's thorough." Her heart thudded in her chest. She hadn't foreseen the outcome of her pushing Cam to stop stalling and give her answers, but that was her job. Why would she give her so much grief about it? Cam acted as though what they'd shared and how they'd opened themselves to each other was no longer her concern. It hurt more than Sarah would have thought possible. She took a wobbly step toward the door, then another. Cam's voice stopped her as she reached for the handle.

"Sarah?" Cam said, then paused. "Good luck with Brace."

She wasn't sure she could trust her voice, so she nodded and walked out. The haze of red kept her from acknowledging Maggie, who stared at her as she pushed open the outer office door and fled.

❖

Cam tossed the pen she'd been tapping incessantly since Sarah had left. She'd handled the confrontation with all the finesse of a cretin, and it hadn't ended well. Sarah most likely thought her initial impression of Cam being a coy, egotistical womanizer had been correct. *Christ. What if she believes all I wanted was to get in her pants?* Wouldn't that be rich. There was no denying she'd briefly thought about her in those terms, but not for a while. Not since Sarah had been the one to broach the subject of taking her to bed, which had been an unexpected result. *Like that'll ever happen again.*

She paced the area between her desk and the windows. The setting sun cast streaks of pink and orange across the expansive sky. A moment of melancholy descended, clouding her mood even further. Watching sunsets alone wasn't how she wanted to see her future. It was one of the reasons she'd let Sarah in. And now she was gone, and all because Cam couldn't handle the possibility of getting hurt if she decided a relationship with Brace was more important than having one with her. What a jackass. She'd handled the ordeal poorly and she knew she'd hurt Sarah with her flippant attitude. Maybe after the situation with Brace was over with, she could try again. Cam could only hope the distance she'd created between them wasn't forever. Forever was a fucking long time.

❖

Sarah curled up in the corner of the couch with a beer. The folder holding the report mocked her from the coffee table. The reason she'd hired Cam was inside the pages. Cam no longer had an obligation to her. The thread that had held them together was gone. *Was that all it was?* She walked away convinced Cam had no intention of contacting her for meals or anything else. Especially not sex. She should be happy to have cleared up their muddy relationship, but she was anything but. If Cam did contact her for sex, which would be crude, then she'd know her original belief about her had been correct. But if so, why had their time together felt genuine? That last night they'd spent together had been real. She knew it.

Had her desire to pursue Cam in a more personal way been a mistake? Her head told her yes, but her heart—that was another matter altogether. The vulnerability in Cam's eyes hadn't been fake. *If I was wrong then Cam deserves to be alone.* She was better off without her. Her heart hammered in her chest. The anger that had risen to the surface following Cam's decree of her contractual obligations having been met had hurt as much as the words had pissed her off. How dare Cam dismiss her so cavalierly?

"Who does she think she is?" Sarah asked aloud. She pulled a long swallow from the bottle, liking the bitter taste, akin to her current attitude. Wasn't she the one who had made sure Cam was serious about doing what she'd been hired to do? Hadn't she asked her time and again if she was stalling or withholding information? What about Cam's explanation? And all the personal details of her childhood she'd shared with Sarah? Didn't that mean Cam hadn't been involved with Sarah only because she was obligated?

The more she thought, the more confused she became. She had no idea where she and Cam stood on a personal level, although it was clear the professional one was over. So, why was she hesitating to read what was in the report? Had Cam really meant it when she said meeting Brace was up to her? She hadn't asked Sarah to let her know when or given her any advice as to how to be careful. If she was honest with herself, Sarah was just as upset about Cam's lack of concern as she was by her not mentioning if she was interested in seeing her again.

"To hell with her."

Sarah ran her hand over the label on the cover. It read: Peters, Sarah. Missing Person. She took a breath, then opened the cover and began reading the first page. She could hear Cam's voice in her head.

This is a comprehensive report compiled under contract agreement between client, Sarah Peters, and the investigative team of Stark Revelations. Contained herein are copies of documents obtained in the search for the client's twin brother, whom she claimed to have no prior knowledge of until the death of her mother.

A retainer of an initial amount of one thousand (1000) dollars was paid at the signing of said contract (see attachment A). A subsequent amount of two thousand (2000) dollars was paid twenty-one (21) days later, the remaining balance of which, if any, will be returned by certified check within thirty (30) days of this report.

Sarah's chest tightened. *This reads like...*she sighed. Like the legal document it was. She wasn't thrilled by all the technical jargon, but she owed it to herself to review it. It deserved more than a cursory glance considering all the time and energy Cam had devoted to her. Was that true? Had Cam given it so much attention because of Cam's feelings for her? She shook her head before standing. If she was going to pore through the more than fifty pages in the bound folder, she was going to need more than a beer. She needed food. The last time she'd had a meal, she and Cam had ended up back at Cam's place and had earth-shattering sex. She had no hope of a repeat. She'd been more or less dismissed after their meeting today.

Sarah couldn't help feeling that Cam hadn't wanted to let her go, but having been reamed out more than once for withholding information from her, what did she expect?

The fridge didn't hold much in the way of sustenance, so she settled for a small bowl of pasta with one leftover meatball. While her plate whirled in the microwave, she heard Cam's voice. First in the throes of passion, then her words of caution as she walked away. She hadn't been able to face her, afraid of what she might see in her eyes.

Her head was perfectly okay with giving Cam a hard time and demanding answers. Her heart...not so much. Cam had somehow worked her way inside and Sarah didn't know how to handle it. The last decade, she'd focused on first college, then taking care of her sick and aging parents. She'd never looked for a woman to share more than her bed. She wasn't sure if she would have recognized interest from her occasional partners or not. There hadn't been time or energy for anything beyond what was already on her plate. Her situation had changed though, and she no longer had her hours filled for her. The ding of the microwave reminded her of the bell at the diner and the look on Cam's face when their eyes had met.

Sarah swiped at her forehead and pulled her food out to set it on the counter, but her appetite was gone.

"Oh, Cam. How did we get here?"

Cam stared at the ceiling. *I should have gone after her.* Then what? She'd already told Sarah she didn't think it was a good idea to make contact with Brace. The report spoke for itself, even if it didn't explicitly state he'd broken the law, it was all in the documents of shady reports and missing evidence.

Was Sarah capable of separating the facts from her desire to talk with him? Cam knew better. Sarah had a stubborn streak a mile long, not to mention her fierce independence. Qualities she found endearing and frustrating at the same time. She only hoped Sarah would read the entire report before deciding what to do.

Sarah might believe that the case was closed, but Cam had more work to do. She almost felt bad about placing the tracker in Sarah's car, but she'd never forgive herself if Brace went after her to physically hurt her. And while she didn't want to see Sarah suffer emotionally, she'd recover from Cam's rejection. At least she hoped so, since she'd done the same thing when trying to keep her feelings in check, unwilling to show Sarah her heart was suffering the effects of their riff.

She was wasting time. Wondering what Brace would do was all conjecture. Maybe Sarah would meet him, he'd tell her to go away, and that would be the end of it.

"Ha." Her voice echoed in the cold room.

If she knew anything about Sarah, she wasn't the type of person to walk away without giving a situation everything she had to give. Which made their parting even more painful. Sarah had challenged her to not let things between them end in paperwork, but she hadn't put up a fight, and not letting Sarah see how badly she was hurting was the only way she knew to maintain enough distance to see this through. If she let her heart take over, she'd lose her edge. The one that kept her sharp and let her see the bigger picture. Sarah was part of her bigger picture, and she was going to make sure Sarah was alive to see how much Cam cared. It might take a long time, but Cam hung on to the hope of having a chance to tell Sarah she loved her.

Cam grabbed the paperweight and hurled it at the wall. *Shit.* She'd have to get that dent patched before someone saw it. Maggie wouldn't be pleased by her lack of self-control, and neither was she. She dropped her head to her arms. She needed to get her act together. She needed to function and act rationally if she planned on being around when Sarah needed her. She half-hoped she wouldn't, but it would be nice to believe she was needed…by someone. No more losing control and no more mistakes. But the lingering thought remained. She didn't want Sarah seeing her confession as a last-ditch effort to keep her from Archer.

She pulled up the app on her computer and breathed a sigh of relief. Sarah was safe in her house, and she was fairly confident that's where she'd stay for the rest of the night. She hated resorting to clandestine tactics like the GPS bug she'd planted in Sarah's car, but she wasn't going to worry about that now. Sarah never had to talk to her again if she didn't want to. The reason she'd given Sarah about not going with her was absolutely true. He'd shut down the moment Cam entered the room, which meant Sarah wouldn't get anything from him. But she also wasn't about to let Sarah handle this asshole alone. Cam closed the laptop and tucked it in her bag. After a stop at the coffee shop to fill her thermos, she was going to do what she did best. Watch and wait.

CHAPTER TWENTY-FOUR

Sarah's hands were sweaty and shaking so much she had trouble hanging on to the phone. She didn't want to sound unsure of her intentions. That wouldn't do. An officer of the law commanded respect for the badge. The jury was out as to whether or not he deserved it. Cam's report had been meticulously detailed; she had to give her props. It appeared she knew what she was doing, and the money she'd given her probably hadn't covered half of the time it must have taken her. Her guilt level raised a notch. She should have said something…anything…to keep the lines of communication open between them. Too late. The only excuse she had was her level of hurt that had quickly turned to anger. She wasn't about to grovel to anyone.

For the third time in as many hours, she set her cell down and wiped her hands on her jeans. Second-guessing herself hadn't ever been her style. She grabbed the phone and punched the contact icon. The first speed number was the one she needed.

An hour later, she sat across from Lisa and her world wasn't off kilter for a change. And to Lisa's credit, she didn't appear to be as deep in thought as Sarah knew she was.

"You let her have the last word, then?" Lisa blew across the surface of her hot chocolate. It was their other "serious discussion" go-to.

"When you put it like that, it sounds almost as bad as it feels." She chased the melting marshmallows around with her spoon.

"And you expect it to sound good how?"

Sarah sighed. "I thought I'd have your support."

Lisa shoved her leg. "You always have my support. And my honesty. You didn't leave Cam much choice."

She nodded. "I know you're right, it's just…"

"You let that damn stubborn streak win over what you really want."

"What do you mean? What I really want is to meet Brace." That's exactly what she wanted.

"No, it's not."

Sarah narrowed her focus.

"Well, yeah, there's that. But what you really want is a relationship with Cam. I just hope you're willing to give her another chance."

Lisa's words cut to the quick of the matter, which was why she loved her. The more she thought about Cam, the more she wanted to move to the next level of their relationship, no matter where Brace fit into her life. If she'd been waiting for an event to push her one way or the other, she'd evidently found it. Or it had found her.

Later, after hugs and promises to get together again soon, Sarah rinsed out the mugs and set them in the dishwasher. Lisa's words replayed in her mind. She dropped onto the couch and put her head in her hands. She knew exactly why her heart ached. Cam. She pulled her knees to her chest and stared ahead. Cam was a given and Sarah was invested in the long-term with her. But for now, she had to take her out of the equation. She couldn't shake the fact she'd paid a lot of money and Cam had provided two blood relatives, more than she'd dared hope for. Maybe Paul hadn't raised her, but if what Cam told her was true, he wanted to meet her. Maybe she could have her own family *and* family members in her life, but she'd never know if she didn't try. If she didn't do anything with the information, she'd never be able to go on. Even though she trusted Cam's report, and respected her thoughts on the issue, she simply had to know for herself. She couldn't move forward with Cam while wondering if she'd made the wrong decision about contacting Brace. Wise or not, she couldn't let it go.

She didn't normally do hard liquor. Her parents had rarely indulged in anything stronger than a glass of wine. She rummaged through the back of the sideboard and discovered a long-forgotten bottle of bourbon, remembering when Cam had asked if she had any. She held the glass and swirled the amber liquid into a whirlpool before taking a healthy swig. The resulting cough took her breath away, and she set the remainder next to her phone.

"Christ." She wiped the back of her hand across her mouth. "How do people drink that shit?"

After the initial heat hit her stomach and the warmth traveled through her limbs to make her toes tingle, she took a deep breath and picked up her cell. She had to do this before she lost her nerve. She entered the number Cam had provided for the narcotics unit, and she prayed she wouldn't have to go through a string of transfers to reach Brace. She wasn't sure how to explain who she was or why she was calling. After the fourth ring, a gruff voice answered.

"Archer."

"Uh, hi." So much for not sounding unsure. "My name is Sarah Peters and I'd like to speak with you. In person."

"What's this about, Ms. Peters?" There were paper noises in the background.

"It's personal."

"I'm sure there's someone in the general division who can help you. This is the narcotics unit." He was starting to sound impatient.

"No." Sarah was up pacing. "It…it has to be you. Please?"

"Fine. I'll be in the office until later tonight."

"I can't meet you there, and it will take me a while to drive to your area." Sarah didn't think revealing who she was while sitting among coworkers would be the most comfortable situation for either of them. She looked at the precinct address. It was at least forty-five minutes away. She scoured her memory for somewhere midway. Somewhere they could talk privately. Then she remembered Cam's warning, and although she hated her hesitation, she considered the possibility there was a good reason. "It's really important."

"I'm sure it is, but—"

"It's regarding your family." Okay, so that was a bit of a stretch since Brace wouldn't recognize her name, but she was running out of ideas. And if she didn't get him to agree while he was still on the phone, she might never have another opportunity.

"What about my family?" The tone of his voice changed from mild annoyance to harsh concern.

"I'll explain everything. I promise." She heard excited voices in the background. "A PI met with you several weeks ago, and I have more information."

"Where?"

The only place that came to mind was the diner. "If it's not too much trouble, I could meet you at Eddy's. Do you know it?"

"One hour." He abruptly hung up without another word.

Sarah chewed her bottom lip. She thought she'd been sweating before, but nothing compared to the cold sweat soaking her shirt. She had the distinct feeling she was going to regret what she'd done. It was too late to worry about it. She would meet Brace, show him a few family photos of when she was young, along with her mother's letter, and hope there was a resemblance. Not all twins looked alike. She glanced at the clock. She had to get moving soon. She should have made the time later, but for a reason she couldn't pinpoint, she wanted there to be more than just the two of them at the diner, and dinnertime would be busy. *I hope you're wrong, Cam.*

Acting on instinct, Cam got in her car and drove within a few blocks of Sarah's house. She'd parked at the end of the next block and spent most of yesterday evening there until she was sure Sarah was staying in for the night. How long would Sarah wait until she'd contact Brace? Cam hoped never but knew there was no chance of that happening. In all likelihood Sarah already had, and that would mean she'd be on the move. If not today, then certainly within the next day or two. She couldn't chance missing her. Even with the GPS bug she'd placed under Sarah's seat, she only trusted technology so much. She'd considered downloading a tracker on Sarah's cell phone until she thought better of it. That was too invasive, even for her, and could destroy any trust that remained between them. Though that would likely end once she told Sarah about the tracker.

Cam hated being sneaky. But the thought of the alternative—something horrible happening to Sarah—left her little choice. She would sacrifice herself if it came to that. The air in Cam's lungs left. There was no doubt left about whether or not she loved Sarah. Truly loved her. Now wasn't the time to tell her. Or maybe it was. She didn't even know if Sarah would talk to her again. The way she'd let her walk out of her office felt more like she was letting her walk out of her life. A sob escaped around the lump in her throat. *What if I've blown any chance at happiness? What if she never wants to see me again?* Cam shook from the chill that ran up her spine. She had to stay focused. Had to be sure she was on top of the situation and paid attention. Nothing else in the world mattered. Come hell or high water, Cam would keep Sarah safe.

She swiped at the errant tear and studied the screen. *Fuck.* Sarah was moving, turning left, then left again, heading directly for Cam. It was too late to hide her car. Sarah knew what it looked like. The best she could hope for was a distraction as she headed her way. Cam slid down as far as she could after tipping her rearview mirror so she could see out the driver side window. Thank God she had done it enough times to know the right angle. As headlights glared inside her car, she watched Sarah's old model car cruise by at the same time she was fiddling with controls on her dash, her attention diverted down and to the right, away from where Cam was parked. As soon as she was half a block away, Cam sat up, fixed her mirror, and got moving. She didn't know where Sarah was headed, but the blip on the laptop kept her a safe distance ahead. All she had to do was remain calm and focused.

❖

Sarah scanned the parking lot for a police cruiser before remembering Brace wasn't a patrol officer and likely drove a nondescript vehicle to blend in with the seedier neighborhoods where drug dealers could be found. Cam had included vivid descriptions of the type of area Brace frequented, and she was grateful she'd added subtle warnings in her report, otherwise Sarah doubted she'd have even thought about her surroundings. Thankfully, there were a number of cars in the parking lot. She wouldn't have to face him in an otherwise empty location.

She'd changed clothes three times before giving up. What did you wear to meet your adult twin for the first time? She'd started with jeans and a sweatshirt, but that's what she wore when she went for a beer. She had finally decided on her favorite skirt and mid calf boots.

"Let's do this." She got out and locked the car, then slung her bag over her shoulder before smoothing her hands down her shell/sweater combination. The bell over the door jingled. The last time she'd heard one, she'd been welcomed by Cam's warm smile, and she wished Cam was with her now.

Sarah looked around at the occupied tables. The last booth held a man staring at her. He was a male version of her own reflection though his coloring was a bit darker. It was an eerie specter, especially since he didn't look all that pleased. Maybe he was in as much shock as she was. Her hesitation began to fade as she approached and he stood. His eyes remained guarded, but at least he was smiling.

Sarah extended her hand. "Hi. I'm Sarah. Sarah Peters. Your sister."

Brace took her hand firmly. "Brace Archer." He gestured to the seat across from him. Once he joined her, he looked around the diner. The murmur of voices was reassuring and the closest customers were a couple of booths away.

"I can't believe I'm finally meeting you." She tried to tamp down her enthusiasm without success.

"By using a private investigator."

It was obvious he was annoyed by her method, but she couldn't have done it without help.

"Yes. I…" Sarah stumbled over how to explain why she'd searched for him. "My adoptive parents never told me I had a twin. I

only found out after my mother's recent death. She left me a letter."
She took in his features, so much like her own. His hair was a darker
shade of blond, but there was no mistaking their similarity. The
confirmation was the color of his eyes. They were blue like her own,
but also a shade darker and even more so since they'd sat down. Her
own eyes did that when she was aroused or upset, and Brace clearly
appeared upset, annoyed even. A waitress came over with menus,
then produced a pad and pen.

"What can I get you?"

Brace stared at her. It sent a chill down her spine, and not in a
good way. He handed the menu back. "Nothing for me. I don't plan
on being here long."

She couldn't hide her disappointment.

"I have to hit the streets in a few minutes." Brace smiled tightly.
"I'm sure you understand. Crime doesn't wait for family reunions, if
that's what you think this is."

Sarah handed over her menu. Her appetite had disappeared.
"Hot tea, please." Perhaps it would help settle her churning stomach.
She looked at Brace again, still unable to comprehend he was her
brother.

"I'm sorry you've come all this way for such a short visit." He
glanced out the window, then back at her. "I don't know how much
stock I can take in believing you're my sister."

Sarah sat back. "Surely you can see the resemblance. It's like
looking in the mirror." She rummaged in her bag for the envelope
containing the letter and pictures. Sarah picked a picture from when
she was six years old with lots of wavy blond hair, big blue eyes
staring at the camera, and held it out for Brace. He looked but didn't
show any real interest. What if her twin *was* a sinister man with
a less than altruistic agenda? Could her desire for a sibling have
been so overwhelming that it had clouded her judgment, causing her
to ignore red flags that might have been glaring back at her in the
report? Should she have listened to Cam after all?

"Look. I'm sorry you don't have a family—"

"I do, and it's you." Why couldn't he see that this mattered?
Didn't he care that he had a sister? Something in Brace's demeanor

changed. She wasn't sure if she was glad or not. For an instant she thought she saw something sinister in his eyes, then it softened.

"I really do have to go, but if you're sure we're related, maybe we can talk again." Brace produced his phone. "Can I have your contact info so I can text you? Maybe meet in a bit more private setting? I have a lot of questions."

"That would be great." She entered her name and phone number, then handed it back. He didn't reciprocate by asking for her phone, and her anxiety rose. He had her info, but he wasn't willing to do the same for Sarah.

"I'll send a text when I can." Brace stood.

Their time together was ending before it had barely begun, but she understood he had a job to do. She was sure she'd hear from him again.

"I'll contact you soon."

"Sure." She stood there, not knowing if she should hug him good-bye. She didn't have long to think about it. Brace stuck out his hand.

"Good-bye."

Sarah was stunned speechless. His cold demeanor and formal handshake spoke volumes, and she hated admitting maybe Cam's warnings hadn't been unwarranted. How much was she willing to cower to her unreasonable need to get to know him if the person in front of her didn't share her enthusiasm? Perhaps she'd take Cam's suggestion and contact Paul. It certainly couldn't be any worse than the standoffish attitude her brother was showing.

"Good-bye, Brace." She held on for a few extra beats, hoping she'd misread him, but when he jerked his hand back, she knew better.

❖

Cam waited until they'd both left the diner and took off in their cars before emerging from the kitchen where she'd watched the interactions between Brace and Sarah. The gun at the small of her back lent a degree of comfort, though she knew she had to remain vigilant. The look of hunter viewing his prey was engrained in her memory. Brace had smiled a few times as he and Sarah talked, but it hadn't reached his eyes. Cam had seen the same look directed at her when she'd met him at the station. As she suspected, Sarah hadn't wasted time in contacting him. Cam walked to the booth they'd been in. The hairs at the nape of her neck stood up. This wasn't good, and there was no shaking her belief Sarah was in danger. She *had* to convince her to not see him again without revealing that she knew they'd met.

"You okay?" Jen, the owner of the diner, bumped shoulders with her. They went back a long way. "The spot between your brows is wrinkled."

"Worried. That guy Sarah was with is scum."

"Hmm. They look a lot alike."

"They should," Cam said. "He's her twin brother."

"Well, I'll be damned. He didn't look too happy to see her." Jen might be a lot older, but she was a sharp observer of her patrons. Cam had relied on her more than once for giving her a heads-up about shady characters.

Cam wished she could tell her why, but the less anyone knew about Brace Archer, the better for their health. "Thanks for letting me hang in the kitchen." She kissed her cheek, smiling when Jen's face colored.

"You go on now." Jen slapped Cam's ass. "Do whatever it is you do."

That was exactly what Cam had in mind.

CHAPTER TWENTY-FIVE

Sarah stood with her hand on the open door. "I thought you were done with me. What do you want?"

Cam stood on the top step. Her gaze held Sarah's steadily and didn't show any of the remorse or guilt Sarah wanted to see. At least then she'd have some idea if they had any chance for a real relationship.

"Can I come in?"

"Why?" Sarah asked.

Cam's eyes softened. "Sarah, please. Can we not do this?"

She didn't trust herself to not say things she would regret. Her parents had told her to hold her tongue when she was angry, to think about her words and the affect they would have on herself as well as the person she wanted to hurt. Sarah stepped back and waved Cam inside.

"I'm not sure what 'this' is." She glared at Cam as they awkwardly stood in the living room. She was still angry at her as she remembered how cool Cam had been towards her when she'd handed over the report. The space felt too inviting for whatever conversation they were going to have. This was the place for family gatherings, relaxing times when she and her parents would watch movies together, or laugh while they played board games at the coffee table. She headed for the kitchen, making it clear Cam wouldn't get her attention unless she followed her. She put on a pot of coffee. Not that she wanted it, but she needed time to mull over how she felt. She missed Cam. Missed their times together and the moments of intimacy they'd shared. She turned to find Cam patiently waiting, her coat still on. She gestured to the small kitchen table.

"Why are you here, Cam? What more could you want from me?" She sucked in a breath, afraid tears would come on the heels of the lump in her throat. "Haven't you gotten all you wanted from me?"

Pain showed in Cam's soulful eyes. The same eyes that had been a greenish-gray earlier now swirled with dark flecks, the green having changed to a stormy dark shade. "I never said we were done, Sarah." She reached across the table, stopping short of touching Sarah's clasped hands. "Brace is dangerous."

"Yes. You've said that before. We're going around in circles, Cam." She didn't know if it was a good idea to tell Cam she'd already met her brother. There wasn't any reason to hold back. "For your information, we've already met. He seems like a very nice person. He was confused at first, but we're going to see each other again." She wasn't about to admit their meeting had been anything but warm, and she wasn't going to give Cam any more fuel for her to stoke the fire about Brace being bad news.

Cam's eyes narrowed. "Don't be deceived by your desire for family. Didn't you read the report?"

"Yes." Sarah got up and busied herself with pouring coffee. She knew what Cam was getting at. Sure, it appeared Brace was dirty, or at least that some of his practices weren't standard procedure, but she was going to give him another chance. He'd probably been just as shocked as she had been to find he had a sister, and… well…maybe he had *some* redeeming qualities Cam wouldn't know anything about. She stood staring out the window trying her best to see things from Cam's point of view. She did this for a living, and she had to give some weight to her words. She took a breath, and Cam's familiar scent filled her nostrils before she felt her hands on her shoulders.

"Sarah, I hope I'm wrong for your sake. Just know that experience has taught me otherwise."

She couldn't think with Cam so close, touching her. She hoped for another chance to talk with Brace before she blew him off as the lowlife Cam believed him to be. Sarah slid from beneath Cam's touch and turned, handing her a mug.

"If you could have seen him…" Sarah began.

"I don't want you to be alone with him." Cam's words were harsh.

"Don't be ridiculous. I'm not a total idiot. We met in a public place. When he contacts me, I'll do the same again, I'm sure."

"Sarah, leave it alone. If you want blood in your life, contact Paul, he's—"

"No." Her anger rose. "You don't get to tell me what to do. This is *my* life and I get to choose who to have in it. You said so yourself when you so ceremoniously handed me the file and let me leave your office." She felt the tears threaten as her eyes burned. Was Cam ever going to understand her internal struggle between accepting what Cam told her about Brace as fact and wanting to form her own opinion of him? It was unfortunate that Cam would never know what it was like to grow up with a loving family. If she were lucky, she might be able to create a family of her own someday. She questioned if Cam would ever be a lasting part of her life, too. For the foreseeable future, she couldn't worry about *their* future, since it appeared unlikely they'd have one. "I'd like you to leave." Sarah moved toward the front door.

"Please don't shut me out. I need to know you're okay." Cam reluctantly joined her at the open door. "I need to know—"

"What, Cam? Why is it always about you and what you want?" Her heart seized in her chest. What Sarah needed, foolish or not, was for Cam to be on her side. To stand by her, and if she failed with Brace, to be there to help her move on. Sarah wanted her support, not her warnings. "If you aren't on board with my decision, I don't know if there can be an us." Sarah watched a sea of emotion on Cam's face before it settled into one of resignation.

Cam nodded. "Promise me you'll be careful. Please." Her plea came on a cracked voice. She leaned in.

Sarah offered her cheek at the last second. She wouldn't be able to trust herself to keep distance between them if she kissed

Cam's inviting lips. The hurt in Cam's eyes was almost too much. Cam turned away and slowly walked down the front steps. Sarah leaned against the closed door. As the tears fell, she slid down the door, regretting things between them had to end this way.

Sarah slept horribly that night. Not only did she feel guilty about sending Cam away without any hope of a future together, she hadn't even let her kiss her good-bye. She wasn't normally mean, but the thought of Cam interfering with her reunion with Brace had caused her to act irrationally. She should have realized after their time together, Cam only had her best interest at heart. Yet, she'd walked away, leaving the decision clearly in Sarah's hands, but isn't that exactly what she'd wanted?

What if everything she'd warned her about was true?

"Shit."

She'd let her usual good judgment be clouded by thoughts of having a sibling, even if he was a total jerk. The more she thought about his actions, the more she had to admit Cam very well could have been right all along. Sarah wondered how much of a smug look she'd have if Sarah conceded and told Cam she'd been wrong to not listen to her. She needed to read the report again and try to be objective. But right now wasn't the time. She had an appointment with a small gallery that had seen one of her pieces and wanted to talk to her. It might be the break she'd been waiting for as far as her sculpting went. Maybe she should show Brace her workshop. Let him see she had her own interests and building a bond between them would only enhance her already fulfilling life. *Ha. That's a good one.* Well, it wasn't a horrible idea, that much was true.

While in the shower, Sarah ran the soapy sponge over her body remembering how Cam had washed her with so much attention, she'd felt loved. Her eyes popped open, the sponge tumbling from her slack fingers. Did Cam love her? Was that why she was so adamant about Sarah not getting involved with Brace? *No. That's just idle speculation.* If Cam loved her, she would have told her. Wouldn't she? Sarah thought back to the conversation they'd had the night she'd confessed about her upbringing. She had looked terrified when she'd told Sarah that Liv taught her she was worthy of love.

"Oh my God." Sarah's hand flew to her mouth. All of a sudden the signs were there, like neon on the Vegas Strip. The way she'd run interference with Maggie. The excuses to spend time together. The frequent texts and calls. The tender touches and the slow, passionate kisses. The more than thorough investigation even when she could have easily stopped. Her persistent worry about Sarah's safety, and the way she'd shut down after she'd been so vulnerable... And what about her own reactions when it came to Cam? Hadn't she sought her out? Made trips to the office when she didn't need to. Had to fight urges to contact her. She'd been the one to take Cam to bed against her better judgment. Or had there been an undeniable attraction between them that she'd chosen not to verbalize until Cam had hinted at feeling the same? Only Sarah'd had tunnel vision. Her goal had been finding a sibling—not a partner.

"Well, Peters, you might have finally fucked up having a family of your own with the one person who had been willing." She had no idea what to do about it.

❖

Cam watched Liv peek out the side window before opening the door.

"What a nice surprise, I—"

Cam let hot tears score tracks down her cold cheeks. Inside, she was numb. Liv said nothing as she pulled her in and embraced her. They stood in the foyer for a long time while she let the anguish take over. She hated running to Liv every time life dealt a blow to her ego, but this was much different. This pain—the pain of losing Sarah—rocked her to her core. She couldn't have stopped the pain even if she'd wanted to. Liv had taught her that real love, no matter what we thought with our head, was guided by our heart. The second Sarah had turned her cheek for her to kiss, Cam's heart had truly broken.

When the sobs turned into softer heaves, Liv ushered her to the well-worn leather couch. She'd spent hours in the same spot she dropped to. They'd talked about all manner of issues, from having respect for herself to Liv's belief she'd been put on this earth for a greater purpose than her own rocky start in the world. Cam had never heard the whole story of Liv's sordid teen years and early twenties, but from the glimpses she'd gotten, she suspected Liv had been into hardcore drugs at one time. She often wondered how she'd risen above that den of despair. Cam needed those answers. Now.

"What happened between you and Sarah?" Liv handed her a bottle of water.

Cam snorted. She met Liv's compassionate look. "I know. You can read me like a book." She trembled as she cracked the seal, then drank. Cam wiped her lips.

"Before I tell you what you already know." Cam smirked. "I need you tell *me* something."

"Okay. Ask." Liv wasn't one to mince words, nor was she one to waste them.

"What happened to turn your life around?" For the first time since they'd met, Liv's brow creased, and her eyes seemed to harden. She swallowed hard before leaning forward, resting her elbows on her thighs and staring straight ahead. The crow's feet at the corners of her eyes deepened. Cam regretted asking. Her scars must run very deep for Liv to allow her to see how much pain she was in. Cam reached across the space separating them to squeeze the solid arm she'd found so much comfort in.

"Liv, I'm sorry. You don't owe me an explanation." Cam had done what she always did when she felt lost. She'd come to Liv for guidance in what she should do. And for answers to questions she'd never had. For some reason, she believed the key to her own future lay in Liv's past. Now she wasn't so sure she hadn't made a mistake by coming to Liv this time.

Liv laid her hand on top of Cam's and squeezed back. "No one's ever asked." She smiled. "I should have known you would one day. You have a curious nature." She smiled. "Serves you well in your line of work, I'll bet." She got up and went to the small cart that served as her bar. It had always been sparse, but the whiskey was her favorite, though Cam had never witnessed her having more than a couple fingers on any given night. She poured half a tumbler before holding the bottle out to Cam.

"Want one?"

"Not that much."

Liv laughed. "Lightweight." After pouring half her amount for Cam, she took a swallow, then set it down. "I was twenty-three when my savior found me. On the street, strung out on drugs. I didn't know what day it was. Hell, I didn't even know what year it was. Not that it mattered. I was going to die on those streets. It's not like I had anywhere to be. No one would miss me."

Cam wanted to tell her she'd felt much the same when she'd met Liv.

"He picked me up from the doorway…"

"He?"

She met Cam's surprised expression. "Not all men are assholes you know. Many, but not all."

"Sorry."

Liv shrugged, dismissing the interruption. "Anyway, he took me back to his apartment. It was in a decent neighborhood. He told me to shower and gave me a stack of clean clothes." Her eyes shut with the memory. "Hot water had never felt so good. When I came out he had a fridge full of food to offer. I ate like it was my last meal and he watched, giving me more of whatever I wanted."

She looked up again and her eyes held the memory with so much tenderness Cam thought back to the night Liv had rescued her, knowing they'd shared a similar experience.

"I was such a jerk, I went through his medicine cabinet, but the strongest thing I found there was ibuprofen. I'd been without drugs for more than a day. My hands were shaking so bad. Eventually, I got through withdrawal and I started to function again."

Cam sipped and gave her time to sort out whatever she was working through.

"Long story short, I owed my supplier some money and a few months later, he came looking for me. He must have found out from street chatter where I'd gone. The scum forced his way in one day while I was looking for a job. I don't think Michael had a chance. The knife…" Liv sucked in a breath before she went on. "It hit his liver. I'm sure he would have been robbed, but something scared the attacker off and he left Michael lying there, bleeding out. I got home just before he died. He wanted me to have everything he owned and gave advice I'll never forget."

She swallowed around the lump in her throat. She'd never seen Liv as vulnerable as she looked in that moment. "What advice?"

"Kindness comes in many forms. It was up to me to save another soul who was struggling."

"You did. You saved me, Liv."

She nodded as a tear slid down her cheek. "Yeah. And I hope you do the same for someone else someday. That's our legacy. Michael. Me. You."

Cam took a shaky breath. "I don't want to lose her, Liv." Liv took her hand, and she felt the strength she'd always found in her simple touch flow between them.

"Then fight for her. Fight with your entire heart and soul. Whatever's happened between you two is temporary." Liv squeezed once more and let go. "Trust your gut, Cam. You won't be disappointed. No matter how it turns out, trust that Sarah was brought to you for a reason." She smiled. "Just like you were brought to me."

On the drive home Cam weighed the pros and cons of each option she was considering. She checked her app and breathed a sigh of relief knowing Sarah's car was home. She drove by to make sure she was alone. The living room light was on and she glimpsed Sarah curled up in a corner of the couch, sipping from a mug, flashes of dark and light from the TV illuminating her face. Satisfied, Cam continued on. She had to come up with a game plan and a contingency. Liv said to trust her gut and her gut told her Brace would never accept Sarah in his life. He had too much at stake. There had to be a weak link in his armor. It was her job to find it and exploit it without Sarah's involvement. *Easy as pie*. If only she could be sure.

CHAPTER TWENTY-SIX

I s this Sarah?"
"Yes." Sarah couldn't quite place the voice, though she'd heard it before.

"It's Brace. Can you meet me tomorrow?"

Her heart pounded with anticipation. "Yes. Where?"

"There's a private club near Pulaski Park that we could go to."

"That doesn't sound very private." Sarah tried to keep her tone light. All she could hear was Cam's voice cautioning her to be careful. *She's projecting her own experiences.* This could be her chance to convince Brace how much she wanted them to be in each other's life, and to be sure she could trust him.

"It is. I'll get us a table away from prying eyes."

She chewed her bottom lip, unsure who would care that he was meeting some woman in a private club of his own choice, but at least there'd be other people and that gave her a modicum of comfort. "Okay. Text me the address and the time and I'll be there." No matter how ridiculous it might be, the idea of seeing Brace again buoyed her spirits. The downside was not being thrilled she had no clue where she was going.

"I'll send it." Brace once again abruptly ended their conversation.

Sarah stared at the screen, willing it to display a message from Brace with the information she'd need to find him. After a few minutes, she gave up. *Maybe he got called away.* It happened with police all the time. She paced in her kitchen as she pretended to fix dinner, and dinner made her think of Cam.

She missed having meals with Cam. They were fun and easy. *Don't go there*. She couldn't get sidetracked by memories in light of the last time she'd seen her. Cam had been so dejected she'd almost changed her mind and asked her to stay before she remembered how mad she was at her for making her feel like an idiot without a lick of common sense. No. She'd done the right thing by sending her away. If Cam couldn't lend her support, then Sarah couldn't be involved with her.

Second-guessing her decision at every turn made her antsy. If she didn't get the text soon she'd go to the garage and work. Sarah sat down with her bowl of rice and veggies and pulled the file on Brace closer. The last time she'd read it, she'd placed a sticky note on the page with Paul White's contact information. Another decision to make. But for the immediate future, she'd focus on Brace and the report. It wouldn't hurt to read it again and see if there was a detail about Brace she hadn't noted before. Just to be safe. The cover page caught her attention. She ran a fingertip over Cam's name.

"Cam, why can't we seem to make us work?" She ached to have Cam's hand hold her own. To feel her long, lean body over hers. She'd believed in the prospect of a future together. She'd even gone so far as to fantasize what it would be like to wake up next to her every morning and fall into bed together each night. Maybe she would be able to tell her things with Brace were progressing and she needn't worry. She sighed loudly, then flipped over the page, hoping against hope there wasn't anything she'd missed on the neatly typed pages. Something that would confirm she wasn't the one being reckless.

At six in the morning, Cam headed to the office before Maggie could show. She didn't want to be quizzed about where she'd been spending her time. Maggie knew Cam didn't have a case at the moment, and it wouldn't take her long to figure out she was doing detective work outside the realm of professionalism. Maggie had raised an eyebrow every time Cam walked out from behind her closed door. She didn't want to admit that she wanted to help Sarah more than any other previous client.

Sipping from the steaming cup of Starbucks calmed her. There were few things over the years that had given her consistent pleasure like the first sip of morning coffee. She opened her email and scrolled. Her heart skipped a beat. Sarah had sent her an email late last night. She stared at the notification line. She didn't want to open it, but she had to. There were only two reasons Sarah would write her an email instead of texting or calling, and neither of them were encouraging.

Sarah's words echoed in her head as she read the email. She explained the reasons she couldn't see Cam anymore if she wasn't able to give Sarah support while she connected with Brace, and although she would never forget their times together, she was sorry things hadn't worked out between them.

It ended with, *"I know you might not understand the importance of what I'm doing, but I can't let this opportunity slip away. I'm going to see Brace tomorrow, and I hope he isn't the ogre you've believed him to be. I promise I'll weigh your caution in my dealings with him. As for Paul, I'll decide when to contact him after things with Brace have settled. You were right. Blood is blood, and I should meet him. Take care, Cam. Don't let your demons hold you back from what truly matters to you. Fondly, Sarah."*

She swiped at her face, knuckling her eyes. Cam's heart was breaking and it was worse than any suffering she'd endured in the thirty-six years she'd been alive. This heartache would last. She'd made such a mess of things, and now Sarah was going to meet up with that maniac again today. She had to make sure she was nearby, even if Sarah didn't want to see her again. At some point she'd have to let go, but it wouldn't be today.

Cam watched the dot move across the screen while Sarah drove to her job site. Then she spent the rest of her day following intel that led nowhere. She was no closer to having what she needed to file an official complaint than before. When she did, it would most likely be the final wedge ending what little, if any, chance remained between her and Sarah, but it was a price she was willing to pay. She reread the email a dozen times, looking for a kernel of encouragement. Anything she could hang on to that meant the door between them had been left ajar.

Bleary-eyed, she finally closed it. There was no question in her mind that she loved Sarah, even if she never got a chance to tell her. With love came sacrifice. Cam would gladly sacrifice herself to ensure Sarah didn't fall prey to Brace's whims. She believed he wouldn't think twice about hurting Sarah if she pushed too hard to learn more about him and his life.

She struggled to breathe and focus. Talking to Liv had helped. It always did. Liv was the voice of reason when nothing in her world made sense. She'd never felt smothered under her guidance or words of wisdom. Since learning Liv's story, their connection felt tighter, if that were even possible. Liv had told her to not let Sarah go. To try to see it from Sarah's side, but at the same time she owed it to herself to tell Sarah how much she cared. To tell her she loved her. Liv reassured Cam that love bridged the widest gulley, as long as she didn't give up. It was up to Cam to show Sarah she was in it for the long haul, and if it included Brace, then she'd learn to deal with it. In light of the email, she wondered if any of Liv's advice would be of use since it was based on Cam talking to Sarah. It was unlikely she'd have a chance, but that didn't mean she wouldn't try.

Sarah wiped at the sweat on her bottle. She was uncomfortable being the only woman in the dark, antiquated space. Brace had barely said more than two words since she'd arrived. The silence had to end. "So, what made you decide to become a police officer?" Sarah met his probing stare.

"You're the one who came looking for me. Don't you think I should be asking the questions?" His tone was even, but she detected an edge of malice.

"Okay. Ask away." She tried to ignore the negative undertones.

"What made you decide to look for me? You've survived all this time without knowing I existed. How can I even be sure you are who you claim to be?" Brace threw back a shot of tequila and held up his index finger to the passing waiter to have him bring another. He didn't even bother asking if she was ready.

"As I said, my adoptive parents died. I want a family connection. We have the same birthday. The same eye color. The same facial structure." When he seemed unconvinced, she went on. "Those things can't be coincidences, surely?"

"Coincidences happen all the time and they're just that." Brace took a sip of his fresh shot and chased it with a swallow of beer. "Why an investigator?"

"I didn't even know your name or how to begin to find you. And the information she found made it clear that we separated at birth."

"And just like that you want to know everything about me?"

Sarah shifted in her seat. This was going nothing like she'd imagined. "How about we start with the easy stuff and go from there?" She shared what she hoped was a genuine smile to make him see she meant it.

"Like?" Brace sat back and crossed a leg over his knee.

If she thought Cam was cocky, she had nothing on her brother. "Where did you grow up and go to school? Do you have other siblings?"

"Pennsylvania. No siblings."

"I'm an ironworker by trade, and I have an—"

"That's a surprise, for someone built like a mouse."

Her hackles came up. Brace was downright rude. "Stature has nothing to do with ability." She looked him up and down. Sarah had wanted to make a derogatory comment of her own until she saw the warning glance. He was starting to give her the creeps. "Have you always wanted to be on the force?"

"No. I did it out of spite, but it's a living."

Sarah didn't find the humor in it, and again, she searched for something to say. "Why out of spite?

"My parents wanted me to be a suit, but that didn't really *suit* me." Brace laughed at his own condescending joke.

"I can't do the same for you, but it would be nice to meet your parents sometime."

And just like that, the darkness in Brace's features returned. *Is he angry with me?*

"I don't think so. I like my life the way it is." Suddenly, he leaned forward and stared her down. "What do you want from me?"

Sarah recoiled, unable to hide her reaction to what had felt like a slap in the face. "I don't *want* anything. I thought we could get to know each other and bond. You know, like a brother and sister." She knew she sounded curt, but she couldn't help it. The more time they were together, the less enthusiastic she became on forming a relationship.

"What'd that dyke you hired tell you? My family isn't going to be a part of whatever scheme you're cooking up. You're not going to get anything from us."

"I swear I only wanted to find you."

Brace was expressionless. It was hard to tell what he was thinking.

"Well, this has been enlightening, but I've got to go to work."

Obviously, he had his own agenda when he'd called, but for the life of her she had no idea what it could have been. She looked at the empty glasses in front of him and wondered if he always drank before his shift. "Maybe the next time we could have dinner."

"Unlikely." Brace sneered, then stood and threw a one-hundred-dollar bill on the table. "The beer's on me."

"Thank you." She felt more awkward now than when she'd arrived. She made an excuse so that he could get away without making her feel any more like an inconvenience he was bored with than he already had. "I have to use the restroom, so you go ahead." She turned toward the dark paneled hallway and hoped she didn't get lost.

"Hey?"

"Yes?" Maybe he'd changed his mind about dinner.

"It's this way." Brace pointed to the opposite direction.

"Right."

❖

Sarah leaned back against the headrest. She'd hung out in the restroom until she felt steady enough to drive. Her second visit with Brace hadn't gone any better than her first, and she'd had a glimpse of something darker in his nature. So far Cam had been right. Maybe seeking him out had been a colossal mistake.

She looked around, trying to remember which of the entrances she'd turned in, when she saw a familiar vehicle parked at the farthest end of the lot.

"It can't be." There were lots of Chargers the same color as Cam's. She was being paranoid. Then there was movement inside. After turning the key, she put the car in gear and looped around the lot in order to come up from behind. As she got closer, there was no mistaking the license plate. It read STARK911. She jumped out and stormed up to the passenger door.

"What the hell are you doing here?"

Cam flicked her eyes from the computer screen to Sarah. "If you must know, I'm on a stakeout." She shoved some papers around.

"Don't give me that crock of shit. Are you following me?" She wanted to be pissed more than surprised, but she was also glad to see her. She missed Cam.

"Did you see me following you?" Cam stated in such a way she was questioning her own judgment.

"No."

"And if, notice I said *if* I was tailing you it would only be because I'm worried and I care about you. Even though you don't know what people like Archer are capable of. But I wasn't, so you needn't make a fuss."

"Really? And you do, I suppose. Because you grew up among people who didn't give a fuck about you. Who only took you in so they could collect a fat check every month." She stared Cam down, convinced she'd been right about Cam following her. "That wasn't my life, and I don't think it was Brace's either. You don't know what it's like to have your family ripped from you."

"You're right. I don't know and I probably never will."

The flat look in Cam's eyes and her lack of emotion confirmed how deeply Sarah's words had hurt her. She'd let her anger take control and now Cam was paying for her rush to judge. Sarah reached through the window, but when Cam flinched, she stopped. "Cam, I didn't mean—"

Cam looked at her with dead eyes. "I think you say exactly what you mean."

"I'm sorry for everything I said."

"Good-bye, Sarah." Cam stared through the windshield. "You've made it clear you want Brace in your life and nothing else matters, not even your own safety." Cam's knuckles showed white, her jaw bunched. "You won't see me again."

She'd brought this on herself. The realization was a hard pill to swallow. Even if Cam *had* followed her, Cam's intentions had always been to keep Sarah safe; there was nothing else. No other underlying scheme to keep her away from her brother, and Sarah had thrown her caring in her face as though it meant nothing.

"Cam…" Sarah's attempt to make eye contact failed. There wasn't much she could do in the way of damage control.

"Please just go." Cam's eyes were shut, as though trying to shut her out, too.

Sarah backed away and the Charger roared to life. She hoped for one last look between them, but the proverbial wall was back up. It left her feeling isolated, the same way Cam had grown up, and Sarah knew she'd lost her. Cam put the car in gear and sped out of the parking lot and, ultimately, out of her life.

Cam pulled up behind a darkened business the first chance she got. She'd been careless letting Sarah see her car. After watching Brace leave, Sarah had remained inside so long she thought she might be having a drink or perhaps eating and was confident she had time to move. Then Sarah came out, and it was too late. She stayed put, hoping Sarah would leave without noticing her.

She hadn't been prepared for the verbal assault Sarah had hurled at her. The pain had sliced her like a knife driven deep inside and then twisted for extra measure. Sarah would never understand how much she was hurting because she hadn't experienced abandonment and abuse. There hadn't been anything she could say in her own defense, and she didn't have the strength to fight anymore. She was bleeding out and no longer convinced love could heal all. She'd refused to let Sarah see her flesh stripped away by Sarah's cutting words. There would never be a woman she could trust. Up until a few minutes ago, she thought that woman was Sarah. How very wrong she'd been. It was Sarah's choice, Sarah's life. She'd done what she could, and it hadn't been enough. Liv was wrong. Sometimes love wasn't worth the pain.

CHAPTER TWENTY-SEVEN

Cam pressed her earbud to connect to her phone. "Camdyn Stark."

"Something's going down," Jimmy said in a hushed tone.

She straightened in her chair. "Where are you?"

"In the car. I can't take a chance calling from the office, he's got moles everywhere." Whatever the new development was had to be important for Jimmy to break his own promise of not contacting her.

"Talk to me." Cam pulled a pad toward her and poised her pen over the paper.

Jimmy told her Brace had been unusually busy at his desk and spending a lot of time on the computer, a habit he hadn't exhibited since his first few months in the division. Word on the street was he was demanding a hit be made, but his usual eager beavers were backing off, saying it wasn't the kind of target they wanted to be involved in.

Her stomach knotted, her bowels turning liquid. For once she hoped her instincts were wrong. "Do you think he's after Sarah?" She'd kept track of her from a distance and through the GPS that was still working. Sarah had briefly met Brace once in the ten days since their last confrontation, but she had no idea how that conversation had gone or whether Sarah and Brace were still talking. She wanted to believe Sarah had given up, but that wasn't who Sarah was. She didn't back down from challenges. Except for building her and Cam's relationship, and that's what really hurt. She pushed her disappointment away and refocused. She loved Sarah too much to turn a blind eye to any apparent threat. Sarah would just have to deal with it.

"Hard to tell, but the activity isn't his usual MO, so I'd have to guess neither is his target."

Cam heard the police dispatch come over Jimmy's car's radio.

"I gotta go. Watch your back."

She remembered the shifty look she'd gotten when she'd challenged Brace. "You do the same."

The line went dead, and Cam clicked off.

"Mags," Cam yelled out her open office door.

Maggie leaned against the frame. "What's up?"

"We've got some work to do. Pronto. Get your pad…" Maggie held up her ever-present steno pad. Cam swore she must have a case of them hidden in her pockets. "Right." She gestured to one of the chairs facing her desk. She needed that elusive ammunition she'd been hunting for if she was going to take Brace down and Maggie, bless her heart, had garnered lots of connections over the years. She didn't like to call in favors, preferring to do the legwork herself, but time was of the essence, and if she had any hopes of getting Brace permanently away from Sarah, she had to move quick.

Maggie tapped her pen on the desk to get her attention. "Let's get to it."

Cam grinned at her. She'd never regretted hiring Maggie, not only for her keen sense of right and wrong, but for keeping her on track.

"It's time we pull out the big guns and take Brace Archer down."

"I like the sound of that."

❖

"Where the hell do you hide your shit?" Cam asked the empty car. She'd been trying to connect the dots between Brace and known drug felons, but she kept running into dead ends. Her hope was to find his stash of either money or drugs, but everywhere she looked left her frustrated. Brace had so many connections in his criminal world he rarely spent enough time with any to give her a chance to follow. Cam tapped her fingers on her thigh as she stared absently out the window. She was missing an important link to the self-proclaimed drug lord. For the life of her she couldn't grasp what it was.

The blip on her computer started flashing, but something was wrong. Sarah's car was traveling in the opposite direction from home. A text message came through her phone at the same time, jerking her attention momentarily away. It was from Jimmy. It glared back at her in capital letters.

SHIT'S GOING DOWN TONIGHT. DON'T KNOW WHERE OR WHEN.

"Fuck, fuck, fuck."

She turned the key, and the engine roared to life. The tires kicked up loose gravel as she sped out of the parking lot. Once she hit pavement, she reached into the glove box and pulled out her handgun. She rummaged in the console until she found her backup and the extra clip she always had with her. If she needed more fire power, she could rely on the semiautomatic hidden in the tire well of her trunk, but hopefully she wouldn't need it. She was five minutes behind Sarah. If she went into an area where she lost the signal, she might lose precious time. She had to close the gap.

Cam turned on her radar detector and pressed the accelerator, whipping past cars as though they were standing still. She glanced at the speedometer and eased back. Going ninety in a forty-five was a surefire way to earn a ticket and blow her chances of getting to Sarah. The voice in her head didn't back down. She *had* to catch up with her. There wasn't any proof Sarah was headed to meet up with Brace, but she couldn't take a chance. Sarah had given up on their relationship, and if that's what fate held in store for her, so be it. Cam couldn't dismiss her emotions that easily. Not since she'd opened herself up to Sarah. She still pictured their future and all the adventures they would have together. If what she believed about Brace was wrong, she'd accept his being in their lives. Her heart told her Sarah was worth a bit of acquiescing on her part. That's what people did for those they loved.

A car honked, bringing her to the present. As luck would have it, the traffic in front of her came to a crawl. Sarah had been far enough ahead that she was still moving. Cam narrowed the screen for a wide-angle view of where she was headed. She glanced up in time to avoid rear-ending the car ahead of her. Sarah was heading into the edge of a drug-infested part of the city. The worst part was she was likely unaware of the danger that lay ahead of her. She had to do something. And quick. She pressed the Bluetooth sync button on the steering wheel and told it to "Call Sarah." The mechanical voice sounded hollow in her ears, matching how her stomach felt. One ring, then another, and another. On the fifth ring, voice mail picked up, and she disconnected.

Cam looked to the right, then left. An opening with barely enough room for her car came into view and she gunned into the lane, then onto the sidewalk. She took the first left and got back on the road, not sure where she was. The map re-centered itself, and she shot through side streets, missing pedestrians by mere inches. She mouthed sorry as she kept her eye on her destination. Sarah's car had stopped moving. She was three blocks away.

She prayed she'd been wrong as to where Sarah was headed, however, tailing her for the past few weeks and keeping track of her whereabouts via GPS told her Sarah stuck to routines. Work then home, or work, garage, and home. She rarely ate out or made more than one trip a week to the grocer's.

Jimmy's warning drowned out the other random thoughts bouncing around in her brain. If Brace was as ruthless as Barnes had intimated, there was no telling how many of his thugs were with him. She'd be out-muscled and out-armed, but maybe she could surprise them by drawing down on them first. She hoped it didn't come to that. She didn't want to die, but the alternative wasn't an option. Sarah deserved a full, happy life…with or without her.

Cam slowed as she made a right turn that brought her into a back alley, the walls lined with gang graffiti, trash, and rotting garbage. Sarah should have known better than to be here, but how could she? She hadn't been raised on the streets. Cam doubted she'd ever had to fight for her survival or face a street gang. Sarah's family life had sheltered her from the abominations of the world that Cam had grown up in. It was Cam's turn to save someone, and that someone was Sarah.

Sarah waited at the red light impatiently. Her phone buzzed on the seat beside her and she glanced over. *Cam*. They hadn't spoken since she'd confronted her in the parking lot, accusing her of following her and lashing out at Cam's vulnerable place. She really needed to try to apologize again. She didn't want things to be over between them, and she'd been naïve to think she wasn't in too deep to end what they had. She'd been so wrong. Sleepless nights and lack of appetite told her Cam wasn't just a diversion or a passing fancy. Sarah had too much on her plate and her mind was muddled by the never-ending decisions she had to make. *What bills should I pay? How many extra hours can I work? What should I do about the gallery owner wanting to see more of my work? How do I deal with Brace and Cam?* Unfortunately, Cam had been the sacrificial lamb of the equation because she had refused to believe Brace was the ass she'd tried to warn her about. She'd convinced herself that the sex had been fun…okay, mind-blowing, but there was no future with Cam and the past that made her leery of relationships. It had been an easy out. At the time, Sarah had thought that Cam was the easiest tie to cut. She swallowed around the lump in her throat. She'd made a huge mistake. Cam hadn't contacted her since, and she had no one to blame but herself.

Still, Sarah couldn't deal with her at the moment. She was heading to meet Brace and she'd finally decided she didn't want him in her life if he didn't want Sarah in his. It felt too much like work. She wasn't willing to entertain how intelligent it had been to let him pick some secluded location. A lot of her recent actions had been out of character. She'd rushed to judgment about Cam. And on several recent occasions, she'd treated her terribly. They were both behaviors she'd never exhibited to anyone, so why Cam? No matter. Her phone buzzed again and she ignored it. *You think I'm being foolish, but I have to tell him in person.* The light turned green and she sped off, her goal clear even if her conscience wasn't. She slowed as she entered a part of town she'd never been in. The chill that ran up her spine was foreboding. If her brother cared at all he would have never suggested she meet him in such a horrible location. She'd tell him she'd been wrong to pursue him and leave as soon as she could.

The numbers on the abandoned-looking buildings were worn. She took her time as she cruised down the deserted street. The few parked cars she passed were missing parts. Gone were tires, hoods, and doors on the ones she could see. *Where the hell am I going?* The voice in her head, mainly Cam's, urged her to turn around. To get out of there while she could. Even with the doors locked, Sarah was convinced she wasn't alone, and her skin prickled with fear. Then she caught movement to her left. Brace appeared in the doorway of a storefront. He smiled at her and she let out a relieved breath. She was going to be okay.

Cam had lost valuable time. She was five minutes behind. She had to find her. She slow-rolled along the darkened street, praying she wasn't too late. The dot on the screen no longer blinked. *Where are you?* Cam peered down narrow alleys and places where the few functioning streetlights cast long shadows. Sarah shouldn't be here. Her heart beat faster as her chest tightened. Desperation threatened to take over, but losing control wouldn't help Sarah. She doused her headlights. First, she had to find her, then she'd worry about her next move. *There.* Halfway down the next block on the left sat the aging car, and Sarah was walking toward a shadowed figure. Her gut soured. It had to be Brace. She stopped the car and waited. Cam fought hard to maintain control. She was used to acting logically. Weighing action versus inaction, and the possible outcome of each. She'd never functioned on pure emotion. Never had a need to rely on anything other than her investigative skills. She picked up her cell. Maybe Sarah would answer it this time. Cam stared at the instrument that had previously kept her and Sarah in touch, but that was before she'd lost Sarah's faith in her. Before Cam had let her emotions win over professionalism. She tossed it down as though it had physically burned her.

"Think, Stark. Think."

She'd always been good at thinking on her feet, so why, when she needed it most, was she hesitating? *Because it never involved anyone I loved.*

Once she was out of the car, Sarah felt more than a little exposed. Brace stood near a building with a rusty sign hanging askew. The dark shadows behind him, obscuring her ability to see, lent to the already creepy atmosphere. She took a couple of steps but couldn't bring herself to get closer. He would have to come to her.

"Hey," Brace called across the distance.

"Hi," she said. Sarah knew he could hear the angst in her voice.

His face grew hard as his eyes narrowed while he waited. Finally, he stepped from the shadows and approached her.

"What are we doing here, Brace?" Sarah refused to look around, but she swore she could hear movement close by.

"I wanted to show you where I spend a lot of my time. You know, since you're so interested." Brace glanced over his shoulder.

"Couldn't you have just told me?" Her laugh was pure nerves, but he must have thought it was for his benefit.

Brace shrugged. "Proof is in the pudding, so they say. Come on, there's some really cool old stuff inside. Maybe you could find something that interests you. You do shit with metal, right?"

The prospect of finding something unique to use as a sample for the gallery was tempting. "You sure it's safe?"

"You're with a cop. Why wouldn't it be safe?"

Something in his smile was off, but she attributed it to a bad case of the willies. That along with Cam's constant badgering about how "dirty" Brace was had caused her to lose her objectivity. *Damn you, Cam.* Sarah took a breath, tentatively stepping closer, giving her time to tamp down her earlier alarm. "Let's see what you've got."

"That's the spirit." Brace seemed pleased. He pushed the worn, peeling door open and stepped inside as he pulled out a flashlight. "There's no electricity, but it's worth having a look around."

She stood near the door, hesitant to go any farther as her initial anxiety returned.

"Here." Brace pointed to a pile of discarded items. "You might find a hidden treasure."

Sarah moved to where Brace pointed as he shined the light over broken racks covered in rust and cobwebs. It looked like they'd been there for decades. When she bent over to take a closer look, she felt him brush against her, and warning bells sounded in her head.

"I don't think I can use any of this." Sarah straightened. She needed to get out of the tight quarters, and she didn't like how much Brace was invading her personal space. He must have sensed her unease because he took a step back.

"Okay. There's a couple of things over here you might like." He took her hand and led her toward the far wall where a thick layer of dust obscured the surface. "Be careful where you step. I wouldn't want you to hurt yourself."

Something in his tone still wasn't right, but at least he was being mindful of her inability to see where she was going. "Thanks." Once they were closer, he aimed his light on an old cash register. It might have been bronze, but it was covered in the same grime as everything else. She was about to tell him she appreciated the offer when he bumped into her, trapping her next to the counter she leaned on.

"Brace. What are you doing?" Panic rose along with her voice.

He held his hands up. "Sorry. It's hard to see in here." He backed away and moved the light to a back corner. "There's a bunch of pewter and bronze plates over there."

"Brace…" She looked at the entrance, wishing she was already outside.

"This is the last of anything good in here." He fanned the light up. "Please? You've come all this way. I was hoping you would find something you could use."

As much as her gut twisted, she wanted to believe Brace was trying to make amends. "Okay, but then I really have to go."

"Sure, sure." Brace grinned a little too wide before swinging the flashlight toward the back of the room.

Sarah moved slowly. The light was directed where Brace had pointed, and she was trying to be careful where she stepped. She tried looking at what appeared to be another pile of junk. "I don't see anything I can use."

"Go a little farther."

Sarah sighed before taking another step, and that's when she felt the floor give way beneath her weight. Her arms shot out to brace her fall and slammed into the floor around the hole she'd dropped into. Her legs dangled in midair and she tried to not panic. Brace stood a few feet away, a sinister grin plastered on his face.

"Help me." Sarah tried to push against the edge of the jagged opening, but she heard the boards creak and stopped.

"Dear sister, what a shame we didn't get to know each other better before your accidental death. Why on earth were you even walking around in a place like this? I guess we'll never know."

Sarah was stunned. Cam had been right all along, and unless a miracle happened, she wasn't going to have a chance to tell her. She'd read about her demise in the obituaries. She might even believe it had been an accident, knowing Sarah collected junk for her sculptures, but she doubted Cam would ever accept it. Sarah imagined Cam going after Brace for revenge. She couldn't let that happen. "Brace, please. Whatever you may think, all I wanted was to find you. If you don't want me in your life all you have to do is say so." Her arms shook with the strain of holding her weight as she hung there, and she imagined if she fell to the floor below Brace would leave her to die. Suffering and alone.

"I can't take the chance. My life is fucking perfect, and that inheritance is mine. My bleeding-heart parents might want to help my poor orphaned twin, but it's not going to happen. Too bad you just couldn't leave well enough alone." Brace's features morphed into a sinister glare. Careful to avoid getting too close, he raised his foot.

Sarah knew then he was going to make sure she would die in the darkness.

"Good-bye, Sarah." Brace shifted his weight and his foot reared back.

"Stop!"

The darkness lessened and Cam's voice echoed in the cold that surrounded Sarah. She'd never been more relieved to hear her.

Brace turned and the flashlight bobbed as he stepped away from Sarah. "What the fuck are you doing here?" His free hand moved to his waistband.

"Don't move." Cam shone her flashlight into Brace's face, her tone strong and confident.

"You think I'm afraid of the likes of you?" Brace sneered.

"You should be. My office has instructions to alert the police if I don't call back in the next five minutes. I have a feeling not everyone in your precinct is your buddy." Cam sounded solemn. "The only choice you have to make is to leave now, or I shoot and end any future threat to Sarah. Makes no difference to me."

Brace hesitated, clearly considering his options. He dropped his hand and moved farther away from her. "I'll get you someday."

"I'll be waiting." Cam kept her gun trained on him until he disappeared out the door. Cam set her flashlight down and reached for her.

"Be careful." As much as she wanted to get out of there, it wouldn't do either of them any good if Cam ended up in the same predicament. It would likely end in someone's death.

Cam tested the floor between them, then reached for her. She grabbed her hand and held on, pushing up with her other arm. Cam pulled until Sarah was able to get her knees under her, then she stood on shaky legs. Cam wrapped an arm around her waist and guided her toward the exit, her gun held out in front of them.

"Are you okay?"

Sarah leaned into Cam's solid body, needing to know she was real. "I think so." They stood by the door, but Cam held her back.

"Wait here. I want to make sure that bastard is gone, then I need to call Maggie." Cam sidled up to the entrance, her gun at the ready, and peered out, then she disappeared from Sarah's view. She picked up the flashlight. Alone, she tried to make sense of what had happened. Not in a million years would she have dreamt Brace wanted her out of his life enough to want her dead. She'd been wrong about Brace from the start, and it had nearly gotten her killed. She could feel the hysteria welling inside, but she took a deep breath and forced it down. She couldn't fall apart, not yet.

"There's no sign of Brace." Cam held the gun at her side. "Let's go."

Sarah stepped outside, breathing in the fresh air, and pulled her jacket tighter, a sudden chill making her shiver. "If you hadn't shown up..."

"Let's not think about that now." Cam leaned against Sarah's car, then ran her hands down her arms. "You sure you're okay?" Concern creased the normally smooth skin between her brows.

She nodded. Now that she'd had a chance to calm down and could think clearly, she had questions of her own. "How did you know I might be in trouble?"

Cam's hesitation was telling. "My informant told me Brace ordered a hit on someone." Her eyes darkened. "I couldn't... *wouldn't* take a chance it was on you."

"But how did you know where to find me?"

Cam blanched. "I put a tracking device in your car."

Sarah was dumbfounded and stumbled backward. "I trusted you." Cam tried to close the distance between them, but she backed away.

"You can, Sarah. I had to know you were okay and the only way I could do that after you sent the email..." Cam looked at the ground.

"Even after I told you to stay away you didn't."

"No."

Sarah was torn between being grateful Cam had followed her, because she'd saved her life, and her anger at Cam acting as though Sarah was the one being investigated. Would she ever really be able to trust her? If they tried to have a relationship—one that would change both their lives—could she be sure Cam wouldn't use her professional means to spy on her? Was that the kind of partner Cam would be?

Sarah met her gaze. "When will the lying ever end?"

What could she say? "I didn't lie about wanting to protect you."

Sarah's jaw bunched. "Get it out of my car."

Cam opened the driver door and reached under her seat. She held out the small black box with a blinking green light.

Sarah looked at the device in her hand, grabbed it, then tossed it with so much force it shattered on the road. Just like Cam's hopes of a reconciliation. "Sarah, I—"

Sarah held up her hand. "Thank you for stopping Brace. I'm sorry I doubted your opinion of him, but that wasn't the way to earn my trust." She pointed to the bits of plastic. She got into the car and shut her door. When she looked up, Cam saw the tears pooling in her eyes, but the worst part was the sadness in them.

"Good-bye, Cam."

As Sarah pulled away, Cam ran to her car. She didn't care if Sarah liked it or not, she was going to make sure Brace wasn't lurking around. She had to make sure she got home safely. She had nothing to lose. She'd already lost Sarah, but she was alive, and that had to be enough.

CHAPTER TWENTY-EIGHT

W hat am I going to do?" Sarah cried on Lisa's shoulder. Lisa rubbed her back for a bit, then held her at arm's length.

"First, you're going to agree to stay away from Brace. You could have died tonight. Don't give him another reason to try. We have to hope he'll think he scared you enough that you'll leave him alone."

Sarah wiped her eyes for the hundredth time since she'd gotten home. She hadn't allowed herself to cry, not really, until she was safe inside. Brace was as dangerous as Cam had suspected. "I have no intention of seeing him again." And even though Cam had pissed her off, once she'd had a chance to calm down, the heartache set in.

"Good." Lisa handed her a mostly melted bowl of ice cream. She'd bought double reinforcements tonight. "And Cam?"

She stared at the contents, though not seeing it, and sighed. All she could see was Cam "She was right, Lisa. I was so blinded by wanting family I refused to see Brace for who he really was, even when it was staring me in the face. Cam..." Her throat tightened. "All she ever wanted was to keep me safe and now I've hurt her again." Sarah looked up. "Why do I keep doing that?"

Lisa put her hand on Sarah's arm. "We're pretty good at hurting the people we love."

"I don't—"

"Oh, please. It's written all over your face whenever you mention her name. Like it or not you love Cam, so what's your plan?"

Lisa was right. She did love Cam and all the little things that made her the person she was. The cockiness. The thorough way she went about her work. The looks of longing Sarah had caught. The fierce way she'd come to her rescue. None of it mattered now. She was certain she'd pushed Cam away for the last time.

"I don't have a plan."

Lisa tapped her spoon against Sarah's dish. "Then it's a good thing I'm here."

Sarah prayed she hadn't thrown away her future in a fit of anger. She didn't like *that* Sarah, and she hoped it wasn't too late to redeem herself.

Cam gathered her things from the passenger seat. It was the farthest she'd been out of the house since the night Brace had—she didn't want to think about what had almost happened. Sarah was okay and that's what mattered. But the closing of the front door reminded her of Sarah's words, both sounded so final, and she dropped the armful of things onto the table. It spilled onto the floor.

"Great." Cam sighed and bent to pick up the files and sweatshirt. A sweatshirt that wasn't hers. Sarah's honeysuckle scent clung to it, making her pause. She missed her already. Even though she hadn't seen her in days, she'd held on to the hope of a reconciliation. The hope was gone and so was her motivation to do something constructive. To somehow make it right with Sarah. She'd fallen hard and fast. Now she was paying the price. It was probably for the best. Sarah had lashed out once too often, using her knowledge of Cam's past against her. Still, her heart was torn. She'd actually believed Sarah was "the one." How could her instincts have been so wrong?

Cam slid her fingers along the neck of the bottle where it rested on her thigh. The tears had dried, but the pain in her heart remained. After the first four beers, she no longer tasted what she swallowed.

She hadn't gone to the office in three days. Maggie had repeatedly messaged her, asking if there was anything she could do. Cam hadn't admitted how badly she'd fucked up her nonexistent relationship with Sarah, instead telling her she'd suffered a killer migraine and needed to rest a few days. She doubted Maggie was buying it.

Cam hadn't showered in two days and couldn't stand herself another minute. She fingered her hair, a nervous habit she'd developed after moving to another new foster home as she waited to see what form of hell awaited her. She caught her reflection in the mirror and stopped the motion. The haunted look was familiar from her youth when she'd almost given up caring. But she did care. About herself. About Sarah.

"Sarah."

Cam's lips trembled. She got into the shower and turned on the water, barely registering the icy needles pelting her skin. She couldn't remember ever loving anyone as much as she loved Sarah. They'd had a rocky start that first day, but it had faded, and although they occasionally butted heads, she refused to believe Sarah didn't feel the constant pull, too. Mechanically, Cam scrubbed away the grime, though the emotional bruises remained. After brushing her teeth and towel-drying her hair, she felt almost human. She slipped on lounge pants and a sweatshirt. She needed to get her shit together. She'd thought about calling Liv until she talked herself out of it. She'd used her as a crutch for far too long and it was time to take control of her life. Again.

Cam picked up the bottle from the coffee table, tipped it to her lips, and downed the last few drops. She considered having another to help drown her sorrows until she heard a car door slam. It sounded close, and her first thought was of Brace finding her home address, not a difficult task for a cop. There was no question he would come after her since she'd poked around in his business. She closed her hand around the revolver lying on the table and cautiously moved to a window at the far end of the living room. She edged the curtain back with the muzzle. Sarah stood on the sidewalk, and Cam's heart trip-hammered in her chest as she slowly climbed the steps, then pressed the doorbell.

Cam didn't admit to the relief washing over her. She hadn't totally forgiven Sarah for using her past against her, and they needed to talk about the lies and the pain they'd each experienced at the hand of the other. She tucked the gun at the small of her back before opening the door.

Sarah looked down before meeting her eyes. "It was cruel of me to say…" Sarah's voice caught in her throat as tears slid down her cheeks.

She pulled Sarah to her and closed the door. Cam held her head to her chest, hoping Sarah could feel all the words she didn't have the courage to say. Several minutes later, Sarah gently pushed away.

"You've probably heard this a hundred times from others. I'm sorry for what I said. I'm especially sorry I hurt you."

Sarah's fingertips trailed along her cheek down to her jaw, then her chin before stopping just below her collarbone. The touch soothed her frantic mind, bringing back memories of their times together. Cam took her hand and brushed her lips across it.

"Rarely has an apology been given, especially one that was sincere." She held Sarah's hand in her larger one. All she'd been trying to do was shelter and protect Sarah. Her heart had been in the right place even if she'd gone about it all wrong. "I shouldn't have interfered."

Sarah shrugged. "It's pretty obvious you did what you thought was best. I'm over having Brace in my life. He's not worth dying for."

"What about wanting blood in your life?"

Sarah gave a small smile. "You found my dad. I think it's time I contact him." Sarah glanced from her face down to their joined hands. Cam led her to the couch and sat, pulling her down with her.

"I shouldn't have followed you." She looked away, unable to trust her voice to say more.

"I'm glad you did. I was already anxious about spending time alone with him, but then when…" Sarah shook her head. "It doesn't matter now. Even though I didn't show it at the time, I was glad you were there."

"You were inside too long. I didn't want to storm in, but when I heard you beg him to help you…" She couldn't finish as a shiver traveled through her.

"Let's not talk about it anymore. I'm fine, thanks to you not letting my stupidity keep you away."

"I couldn't stay away." She pulled Sarah closer.

"So, now what, PI Stark?"

She tipped her head. "I'm not following."

"Us. We've had some rough moments, but here we are again, so now what do we do about it?"

Cam still didn't know what she was going to do about Brace, though she'd been compiling everything she had on Brace's suspected drug activities. She'd file a complaint in the next day or two. The sooner the better. But talking about that right now could put another wedge between them, and she wasn't ready to go there. She was certain Sarah wouldn't press charges against him, and there was no telling who they could trust on the force right now anyway. That conversation could wait.

She would have liked to make love, to physically show Sarah how she wanted to take care of her, make her happy. The idea that sex could substitute for her need of confirmation that Sarah was unharmed overwhelmed her desire to touch and be touched.

"I want to hold you all night if that's okay."

Sarah kicked off her shoes, then moved into Cam's embrace. "I'd say that would be perfect."

Cam thought so, too.

Sarah inhaled then sipped the dark roast. She hummed as she moved around the kitchen, throwing together veggies and eggs for breakfast omelets, a food that had become one of her favorites. This morning, she'd awakened to Cam draped around her as she leaned on one arm, watching her. There'd been no mistaking the look of adoration and love in her eyes—a look she could definitely get used to. After going to bed and talking for a while, they'd made love. It had been languid, passionate, and tender, reaffirming what she already knew in her heart. She'd been slowly falling for Cam, even when they argued or disagreed on important issues, like Brace.

Every couple had moments when they disagreed, and this had been theirs, but if they were serious about having a long-term relationship, they'd get through it together.

She heard soft footfalls behind her as she stirred the contents in the pan. Strong arms wrapped around her waist and warm lips nuzzled her neck.

"Mmm…you smell so good," Cam whispered.

A tingle shot through her. It happened every time they were together. She loved how her body reacted to Cam's touch, and her soft voice provided another kind of caress. "Are you hungry?"

Cam reached around her and picked up the carafe to fill her mug. "Starved," she said as she looked over her mug and sipped, a sheepish smile on her face. "I worked up an appetite."

Sarah giggled. "We both did. Can you put the toast down? This is almost ready." Something about them working together in the kitchen filled her with a sense of what their life would be like. Lazy weekend mornings of making love, having meals, and taking it slow. The more they shared the more Sarah knew she'd found her future family. Maybe Cam would never let down her guard when it came to Brace and now she understood why it had been so difficult for her. She would call Paul and see where it led.

She slid half the folded concoction onto each plate as Cam buttered toast. Sarah pulled the jug of orange juice from the fridge and poured into a tumbler. "You want some?"

"Yeah. I need to keep my strength up."

Sarah lifted a brow.

"I'm banking on more mornings like this."

Her hand trembled. She couldn't imagine how hard Cam's life had been as a youngster and still she found the courage to be kind, strong, and gentle. Most likely she still battled demons of her past while facing reminders with cases like hers, and Sarah's admiration of Cam grew with each passing moment. Cam reached across to steady the jug and took it from her.

"What's wrong? Did I say or do something?" Cam lifted her chin with her fingers until their eyes met.

"I'm scared. There's Brace and thinking about what he might do. And…you and I are from such different backgrounds. I'm afraid to look ahead too far."

Cam rubbed her thumb across her cheek, then lightly held her chin. Cam's cell phone dinged but she ignored it. "I'm not asking for a promise of next month, or next year. All I want to hear you say is that you're willing to give us a chance."

Cam's lips covered hers as she cupped the back of her head and pulled her close. Sarah no longer doubted she wanted a future with Cam in it. And maybe, just maybe, if she loved Cam with her whole heart, she could leave her past behind for good. Cam broke away, staring into her eyes.

Sarah needed to open up, too. She was about to tell Cam she'd been thinking much the same thing when Cam's phone rang, and the words died on her lips.

"You'd better get that. It must be important." She stepped back, not missing Cam's disappointment.

"You better hope there's a good reason for calling." Cam's tone was abrupt as she answered. She watched Cam's face go from annoyed to concerned as she listened. "All right. Thanks, Mags." She ended the call before closing the distance between them. Cam gently held her shoulders. "There's been a big drug raid. Brace was involved."

"What?" She searched Cam's face.

"Brace was shot. If you want, I'll drive you to the hospital."

Extreme emotions ran through her head. She didn't wish harm to anyone, but she admitted she was relieved Brace wouldn't be able to come after them. With his attempt to kill her, she shouldn't care what happened to him, but that wasn't the person Sarah was. If there was a possibility Brace had suffered a traumatic experience when he was young, similar to Cam, that made him the way he was, then she could feel empathy, even if she'd never forgive him. She didn't need to see him, though for some odd reason she did want to know he was alive.

"I know I shouldn't care what happens to him, but I'm not him, and I do." Sarah gathered her purse and jacket while wondering what else fate was going to throw at her.

CHAPTER TWENTY-NINE

The ride to the emergency room was a blur. Sarah watched the scenery race by without any of it registering until Cam grasped her hand.

"Go ahead. I'll park the car and meet you inside." Cam gently squeezed before letting go.

All she could do was nod; grateful she hadn't had to drive herself. Her legs shook when she stood at the entrance, and she took a moment to prepare for whatever the news might be. She knew Brace was warped, but she couldn't ignore he was part of her, and she of him. *She* wasn't an insensitive monster whose need for power—control—wiped away whatever good was inside him. The sliding doors opened, and she stepped into the chaos of a sea of navy blue uniforms and others in bulletproof vests. They stood around in small groups, talking quietly among themselves and glancing every few seconds toward the emergency department doors. A few of them stared at her, and she vaguely wondered if it was because she and Brace were near carbon copies of each other. The swoosh of the sliding doors was followed by Cam stepping beside her and wrapping an arm around her waist. She leaned into the comfort of her solid support.

"Do you want to try to see him?"

She nodded, unable to put to words why doing so even made sense.

"Let's ask about getting you inside." Cam guided her forward.

The woman at the desk looked up, a weary but kind smile in place. "Can I help you?"

"Hello. I'm Cam Stark and this is Sarah Peters. We're here because Sarah's brother is one of the officers involved in the police raid tonight and we've been told he was injured."

"What's the officer's name?"

"Brace Archer."

She typed on her keyboard and looked at the screen. "I'm sorry. Officer Archer is in surgery. You can have a seat in the waiting room and I'll let the staff know you're here."

Her stomach churned. "Is he…"

"I'm sorry, Ms…Peters is it?"

"Yes."

"I can't tell you any more until he's out of surgery. I'll be sure to find you."

"Thank you. We'd appreciate knowing as soon as possible." Cam guided her to a couple of empty seats on the far side of the waiting area. She kept a physical connection between them as though sensing how lost Sarah felt. "Whatever the outcome, you won't be facing it alone."

God, she loved this woman. Consciously acknowledging her love for Cam gave her a quiet sense of peace. She wished she could tell her, but this wasn't the time or the place for such an important confession. They'd have other moments. *Please let there be other moments.*

❖

Cam longed to find a way to dispel the angst Sarah was going through. She'd found and lost a sibling, though she'd reassured Cam she wanted nothing more to do with him. Nonetheless, if she knew anything about Sarah's character, she was shaken by the abrupt news. Liv was the only person she'd ever considered real family, and she couldn't imagine how she would deal with bad new concerning her. She hated Brace and everything he stood for, but she could never turn her back on Sarah.

"Do you want anything? Water or coffee?" She'd held Sarah's hand for the last two hours, ignoring the cramp in her bicep at the awkward position she was in.

"No, thank you." Sarah shared a weak smile. "It feels like I'm on an emotional roller coaster. First excited to find him, then worried I never would. You telling me he was a criminal with a badge, and me not believing you. And then the look in his eyes when I fell through the floor…"

"It's okay. None of that matters as long as you're here with me." Cam inhaled deeply. "Sarah, I lo—" She didn't have a chance to finish as the doors opened and several doctors dressed in surgical scrubs stepped into the waiting room. Sarah stood when she heard her name called among the cacophony of voices.

"Here. Sarah's here." Cam pushed through the crowd and brought Sarah to the front. The doctor's eyes softened, but the sadness was unmistakable.

"You must be Officer Archer's sister. I'm sorry to have to tell you that he didn't make it."

"What?"

The hush around them was deafening.

"There was too much damage to his internal organs. I'm very sorry."

Cam led Sarah back to their seats and she sat very still. She glanced up in time to see an older couple with a worried look stop one of the uniformed officers. They spoke for a minute before the woman gasped, her hand going to her mouth to muffle her anguished cry. The man nodded to the officer, then wrapped a protective arm around her before they sat.

Behind them, officers began to talk in hushed tones as the news of Brace's death passed among them. Cam instinctively pulled her closer and Sarah let out a long sigh.

"It's over, isn't it?"

"I'm sorry Brace's life ended this way, but I'm not sorry he's no longer a threat to you." She kissed Sarah's forehead.

"It's kind of surreal. Yesterday I was begging him for my life and today he's gone."

A few minutes went by before she realized the couple stood close by. "Excuse me." He looked to the woman whose hand he held. "We're Brace's parents. I'm Jack Archer, and this is my wife, Nicole." He looked between Cam and Sarah. "Do I know you?"

"Cam Stark," she said. Sarah took a minute, then stood beside her and held out her hand.

"I'm Sarah Peters. I'm Brace's twin."

Jack helped his wife to the bench and Sarah sat beside her. "I know this is a shock. It was for me, too. I recently found out we were both given up for adoption." Sarah took Nicole's hand. "I'm sorry for the loss of your son."

Nicole dabbed at her eyes and stared at Sarah before sharing a sad smile. "Sometimes loss and discovery are one and the same." She lightly touched Sarah's face. "You're pretty. You have—" Nicole's voice cracked. "Had the same eye color." Jack reached for her.

"Honey, we should ask if we can see him."

Nicole nodded, then stood. She turned to go, then stopped. "Would you like to go with us?"

Cam watched the exchange between strangers and couldn't help comparing their kindness to Sarah and Liv's kindness to her.

"Thank you, but no. I didn't really know him." Sarah watched them go to the glass enclosure before they disappeared behind the electronic doors.

She was going to ask if Sarah was ready to go when someone held out a bottle of water. Cam looked up to find Jimmy Barnes.

"Thank you." She cracked the seal and held it out to Sarah. Cam still needed to thank him for making sure she was in the right place at the right time last night, but she didn't want to do it with so many eyes watching. He gave her a brief nod, and she knew they were good.

After he walked away, Sarah turned and faced her. "Take me home?"

❖

Sarah sat in silence as Cam drove to her house. She was glad Cam sensed she couldn't talk about the last few hours. Brace's appearance in her life had been brief, and she believed that if they'd been adopted together he would have turned out differently. She'd witnessed firsthand how Cam had found a way to take the higher road. To rise above the torment of her youth to spend her days helping others. And she had—for her and likely countless others. And then again, Brace's adoptive parents had seemed kind. Maybe he'd just been born a bad seed, and nothing would have changed that.

The lump in her throat threatened to choke her. She glanced over at Cam as she maneuvered the car around heavy traffic. They stopped for a red light, and Cam turned to her, love clearly written in the way she looked at her.

"It won't be long till you're home." Cam shortened the distance between them by resting her hand on Sarah's thigh, and the warmth from the contact spread through her and dispersed the chill she hadn't been able to shake since they'd left the hospital.

It was a few more blocks before Cam pulled into the driveway of Sarah's parents' home. *My home.* Cam sprinted from her side to round the front and opened her door, extending her hand. Sarah was grateful for the help. The adrenaline rush she felt when she arrived at the hospital, and then again at the news of his passing, had left her drained. Cam pulled her closer until their hips met, her arm wrapped protectively around her. Together they walked to the front door, and when her hand shook as she tried to unlock it, Cam took the key. She handed it back to Sarah from where she stood on the top step.

"I'll drop your car off in the morning if that's okay." Cam looked at the ground and toed a pebble off the landing.

"Are you leaving me?"

Cam's head snapped up. "No, I...I thought maybe you'd like time by yourself. I don't want to intrude."

Sarah reached for her hand. "Come inside. Please?"

Cam laced their fingers. They fit together naturally, her smaller ones meshing with Cam's long, slender ones. "Okay. If you're sure."

She gave a little yank. "Don't make me beg."

Cam smiled, and Sarah's heart melted as she stepped inside. "You never have to beg me for anything. Whatever you need, that's what I want to give you." She brushed the back of her fingers over the side of her face.

Sarah held her breath. She wanted to reassure Cam she would have a lifetime to do just that. If last night had taught her one thing, it was there wasn't any guarantee of tomorrow. She didn't want to leave this earth without telling Cam how she felt. She shut the door and locked it, tossing her keys on the table before leading Cam down the hallway to her bedroom. Maybe it was wrong of her to want to make love after the news she'd just received, but she couldn't face the possibility of Cam not knowing for one more day how she felt and the role she had taken in Sarah's life. She stood beside her bed knowing there was no turning back. She was about to give her body to Cam and tell her she also had her heart.

Slowly, with her eyes on Cam's, she unbuttoned Cam's shirt and pushed it off her shoulders. She placed a soft kiss between her breasts, then reached behind her and unclasped her lace bra before guiding it down her arms. She was tempted to take a pointed nipple in her mouth but forced herself to wait. She unclasped the fastening of her khaki slacks, and Cam slid her shoes off. Sarah pulled the zipper down, then peeled both layers over Cam's narrow hips. She kissed the top of one thigh, then the other.

"Lie down, baby."

Cam moved onto the bed, resting on her elbows, waiting for her. She had every intention of shedding her own clothes with slow precision, but Cam's body called to her, and she made short work of joining her, kissing her way up her stomach until she lay on top of her, their warm flesh melding together. Cam's mouth met hers and her passion burned hot, setting her body and soul on fire.

Cam slipped her tongue over Sarah's lips, savoring the intensity of the heat of her mouth. It wasn't enough for Sarah to surrender her body to Cam. She wanted her heart and her mind to join the fray. If her battered and bruised soul could surrender to love, surely Sarah's could, too.

Sarah's lush body slid along hers, the heat between them coating their skin in a light layer of sweat. The salt on her lips when she sucked the pulse point of Sarah's neck stoked the fire. Sarah pressed her fingers through her slick folds until they were coated with her essence, then entered her. She groaned and moved to meet her thrusts. *I'm so close already.* Sarah closed her mouth over one of her hardened nipples. Between sucks and licks, Sarah withdrew and slid over her extended clit, making her squirm. Sarah's voice cut through her lust-filled haze.

"Look at me, baby." Sarah shifted until she captured Cam's thigh between her own. She entered Cam again, driving in deeper before backing almost all the way out.

Cam surrendered to the demand of Sarah's fingers as they found their mark over and over again.

"Let me see you come," Sarah said.

Cam fought to keep her eyes focused on Sarah's beautiful face as the tension built in her abdomen before moving lower. Her walls contracted before the flash of her orgasm drove the breath from her chest and she cried out in pleasure, her body bucking in rhythm to Sarah's steady strokes as they drew out consecutive waves. Cam collapsed, sinking into the bed. That's when she heard the words she'd longed to hear.

"I love you, Camdyn Stark."

Tears ran from the corners of Cam's eyes as she rode out the spasms, then she reached for Sarah until their mouths met in a kiss more passionate than any Cam had ever experienced. She had no idea how long they were locked in the fierce embrace. When they broke away in desperate need of air, she held Sarah's face.

"I didn't think I'd ever be able to love someone the way I love you, Sarah. All I want is to make you happy. Every day we're together." Cam wrapped her arms around her and rolled them over. "I'm going to show you how very much I love you."

Cam took her time kissing every inch of Sarah's body, then she did exactly what she promised to do. Over and over again.

Chapter Thirty

Rays of sunlight cast stripes across Sarah's body, reminding Cam of a tiger, but Sarah wasn't anyone she wanted to tame. Sarah's lovemaking had been tender and fierce at the same time, and she'd reveled in the ardor of her love. This morning, more than all the ones that had come before, was the culmination of impossible dreams and desires. It was still hard to believe Sarah loved her. Not that she hadn't hoped against all odds that Sarah would find her worth loving, but to hear the words out loud had put her on cloud nine.

Sometime in the night while Sarah slept, she made peace with her angst about Brace. If it weren't for him, her chances of finding and falling in love with Sarah, who was nestled in her arms, would have been slim. She made a silent promise to forgive more easily in the future. Cam was relieved Sarah would be spared having to deal with Brace and his dark side.

She watched Sarah breathe in a slow, steady cadence, and she brushed a lock of blond curls from her forehead. Her breathing changed as she roused. The dark lashes fluttered against her cheeks before her eyes opened, and she stretched languorously.

"Mmm...good morning."

"Yes, it is." Cam pulled her in closer to her, a place she would never tire of Sarah being. "It's a very good morning."

Sarah snuggled against her, snaking a leg over her hip and pressing her center against it. The searing hot heat of her scorched Cam's skin pleasantly.

Even though Cam's sex was swollen and sore, her body responded, and she became wet. She kissed Sarah's forehead.

"We have to get out of bed at some point today."

Sarah turned to face her. "Why?"

Cam chuckled. "For one thing, we need to eat. Woman cannot live on sex alone."

"Maybe you can't, but I certainly can." Sarah's face was serious until Cam caught the twinkle of mischief in her eyes. Sarah giggled.

"Shower with me?"

"Uh-huh. Then what?" Sarah's fingers played dangerously close to her breast, and she held her hand to her chest, not trusting herself to resist if Sarah went any further.

"After I get a change of clothes there's someone I'd like you to meet." She'd promised Liv if she and Sarah ever got together Liv would meet her, and she had every intention of keeping that promise.

"Okay." Sarah moved to get up, but she pulled her back down.

"Are you…" Cam's vison bore into Sarah's eyes needing to know there were no regrets the morning after confessing her love.

Sarah tipped her head. "Am I what?"

Cam held her breath. "Are you okay? I know yesterday couldn't have been easy and…" Cam braced against the possibility that Sarah might have confessed simply because Cam had been there during a stressful time. "I need to know if you still feel the same as you did last night."

Sarah sat up and brought Cam with her. "I meant every word last night, and this morning, and all the tomorrows to come. I love you." Sarah kissed her hard, letting her know she was serious. "And unless you do something to seriously fuck this up, I'm in it for the long haul."

Cam sighed a breath of relief. She had a feeling she was going to have a lot of mornings, and nights, to celebrate life and love. Something she'd never believed was in the cards for her until she'd met the beautiful creature in her arms. The one she planned on sharing the rest of her life with.

EPILOGUE

Nine months later…

Cam leaned against the counter and watched her two favorite women prepare dinner. Sarah's hearty laughter made her smile. Liv turned to the refrigerator and winked at her. Liv had taken an instant liking to Sarah and told Cam she'd found a partner who would keep her in check. That had made *her* laugh, and it was true. Even though they were still in the "honeymoon" stage, Sarah's ire reared up every so often, and Cam remembered her fire was one of Sarah's most attractive characteristics.

She was relieved Sarah had made peace with not only the loss of her brother, but she'd also accepted the truth about his involvement with drugs. It hadn't been easy for her until the police arrested the man responsible for shooting Brace, and he'd confessed he did it because he was sick of Brace taking his cut off the top, leaving the spoils for the runners. It had been even harder for the Archers. They knew their son had always had a dark side, but they believed he'd changed after he joined the force.

The doorbell rang and she went to answer it.

"Hi, Cam. I hope we're not too early. Nicole must think we're driving cross-country." Jack grinned.

"It's never too soon to see you two. Hi, Nicole. How have you been?" Cam gave her a warm hug. There was still a glint of sadness in Nicole's eyes, and she imagined it would remain for quite some time. Losing a child must be the hardest thing a parent had to face.

They'd contacted Sarah after the funeral and asked if they could talk. Get to know one another since they'd both suffered losses. Sarah had asked if she'd mind if they all got to know one another better, and Cam had done much the same with Liv, including everyone for dinner, or a cookout, whenever they had the time. The doorbell rang again, and Sarah went to answer it.

"Hi, Dad." Sarah gave him a hug. "Glad you could make it."

"You know I'd never miss a family get-together." Paul handed Cam a still warm dish. "Blueberry pie."

She rolled her eyes and pulled him to her. Paul was a decent, kind man. He had begun to treat her as his own shortly after Sarah had contacted him. "Good thing you showed. I think Liv was ready to bolt the door." Cam smiled at Liv. "She used to do that to me when I was late."

"Damn right. This isn't a restaurant you know." Liv laughed and everyone joined in.

Cam glanced around at the people that had become part of her family. Like all of the pieces of her and Sarah's life that had fallen into perfect place. Last month, the Archers had given Sarah enough money to pay off her debts and then some. Sarah, of course, had refused at first, but when they said it had been put aside for when Brace started a family and they couldn't think of a better legacy of their son but to help his sister's family, she finally relented. They'd even introduced her to several of their friends who were gallery owners in New York City. Cam knew those connections had thrilled her more than the money. She'd continue working construction during the busy season, but she'd talked about taking off the winter months to concentrate on her sculpting. Cam would continue to do what she enjoyed—investigating was in her blood. With her influx of cases and Sarah's upcoming art show, neither had a lot to give, but family was important to them both, so they made a point to make them a priority.

She held Sarah's hand as Liv led a short, modern day form of grace. Tonight, she was going to ask Sarah how she felt about starting their own family, and the idea of raising a child...or two... was both exhilarating and frightening, but she wouldn't be doing it alone. Sarah would show their children what it was like to grow up with nurturing and love, and Cam would give her children inner strength, street smarts, and a curious nature.

Cam never thought she'd ever want a family of her own, but her views of family had changed. Her life had changed, too. And best of all, *she* had changed. The nightmares still made an occasional appearance, but with Sarah by her side, they quickly faded. Even her migraines had lessened in frequency and were no longer crippling, though she had her meds—just in case. She no longer hid from her past, content knowing she'd risen above those times, and put them behind her. Now she focused on the future, the one *her* family would build together.

About the Author

Renee Roman has lived her entire life in upstate New York and can't see herself living anywhere there isn't a change of seasons. She works at a local college and writes lesbian romance, intrigue, and erotica in her spare time. She states her first two novels, *Epicurean Delights* and *Stroke of Fate*, are just the beginning of a long list of stories waiting to be told. You can follow Renee on Facebook, at her website www.reneeromanwrites.com, or you can contact her at reneeromanwrites@gmail.com

Books Available from Bold Strokes Books

Blood of the Pack by Jenny Frame. When Alpha of the Scottish pack Kenrick Wulver visits the Wolfgangs, she falls for Zaria Lupa, a wolf on the run. (978-1-63555-431-1)

Cause of Death by Sheri Lewis Wohl. Medical student Vi Akiak and K9 Search and Rescue officer Kate Renard must work together to find a killer before they end up the next targets. In the race for survival, they discover that love may be the biggest risk of all. (978-1-63555-441-0)

Chasing Sunset by Missouri Vaun. Hijinks and mishaps ensue as Iris and Finn set off on a road trip adventure, chasing the sunset, and falling in love along the way. (978-1-63555-454-0)

Double Down by MB Austin. When an unlikely friendship with Spanish pop star Erlea turns deeper, Celeste, in-house physician for the hotel hosting Erlea's show, has a choice to make—run or double down on love. (978-1-63555-423-6)

Party of Three by Sandy Lowe. Three friends are in for a wild night at billionaire heiress Eleanor McGregor's twenty-fifth birthday party. Love, lust, and doing the right thing, even when it hurts, turn the evening into one that will change their lives forever. (978-1-63555-246-1)

Sit. Stay. Love. by Karis Walsh. City girl Alana Brendt and country vet Tegan Evans both know they don't belong together. Only problem is, they're falling in love. (978-1-63555-439-7)

Where the Lies Hide by Renee Roman. As P.I. Camdyn Stark gets closer to solving the case, will her dark secrets and the lies she's buried jeopardize her future with the quietly beautiful Sarah Peters? (978-1-63555-371-0)

Beautiful Dreamer by Melissa Brayden. With love on the line, can Devyn Winters find it in her heart to stay in the small town of Dreamer's Bay, the one place she swore she'd never remain? (978-1-63555-305-5)

Create a Life to Love by Erin Zak. When sixteen-year-old Beth shows up at her birth mother's door, three lives will change forever. (978-1-63555-425-0)

Deadeye by Meredith Doench. Stranded while hunting the serial predator Deadeye, Special Agent Luce Hansen fights for survival while her lover, forensic pathologist Harper Bennett, hunts for clues to Hansen's disappearance along the killer's trail. (978-1-63555-253-9)

Death Takes a Bow by David S. Pederson. Alan Keys takes part in a local stage production, but when the leading man is murdered, his partner Detective Heath Barrington is thrust into the limelight to find the killer. (978-1-63555-472-4)

Endangered by Michelle Larkin. Shapeshifters Officer Aspen Wolfe and Dr. Tora Madigan fight their growing attraction as they work together to destroy a secret government agency that exterminates their kind. (978-1-63555-377-2)

Incognito by VK Powell. The only thing Evan Spears is focused on is capturing a fleeing murder suspect until wild card Frankie Strong is added to her team and causes chaos on and off the job. (978-1-63555-389-5)

Insult to Injury by Gun Brooke. After losing everything, Gail Owen withdraws to her old farmhouse and finds a destitute young woman, Romi Shepherd, living in a secret room. (978-1-63555-323-9)

Just One Moment by Dena Blake. If you were given the chance to have the love of your life back, could you ignore everything that went wrong and start over again? (978-1-63555-387-1)

Scene of the Crime by MJ Williamz. Cullen Mathew finds herself caught between the woman she thinks she loves but can no longer trust and a beautiful detective she can't stop thinking about who will stop at nothing to find the truth. (978-1-63555-405-2)

Accidental Prophet by Bud Gundy. Days after his grandmother dies, Drew Morten learns his true identity and finds himself racing against time to save civilization from the apocalypse. (978-1-63555-452-6)

Daughter of No One by Sam Ledel. When their worlds are threatened, a princess and a village outcast must overcome their differences and embrace a budding attraction if they want to survive. (978-1-63555-427-4)

Fear of Falling by Georgia Beers. Singer Sophie James is ready to shake up her career, but her new manager, the gorgeous Dana Landon, has other ideas. (978-1-63555-443-4)

In Case You Forgot by Fredrick Smith and Chaz Lamar. Zaire and Kenny, two newly single, Black, queer, and socially aware men, start again—in love, career, and life—in the West Hollywood neighborhood of LA. (978-1-63555-493-9)

Playing with Fire by Lesley Davis. When Takira Lathan and Dante Groves meet at Takira's restaurant, love may find its way onto the menu. (978-1-63555-433-5)

Practice Makes Perfect by Carsen Taite. Meet law school friends Campbell, Abby, and Grace, law partners at Austin's premier boutique legal firm for young, hip entrepreneurs. Legal Affairs: one law firm, three best friends, three chances to fall in love. (978-1-63555-357-4)

The Last Seduction by Ronica Black. When you allow true love to elude you once and you desperately regret it, are you brave enough to grab it when it comes around again? (978-1-63555-211-9)

Wavering Convictions by Erin Dutton. After a traumatic event, Maggie has vowed to regain her strength and independence. So how can Ally be both the woman who makes her feel safe and a constant reminder of the person who took her security away? (978-1-63555-403-8)

A Bird of Sorrow by Shea Godfrey. As Darrius and her lover, Princess Jessa, gather their strength for the coming war, a mysterious spell will reveal the truth of an ancient love. (978-1-63555-009-2)

All the Worlds Between Us by Morgan Lee Miller. High school senior Quinn Hughes discovers that a broken friendship is actually a door propped open for an unexpected romance. (978-1-63555-457-1)

An Intimate Deception by CJ Birch. Flynn County Sheriff Elle Ashley has spent her adult life atoning for her wild youth, but when she finds her ex, Jessie, murdered two weeks before the small town's biggest social event, she comes face-to-face with her past and all her well-kept secrets. (978-1-63555-417-5)

Cash and the Sorority Girl by Ashley Bartlett. Cash Braddock doesn't want to deal with morality, drugs, or people. Unfortunately, she's going to have to. (978-1-63555-310-9)

Counting for Thunder by Phillip Irwin Cooper. A struggling actor returns to the Deep South to manage a family crisis, finds love, and ultimately his own voice as his mother is regaining hers for possibly the last time. (978-1-63555-450-2)

Falling by Kris Bryant. Falling in love isn't part of the plan, but will Shaylie Beck put her heart first and stick around, or tell the damaging truth? (978-1-63555-373-4)

Secrets in a Small Town by Nicole Stiling. Deputy Chief Mackenzie Blake has one mission: find the person harassing Savannah Castillo and her daughter before they cause real harm. (978-1-63555-436-6)

Stormy Seas by Ali Vali. The high-octane follow-up to the best-selling action-romance, *Blue Skies*. (978-1-63555-299-7)

The Road to Madison by Elle Spencer. Can two women who fell in love as girls overcome the hurt caused by the father who tore them apart? (978-1-63555-421-2)

Dangerous Curves by Larkin Rose. When love waits at the finish line, dangerous curves are a risk worth taking. (978-1-63555-353-6)

Love to the Rescue by Radclyffe. Can two people who share a past really be strangers? (978-1-62639-973-0)

Love's Portrait by Anna Larner. When museum curator Molly Goode and benefactor Georgina Wright uncover a portrait's secret, public and private truths are exposed, and their deepening love hangs in the balance. (978-1-63555-057-3)

Model Behavior by MJ Williamz. Can one woman's instability shatter a new couple's dreams of happiness? (978-1-63555-379-6)

Pretending in Paradise by M. Ullrich. When travelwisdom.com assigns PR specialist Caroline Beckett and travel blogger Emma Morgan to cover a hot new couples retreat, they're forced to fake a relationship to secure a reservation. (978-1-63555-399-4)

Recipe for Love by Aurora Rey. Hannah Little doesn't have much use for fancy chefs or fancy restaurants, but when New York City chef Drew Davis comes to town, their attraction just might be a recipe for love. (978-1-63555-367-3)

Survivor's Guilt and Other Stories by Greg Herren. Award-winning author Greg Herren's short stories are finally pulled together into a single collection, including the Macavity Award nominated title story and the first-ever Chanse MacLeod short story. (978-1-63555-413-7)

The House by Eden Darry. After a vicious assault, Sadie, Fin, and their family retreat to a house they think is the perfect place to start over, until they realize not all is as it seems. (978-1-63555-395-6)

Uninvited by Jane C. Esther. When Aerin McLeary's body becomes host for an alien intent on invading Earth, she must work with researcher Olivia Ando to uncover the truth and save humankind. (978-1-63555-282-9)